We hope you
fun reading th
writing it.

Betsy Riffle

Happy birthday
from Clara

Love Wally

INCIDENT
AT THE BACK GATE

Wally Vore and
Betty McCord-Riffle

Incident at the Back Gate

ISBN: 978-1-54399-670-8 (Print)
ISBN: 978-1-54399-671-5 (eBook)

Preface

We like to say our story is loosely-based on many true stories. The incident actually happened. Wally, the author, was the driver on duty that night. The blood and matter he witnessed traumatized him, although he didn't realize it at the time. He buried his feelings. Afterward, he never understood why the sight of people getting hurt bothered him so, until we started working on this book. Writing about the incident has been cathartic in helping him realize he had a problem.

Wally, the author, wants you, dear reader, to know if you have been through a traumatic experience of any kind and now have unexplained anxiety in certain situations, consider the possibility of a connection. Recognition is half the battle. Then you can begin to move forward.

After the description of the incident, the rest of Wally's character is fiction, as are all the rest of our characters. However, most of our characters have elements of people we have known in our lifetime.

The account of events at the trial are fictional. The outcome of the trial is as it actually happened.

The description of the reservation is a true description of a reservation in the author's experience. It was not the Minnesota reservation. Eventually the U.S. government made good on what was owed the tribe of the reservation the authors describe, and conditions did improve greatly.

We took liberties with the Ojibwa beliefs, including beliefs from other tribes as well. Burial customs described in this book are real customs from long-ago times and, to the best of our knowledge, no longer practiced. We included them because we found them quite beautiful.

Lucinda's story of the Christian School is also true, but the identity of the Native American lady who told this story has been altered.

The stories our characters tell are true, although some have been embellished a bit. Some came from our own experience, and others came from people kind enough to share. We hope you enjoy them. We hope they spark memories of your own.

We would like to thank the Writer's Club in Richmond, Michigan, and especially Gretchen for helping us develop computer skills and lending moral support. We'd also like to thank brother, Tim, a lawyer who helped us get the legal terminology correct. And we'd like to thank daughter Cherie for doing our proofreading and untangling our computer glitches (mostly caused by our ineptitude). We couldn't have done it without you.

Lucille Ball once said if you write one page a day, in a year you will have a book. We believe everyone has a story. Maybe someday we will be reading yours.

Chapter 1

Nothing interesting ever happens at 1:00 in the morning. That's why they call it the dead of night. This night there was fog and a chill in the air. The night breeze that came off of the Bay penetrated PFC Wally's Marine Corp Eisenhour jacket. As the duty driver at the San Francisco Naval Shipyard, Wally was making his customary rounds. He needed to use his windshield wipers to peer through the murky fog.

At that time of night, it is always quiet, with hardly any traffic by the back gate. As Wally's truck approached the brightly-lit gate, he could only see one of the two Marines who should be standing guard that night. Normally, on a night like this, the guards would be inside the guard house. The one guard he could make out was outside and appeared to have a .45 in his hand.

Puzzled by what he was seeing, Wally slowed, bringing his truck to a stop at an angle in front of the guard house. In this way he could use the truck's body as a shield, if needed. Wally was having trouble figuring out what was going on. Why did John have his .45 out? That should not be. Was there some danger out there in the fog? Had they heard something? Where was the other guard? This wasn't good! Slowly and quietly Wally opened the truck door. He carefully slid out of the seat and stood behind the open door.

In an authoritative voice Wally called out "John! What's going on?" When John did not answer, Wally called to him again "Hey, Buddy, what's going on?" Silence.

Leaving the safety of the truck, with his .45 in hand, Wally cautiously approached. His heart was beating so fast. He inched closer to the guard house. All the while he was listening for something out of the ordinary. But he heard nothing. He kept looking in all directions. Nothing. His senses were on high alert. Something was terribly wrong here. But what?

Wally also was keeping a close watch on John. John was seemingly unaware of Wally's presence. He was walking in baby steps, forming small circles. He appeared dazed. Wally realized he couldn't see Nick, the other guard, so he asked John where Nick was. John, in a choked voice, replied "In the guard house."

The guard house at the back gate was made of reinforced concrete, with sliding doors on each end. It was just large enough for two marines; one to watch incoming traffic, the other, outgoing. Looking in the door, Wally could see Nick sitting on the floor with his back to the wall, legs splayed out in front of him.

Wally, anticipating a prank, entered the guard house, expecting Nick to reach out and grab his ankle. But Nick did not move. He just stared straight ahead. "O.K Nick, joke's over. Get up." There was no response. When Wally reached down to give Nick a shake, he slid sideways. It was then Wally could see the wall and, to his absolute horror, what was on it. A tsunami of blood and matter was splattered and smeared there.

Wally, in all of his twenty years, had never seen a dead person before. But this wasn't just any person. This was his bunkmate and best friend, very much alive just one hour before. His first reaction was disbelief. His friend. All that blood. The hole in his chest. Bile rose up in his stomach. He thought for a moment he was going to be sick. No time for that. Wally's training kicked in. He quickly assessed the situation. Nick had been shot, and John was apparently the only other person in the area. John had his weapon drawn. Why did John draw his weapon? Was there another shooter? Or was John the shooter? John was acting bizarrely. Completely out of character for him. Wally decided the safest thing to do would be to first disarm John and then see if he could talk to him and find out what had happened.

Using the protective cover of the guard house, he gently asked John to place his weapon on the ground. When John did not comply, Wally used a more commanding tone, again telling John to place his gun on the ground. Aroused from his stupor, John asked Wally, "Is Nick dead?" In order to convince John to drop the weapon, Wally again said, "Place your gun on the ground and we are going to call an ambulance."

At that, John did drop the gun. Wally asked him what had happened. Instead of answering Wally, John stood in front of him making little whimpering sounds, almost like a cat meowing. Seeing he would not be able to get any information out of him, and understanding something was seriously wrong with John, Wally told him to go over and sit on the curb, giving him the task of watching for the ambulance. As soon as John moved away from his weapon, Wally retrieved it.

Quickly returning to the guard house, Wally placed the gun on the ledge where the log book was kept. Using the telephone above that ledge, he called Corporal Keno, the Corporal of the Guard. He was shaking so much he could hardly dial. As he dialed, he double-checked John's position; he was sitting on the curb, watching for the ambulance, as Wally had told him to do.

"Corporal Keno, we need...I mean...Nick is, Nick is—uh—no longer with us."

"*With* us???"

"What I mean, well, it looks like John shot Nick." Stumbling out the words, Wally added "He's dead. Corporal Keno, and I think John needs a doctor."

"Why do you say that? Is he injured as well?"

"No, Corporal Keno, I think he is in shock. I think you need to get here *now*. This is bad"

In no time there was a cacophony of sound breaking the silence: sirens, screeching brakes, doors slamming, orders barked. Red and blue flashing lights lent an eerie surrealness to the guard house area as men hurried to their assigned duties. The gate area was immediately sealed off with crime scene tape. There were military police, civilian police, ambulances, and several officers filtering in.

Documentation of the scene began at once. John was surrounded by police and medics. A medic was giving John a cigarette. Someone else was lighting it for him. Something about that scene bothered Wally, but the thought was fleeting. At that moment there was just too much going on. As Wally was being interviewed, white lights flickered over the area from both flashlights and photographers. Because he was successively questioned by several different officials, Wally's informal interviews lasted until dawn.

Even after the interviews concluded, Wally was still wondering what had happened. He was shaken down to his bootlaces—to see his friend with such a large hole. Nick was more than a friend. Wally looked to Nick as his mentor. Nick was the only Native American in the barracks. He seemed to Wally to have wisdom well beyond his years. Wally found him to be very intelligent and considered himself fortunate to be Nick's friend. Master of the put-down, no one could get the best of Nick. Wally, however, had never felt the sting of his barbs. Nick was always kind to him.

John was a big easy-going farm boy from Indiana. He was the kind of guy often overlooked. Quiet, unassuming, about his only distinguishing characteristic, apparent during shower time, an unusually large package—the envy of many. The incident made no sense to Wally. How could this have happened?

Once Wally's interviews were completed, he was allowed to return to the squad bay. Arriving there he could see this would not be a usual day. On normal week days the squad bay would be in perfect order, with bunks made up so tightly a quarter would bounce off of them. But today looked more like a weekend; beds less precisely made, men not in uniform. Everyone was milling about or talking softly in small clusters.

As Wally entered the squad bay, the talking ceased. Then faster than a machine gun volley, he was bombarded with questions about Nick and John. However, during the on-site interviews Wally had been instructed not to talk about the incident until after the trial. He could only tell the men he was not permitted to answer their questions at that time. They reluctantly respected that.

Although Wally had been up all night, it was time for morning chow. He went to Tom, saying "Let's go to breakfast. I have some things to talk over with you." Tom was another of Wally's good friends. He was tall and strikingly handsome. Nick used to taunt him saying he had a penis the size of a bee's stinger. But Nick liked having him around because he was a genuinely good guy and, as Nick used to say, a real chick magnet.

As they ate, Wally and Tom discussed the girlfriends of Nick and John. Both women lived off-base. Nick's girlfriend, Betsy, lived with her parents. All they knew about John's girlfriend was that her name was Angie. They decided they probably should notify the two women, since it was unlikely anyone else would think of that. Wally would take on the task of calling Betsy since he had met her a couple of times, and since that would be the more difficult call. Tom would try to locate Angie's phone number and contact her.

After chow, Wally went to Nick's wall locker. He found Nick's personal phone book and copied down the needed number. He then returned the book to Nick's locker. In the meantime, Tom asked around among the guys about Angie's phone number. Apparently, several of the guys had it and one joked about it being on the wall in the Red Garter Saloon men's room as well.

The men made their way to the pay phones. After dialing Betsy's phone number Wally wearily sat on the little seat in the booth. As he closed the bifold doors, he realized how small and cramped the booth was. He felt hot and constrained and reopened the door to get some air. Betsy answered on the third ring with a pleasant "Good morning".

"Betsy this is Wally, Nick's friend. I'm afraid I have some bad news I have to tell you about Nick. I...."

"Oh no, what's happened?"

"Nick.... Nick," Wally was having difficulty finding the right words. "Um.... there's been a shooting on base. Nick was shot. Betsy, he didn't make it. I'm so sorry. If there is anything I can do..." Even as he spoke, he could hear Betsy's strangled cry over the phone. He was at a loss as to what to say next.

Before he could say anything more his name came over the loudspeaker summoning him to Gunny's office. "Betsy, I'll have to call you back. I just heard them call my name. I've got to go see the duty officer. I'm so sorry to have to break off this call right now, but I promise I *will* call you back as soon as I can."

Making his way to the duty office, Wally stepped inside the open door. The gunny sergeant was in the process of chewing ass. In all the confusion of the morning the base flag had not been raised and it was already 0900. At first, he wanted the corporal of the guard to get that flag up. But then he hesitated, not knowing if perhaps the flag should be at half-mast. Gunny Sergeant directed the Corporal of the Guard to raise the flag as usual and if it needed to be lowered, that could be done later. "Get your ass out of here. That flag is already two hours late."

The Gunny Sergeant then turned his attention to Wally. "Have a seat. What happened out there, son?"

"All I know is that John had a gun in his hand and Nick was in the guard house dead. I am so confused right now. I feel really sick. Would it be possible to go to sick bay?" The Gunny Sergeant called over the speaker for the duty driver.

He then stood and checked to see that the flag had been raised. Still facing the window, he said to Wally. "I've witnessed the death of Marines in the field. If anyone could relate to how you are feeling, it would be me. I'm here if you ever want to talk. I realize you've been up over 24 hours. There is an extra bunk in Sergeant's quarters. Go and get some rest after sick bay."

Leaving sick bay, Wally walked through squad bay and toward the Sergeant's quarters. Tom approached him from behind and touched him on the shoulder. "Are you OK?"

"Yeah, just tired. Did you get ahold of Angie?"

Tom replied he hadn't yet. Her roommate said she was out. He promised to try later. Wally explained he was going to get some rest. The two men agreed to meet up later.

Wally settled into a bed in the Sergeant's quarters. But sleep evaded him. He kept reliving the events of the previous night. Why was John acting so strangely? Was it an accident, or was there some darker motive? Did I say the right words to Betsy? Probably bungled it badly... Finally, he drifted off into a troubled sleep. But in a few minutes, he snapped awake again covered in perspiration. Realizing sleep would be impossible, he decided to get a shower. He suspected tomorrow would not be a routine day.

Chapter 2

As Wally finished his shower his name again came over the loudspeaker, summoning him to the Duty Office. There he found a very distraught Betsy. She had driven to the base and been given a day pass to come aboard. Sympathetic to Betsy's reason for coming, Gunny suggested Wally take her to the canteen for coffee. He reminded Wally that he would not be able to discuss the details of the incident.

At the canteen Wally asked Betsy what she would like to eat. All she wanted was water. Wally ordered a hamburger and some coffee. Once seated, however, he found himself unable to eat, even though he was hungry. And he was perplexed as to how to talk to this beautiful young woman seated across from him.

For the first time, Wally really looked at Betsy. She was petite, with startlingly green eyes and the complexion of a porcelain doll. Her light blond hair was shoulder-length, with a slight curl at the end; the kind of hair you'd like to reach out and touch. She was simply dressed in a white knit top, dark slacks, and sandals. No makeup. She was slender, almost giving the impression of being fragile. Her beauty shone through despite the eyes that were red and swollen from crying, despite the red nose, despite the sadness in her eyes.

Talking, as it turned out, was pretty much impossible in the noise of the canteen. There was conversation and laughter all around them, as well as the clinking of silverware and glasses and the clanking of trays and pans in the kitchen. Additionally, it was obvious Betsy was fighting to hold back tears in such a public place. Wally's heart went out to her.

"It is so difficult to talk here," He suggested they go for a walk. The two left the canteen and began strolling toward the softball field. As they walked, they made small talk; the cool breeze coming off the bay, the warmth of the sun, the brilliant blue of the sky contrasted with the white puffy clouds, seagulls making a racket overhead. It would have been a perfect day, if not for the somber mood Nick's death had cast over them. Betsy politely asked if Wally had gotten any sleep since last night. Wally admitted he had not been able to sleep.

When they reached the wooden benches at the softball diamond, Betsy sat down. This was an area of the base she had never seen. It was smaller than she expected, with only a few bleachers. On the bay side a barrier had been erected to keep ground balls and line drives from going into the water, but a high fly would occasionally go over it.

Wally was too restless to sit down at the moment. He paced, explaining to Betsy that this was the field where Nick played. Nick was a good player, but he was even better at taunting the opposing players to the point where they would lose focus. Betsy agreed that was one of Nick's less-endearing qualities.

Suddenly Betsy stood up. All the emotion she had been holding back came tumbling out. She could contain it no longer. It exploded out of her. "Wally—I'm pregnant. It's Nick's. I don't know what to do!" With that, she burst into huge gasping sobs.

Wally was astonished by this information, and even more so that she would trust him with it; someone she barely knew. He instinctively put his arms around her. As she quieted down, Wally suggested they sit on the bench and talk.

"Did Nick know?" Wally's first question.

"Yes. We had just told my parents. We were planning on telling his mom. We were getting ready to set a date for our wedding. We had such plans for our future together." This memory brought a new set of sobs from Betsy; the future that would now never be.

"How are you feeling?" Wally's next concern.

Betsy again jumped up and paced nervously. "Wally, I was so excited when I learned I was pregnant. I loved Nick very much and he loved me. We had agreed to wait until we were married and have a real wedding night, but then there was a night when our emotions just got the best of us. When I found out I was expecting Nick's baby, I was so happy. He was too. We even tossed around some names for the baby. And now I've lost him and I don't know what to do!" Once again Betsy was crying so hard her entire body was shaking. She sat down on the bench and covered her face with her hands.

Wally awkwardly reached out and put his hand on her shoulder to console her. He couldn't help feeling sympathy for the situation she was in. Again, he asked, "What can I do to help?"

Betsy answered, "I don't know. I don't know what to do! Do you think I should tell Nick's mom about her coming grandchild? What will they think of me? Will they accept the baby?"

"Betsy, I can tell you this much. Nick and I were the only two people who never went out for mail call. We never got any mail. So, Betsy, I don't know much about Nick's mom except for the fact that she didn't write. I do know they lived on the reservation."

"Nick never talked much about his family. How am I going to tell them about the baby? What will they say? I'm so scared. Wally, what can I do? I don't know what to do!"

Just then Betsy leaned back, grimaced with pain, grabbed her stomach and groaned. Alarmed, Wally asked "Betsy, are you OK? What's wrong?"

"I don't know. It hurts. It hurts. Oh no, what's happening! Oh my God, the pain!" Betsy's face was pale and her eyes were wide with fright.

"I'll get an ambulance." Wally ran for the closest gate, the main entrance. In no time an ambulance was picking Betsy up and racing her to sick bay.

Betsy was still having serious pain as she was wheeled into the clinic. Wally waited outside. Time seemed to crawl by. Then the door opened and in came Gunny and his duty driver. "I want to stay on top of this. I was informed the girl was in here. What is going on?"

"Gunny, I need to talk to you privately." Gunny directed the duty driver to wait in the car. Wally then told Gunny everything that Betsy had told him, knowing Gunny would understand the information would be kept confidential. He then explained that the sudden pain Betsy had experienced was the reason she was brought to sick bay.

Gunny took in all that Wally had to say without comment. He put his hand under his chin and appeared to be mulling something over. Then he said "I have two questions for you. First, are you all right?"

"I'm OK" Wally replied. "I tried to sleep, but I guess I was just too keyed up. I'm sure I'll get some rest tonight."

"They will be shipping Nick's body back to Minnesota in the morning," Gunny said. "As you know, it is customary to have two Marines accompany the body home and stay until after burial. You were his bunk mate and friend. Would you be willing to be one of those Marines?"

Wally never hesitated. "Of course!" He felt it was the least he could do for a friend to whom he owed so much. It was Nick who had taken him in hand and taught him how to be the most squared away, how to have the shiniest brass, shoes, and helmet possible. He tutored Wally in even the smallest details, such as getting his uniform pockets sewn shut so they would lie flat. He even showed him how to keep his cigarettes in his sock. All Marines did that so there were no bulges in their uniform. They had often double-dated, but that was before Betsy came into the picture.

Gunny had one more question: "Could you recommend someone to go with you?" Wally immediately thought of Tom. He knew Tom's calm, steady manner would be a tremendous asset on such a trip. And so, it was agreed Tom would be the second Marine.

Just as they settled on the assignment, the door opened and the nurse came out to talk to the men. She explained they couldn't do much for Betsy at sick bay. She needed to see her own doctor, but she was in no condition to drive herself. Wally was given permission to drive her to her doctor. Her parents were going to meet her there. Gunny agreed to stay at sick bay while Wally went with the duty driver to pick up her car.

As Wally drove Betsy, he realized he didn't have his military driver's license with him. No time to stop and get it now. The doctor's office was halfway between where Betsy lived on Half Moon Bay and the base. Betsy's pain had eased somewhat, but she still needed to be seen.

In the car, Betsy had questions. She asked Wally what would be done with Nick's body.

"When Nick's body is released, Tom and I will be his military escort back to the reservation in Minnesota. I don't know any more than that until I get further orders."

Suddenly a car came whizzing by, passing them on the left. It was a red convertible with a mattress sticking up out of the back seat. "What an odd way to transport a mattress!" Betsy said. "Don't you wonder why he's in such a hurry?" Despite her pain, Betsy was trying to lighten the situation.

"Yeah," said Wally, catching her attempt at humor. "If that mattress blows off, it could ruin his weekend."

"Maybe he's a psychiatrist making a house call." The silliness seemed to break the tension. It was followed by a few minutes of comfortable silence. Betsy's labored breathing and clenching hands were the only indications of the pain she was still having.

Betsy wanted to know if there was a way she could also go to Minnesota. She wanted to see where Nick's final resting place would be and spoke of other reasons she wanted to go.

Wally replied, saying he didn't really know. So far, he had not been given details on the trip. "But", he reasoned, "I don't see how they could stop you if you pay your own way." Wally promised to stay in touch as soon as he found out the plans.

"Wally, will you do a favor for me? My father was a Marine, and I know there is a special brotherhood between Marines. Would you be willing to talk with him about my going to Minnesota?"

"I have your six," Wally replied.

"I don't understand. What is that?"

"If something is coming at you from the front, it is 12:00. If something is coming at you from the side, that would be 3:00. But if it is coming from behind, it is six. I know your dad would understand that I will protect you and keep you safe."

Pulling into the doctor's parking lot, Betsy found her parents there and anxiously waiting for her. Giving both a quick hug, and introducing Wally, they hurried Betsy into the office. Betsy was immediately taken to a room. Her mother went with her. Wally and Mr. Miller settled in to the reception area to wait.

"Were you with Betsy when she went to the sick bay doctor?"

"Yes sir."

"Please call me Joe. What brought this on? What happened?"

"I'm not sure, Mr. ...uh, Joe. All I know is that she was very upset about Nick's death. She told me about the pregnancy. She was crying very hard and suddenly she was in extreme pain. I was worried about her and wanted to get her medical attention right away."

"I thank you for your concern and prompt action." As Joe was saying this, a young boy was being wheeled in. When the boy came closer, Wally could see a makeshift dressing on his foot. Blood was seeping out through the dressing. Wally's mind immediately flashed back to the horrific scene in the gate house and he felt sick. He closed his eyes.

"Are you OK son?" Joe asked.

"I'm OK"

Joe was aware that something else was going on, but kept it to himself.

"Betsy wanted me to ask you something. She wants to go to Nick's funeral in Minnesota. She seems to have a deep need to see where Nick is to be buried. She wants to see where he grew up. She wants to meet his family and understand his culture. She wants these things for her child. But you needn't worry if she goes. Betsy told me you were a Marine, so you know two Marines always accompany the body back to the deceased's home. I will be accompanying Nick. I can see you are a caring father. I can assure you I will watch over her and keep her safe."

"When do you leave?"

"I don't know yet. When I get back to base, I will check with Gunny and when I know more, I will call you."

The nurse came out and told Betsy's father that she was getting dressed and could go home. "It was nothing serious," she explained soothingly. "Just a bad case of nerves. Understandable after such upsetting news."

"How are you getting back to base? Do you need a ride? I would be happy to drive you. Betsy's mom can take her home." Wally was very appreciative of the offer.

On the way back to Hunter's Point Naval Shipyard, Wally asked Joe about his time in the Marine Corps. "I was a house mouse in boot camp, so when I got stationed in Camp Pendleton, I had a similar duty in Supply." Wally knew a house mouse was a very special duty. Where most men would come out as Private, the two men chosen for this duty would come out as Meritorious PFC, the next rank up. When Wally would go to the DI's Quonset hut, he would see the house mouse doing various clerical tasks. It was a duty that required trustworthiness because some of the information they handled had to be kept confidential. As the second world war saying went, "Loose lips sink ships."

"One day," Joe continued, "I was not feeling well, so I went to the Camp Pendleton sick bay. There I saw the most beautiful woman I ever laid eyes on. It was Betsy's mother and she was my nurse. I am always telling her she was so lucky I got sick that day. But she says I was lucky she was on duty. All I know is I won the lottery that day. She is a very special lady. By the way, don't forget to call us once you know about Nick's arrangements?" Wally assured him he would call. Joe dropped Wally off at the gate.

Returning to the Marine barracks, Wally lost no time in reporting to Gunny's office. "Sit down", Gunny said. He first asked about Betsy and was relieved to learn it was nothing serious. "Well son, earlier today Nick's mother was notified. She said she wanted Nick buried on their reservation and according to their traditions. I have decided, due to the delicate nature of Nick's death that I will send Lt. Good with you. He will meet with the tribal chief and coordinate plans in accordance with the military funeral Nick is entitled to and the tribal traditions the family wants. You will be leaving in the morning with Nick's body. When you return, you will have your formal interrogation. John's court martial will follow in approximately 6 weeks."

Gunny noticed Wally was looking very tired. "Did you get a chance to eat?" Learning Wally had not eaten and knowing chow time was just concluding, Gunny called over to the mess hall to tell them to hold dinner for Wally. "I want to see you and Tom in the morning before we leave. Go now, eat, and get some rest.

When Wally returned to the squad bay, tired though he was, he checked in with Tom. "I just saw Gunny. Nick's body will be shipped out tomorrow. Gunny wants to meet with us in the morning before we go. Nick's girlfriend came to the base to talk to me this morning. She was pretty upset and I wound up taking her to her doctor. She is OK, just really rattled. It looks like she will be going to Duluth for the funeral. Oh shoot, I still have to call her! How did you do with Angie? Did you get ahold of her? How did she take the news?"

"She was stunned. She asked me where he was. I told her he was taken to the brig on Treasure Island. She wanted to know if she could go visit him. But I didn't know that. I didn't know of anyone who had ever gone there."

Tom had promised Angie he would keep her informed, so he accompanied Wally downstairs to the pay phones.

Afterward, Tom and Wally discussed their phone calls. Wally asked how Angie was doing. "To my surprise, she was laughing and talkative. She even asked if we could meet up sometime. Wally, do you think she is just a gate girl?"

"I don't know, man. I know John thought a lot of her"

Tom asked about Betsy. "Her dad said she was doing much better. She is really looking forward to seeing the reservation and meeting Nick's people. Her mom offered to go with her, but Betsy felt this was something she needed to do alone."

As the two men ascended the staircase, taps came on over the barracks loudspeaker. "Taps, taps, lights out." The exit light over the door provided just enough illumination for each man to get to their respective bunks.

It seemed odd to Wally that Nick was not above him. Then with a little macabre humor he realized Nick just *might* be above him—way above him. His last thought was that he hoped so.

Chapter 3

The next thing Wally heard was reveille—the trumpet that announced "You gotta get up. You gotta get up. You gotta get up in the morning." Wally jumped up and raced for the shower, hoping to beat all the other guys headed that way. He knew his day would be busy and unpredictable.

Gunny's voice came over the loudspeaker. "In the barracks. In the barracks[1]. We will be providing a bus for all men not on duty who would like to go see Nick off. Summer khaki uniforms are required for those who choose to go. Class will be suspended for today. The bus will leave at 0900."

Next stop for Wally and Tom after chow was Gunny's office. Lt Good had already arrived. Gunny began "The transport plane is scheduled to leave at 1000. It should get into Minnesota at 1800. Join me on the bus at 0900. Wear your summer khaki's, but pack your dress blues." Now addressing Lt Good, Gunny said "We contacted a hotel yesterday for your stay. As far as

---

1 *Military speak for "Listen up, listen up."

chow goes, we are going to cut you a check. It shouldn't exceed $15 a day per person."

Wally asked for the name of the motel so he could give it to Betsy, if permitted. "The Totem." Gunny replied. Wally and Tom were dismissed so they could go and pack.

Wally squeezed in a short phone call to Betsy to let her know they would be staying at a hotel called The Totem. Once she arrived, she could check at the front desk for their room number. He explained departure would be at ten o'clock and arrival about three. As far as he knew nothing would happen until the next day.

Betsy's voice broke a bit as she said "You don't know how much I appreciate all you have done. I never thought I would ever wind up in such a circumstance, but I believe this is God's plan for me."

Wally was touched by her earnestness, but all he could add was a lame "If there's anything I can do...I've got to go get on the bus now. Hope we can connect up in Minnesota."

As Wally was boarding the bus, he glanced at the flag. It was at half-staff in Nick's honor.

The bus took them to the airport. The men filed off and lined up behind the hearse. Gunny selected six men plus Wally and Tom to carry Nick's casket, and directed their placement around it. Lt. Good would follow the casket.

At Gunny's command "Forward, half-step, hooh." Slowly and carefully the casket was carried to the back of the transport plane, up the ramp, into the cargo bay. Gunny's command to halt could be heard outside. Next came the command to lower, then "Step back." Gunny then dismissed all but Lt. Good, Wally, and Tom. He turned to the three men and said "I have been in the Marine Corps twenty-three years. I have never encountered a situation like this. I know you men will conduct yourselves to the highest of Marine Corps standards. This is an especially delicate situation, but I have complete confidence that you will make me and the Corps proud of you." With that Gunny departed from the plane.

The flight crew came back and told the men to take a seat up against the bulk head. They then proceeded to tie down the casket and went through the usual preflight instructions with them.

Soon they were airborne. Talking in the noisy, barely insulated aircraft was all but impossible. Soon all three men took advantage of the opportunity to get some extra shuteye.

The floating sensation of the descending plane awakened them. Wheels hit the tarmac and soon the plane was taxiing toward a group of people, which included a regiment of local Marines.

The Marines entered the cargo bay and with precision removed Nick's casket and placed it in the transport vehicle. Going down the ramp, Wally could see a number of people, probably mostly from the reservation. Some looked to be Nick's age, others were older dignitaries. Even the newspaper photographer was present. Lt. Good asked about the chief, and was taken to a tiny distinguished-looking older man. Although he was very weather-worn, he was somehow quite handsome. Introductions were made and a short discussion ensued.

Lt. Good stood at the podium, gave a short eulogy, then turned the mike over to Chief White Horse. The Chief acknowledged the people who came: Nick's family, friends, and classmates. He explained there will be a regiment of Marines who will stay with Nick's body until burial. This is the Marine custom. But Nick's funeral and burial would be according to tribal traditions. Perhaps the Chief would have said more, but a clap of thunder from the threatening sky probably changed his plans. He suggested everyone should go to a safe place before the storm hit. He and Lt. Good got into a waiting car.

Tom, Wally, and the other Marines got into the two cars which followed the transport vehicle.

The casket was then taken to the reservation tribal center. Since other Marines would stay with Nick's body for the time being, Tom and Wally were given a car to take to The Totem hotel. Lt. Good stayed at the tribal center to talk with Chief White Horse.

"Sir, would you like us to wait for you?" Tom asked.

"The car you came here in will be yours to use during your stay, courtesy of the local Marines. Go check in and then go get something to eat. Pick up something for me, as well. I will join you later this evening."

No one was at the desk in the motel. Wally rang the bell. While they waited, they looked around. On the wall was a picture of Roy Rogers and Dale Evans, done in colorful little tiles. When the clerk came out, they asked about the picture and were told that the couple once spent the night there. The owner wanted to commemorate the visit in that way. After getting their room assignment, they asked for a place to eat—not fancy, but good food. The clerk suggested Singin' Sandy's. Wally asked if there was a reservation for Betsy Miller. "Yes, she is due in tomorrow about 2:00 p.m."

Singin' Sandy's was a pleasant surprise. It was homey, with a friendly vibe. There was a magazine rack with the daily newspaper for patrons to sit a spell with coffee and perhaps a piece of pie or a pastry. Instead of being shut away, the kitchen was in plain view, separated by just a half wall and the chef visible as she prepared the orders. It was nearly closing time, however, and the place was almost empty. The chef was singing as they walked in. The waitress, high school age at best, came immediately to take their order.

"Do you have any chow left for two hungry Marines?"

When the chef heard that, she immediately stopped singing and said "Anything you want, honey. You name it; I'll fix it. Then she started singing "You're in the Marine Corps now; you're not behind a plow. You'll never get rich by digging a ditch, you're Marine Corps now." A takeoff on the World War One song "You're in the Army now…"

As the waitress handed Sandy the order, she switched to "Get out in that kitchen and rattle those pots and pans…" Sandy's songs were always just snippets of the original, sung loud and slightly off key. But it didn't matter to her—she loved to sing. And it didn't matter to her regulars. They loved Sandy.

Wally paid for their orders, picked up Lt. Good's order and headed for the front door. Since they were the last customers to leave by then, Sandy came out of the kitchen and gave each of them a hug and a box with some extra homemade cookies. "These are my mom's incredible edible chocolate chip, peanut butter, oatmeal cookies. Y'all come back now!" They promised her they would do just that.

On the way back to The Totem, Tom chuckled. "Did you see how Sandy was dressed? The bell bottoms, the tie around her forehead? She looked like something straight out of North Beach. She seems to have a great sense of humor. I have a feeling she would be a lot of fun to know. Not too shabby on the eyes, either."

Wally agreed. "Yeah, she seems nice."

Once in their room, the two men got squared away and then prepared for bed. There was a knock at the door and Lt. Good stepped in to bring them up to date. The men sat on their beds, giving the Lieutenant the desk chair so he could eat as he talked.

Lt. Good gave them a brief outline of what would happen the next day. "Even now there is a wake being held at the Tribal Center. Family members will take turns holding vigil there. There is a bonfire outside and that, too, will be maintained by family from now until Nick's burial. Two Marines are currently stationed with the body. You two will relieve them at 0800 tomorrow morning. Your duty will last until 0400. You will then be relieved again by local Marines. Wear your dress blues. That will be our schedule until the morning of Nick's funeral. Outside, there will be a big feast and you have been welcomed to share the meal with tribal members. You can take turns eating. There will be music. People will be coming and going."

Both Wally and Tom had been concerned about how the tribal members would view their intrusion onto the reservation, given the probability that Nick had been shot by a fellow Marine. They asked Lt. Good about how he was being received by Chief White Horse. "He has been very grateful that we brought Nick's body back. He appreciates how well the Marines take care of their fallen. He anticipated there might be resentment by some, and he has already addressed that. He appears to be highly respected, almost revered, among the tribal members. I have been surprised and pleased by the level of cooperation

I have experienced with him. He is a very intelligent man. I did promise him we would send a full report after the trial."

With that, Lt. Good took his leave, wishing each a good night.

Chapter 4

The next day was a pleasant surprise for Tom and Wally. As the two men stood at their station, many tribal members came up and greeted them warmly. Most expressed appreciation that the military would so thoughtfully return Nick's body to his tribe. A few asked for details about what happened to Nick, but were understanding when told it was not something they could talk about until after the trial. There even were questions about how to join the Marines, what daily life was like, etc. These questions Wally and Tom were happy to answer.

About noon, two women and a young girl approached them and introduced themselves. The older woman was Nick's mother. She was the kind of person one would instantly like. She had a big smile and affectionately greeted each man with a hug; first Tom and then Wally. She invited both men to come and have lunch with them. Wally said he would go first, and that would give him a chance to talk with Nick's mother.

Tom explained to the mother he would stay until Wally returned. As Wally left, Tom was already deep in conversation with the lively young woman who had introduced herself as

Becca, Nick's sister. The little girl, Annie, accompanied Wally and her mother out to the tables filled with potluck food. Annie's forehead was smeared with something black. This puzzled Wally, but he was too polite to ask about it. He noticed all the children were similarly marked. He supposed it was some traditional symbol of mourning.

The tables were groaning with food. There were foods prepared with venison, fish, wild rice, and many other casseroles on the tables. They filled their plates and sat down to eat.

Nick's mother asked Nick to call her Minnie. She explained that it was tribal custom for each family to contribute food each day until the funeral. They would be welcome to eat there at any time.

Wally told Minnie about the deep friendship he had with Nick, and how much Nick had meant to him. Right from the first day they had hit it off. He told how he would have felt lost if Nick hadn't taken him in hand and showed him how to be the best Marine he could possibly be. "Nick had the shiniest shoes, brass, rifle stock, and he showed me how to do the same. In the Marine Corp we call that being 'squared away'. I miss him very much and I know I will never forget him."

At this Minnie nodded. "Yes, that sounds like my Nick. He always tried to be his best. After his father died, Nick took over the responsibilities a father normally would do. He watched over his sisters, did little repairs around the house, and tried to take good care of me. He always was ambitious, wanting something better for us. There isn't a lot of work here on the reservation, and we didn't have a car so he couldn't get a job off the reservation. He joined the Marine Corp because he saw it as a way to earn an income. He sent us a little money every month. He would call us once a week. He was always asking about this one or that one and giving me advice on how to handle a problem I might have had. And, yes, he did mention you. He thought a lot of you. He was more than a beloved son. Some people leave a hole in your heart that can never be filled. He was such a man."

"Did Nick ever talk to you about having a girlfriend?" Wally asked. "Betsy? Oh yes! All the time. He loved her so much, and he promised me I would be meeting her soon. I regret now that I never will. She was such an important part of his life."

"Well, actually, Betsy is coming here for the funeral, if that would be all right with you. She should be here about two o'clock. I know she wanted to meet you and all of Nick's family. Would it be convenient if I brought her to your house after dinner tonight? I'm sure you would like her once you meet her."

"Oh my—I would be delighted to meet her! From all that Nick has told me about her I already know I will like her. It will be like getting something of Nick back. Please do bring her."

All during their conversation, people were stopping by and giving Minnie hugs and pats on the shoulder. They were too polite to interrupt, but Wally realized Minnie had other people to see and other things to do. Getting contact information from her, Wally excused himself and relieved Tom so he could go get some lunch. Becca and Tom were still deep in conversation as she accompanied him out to the tables.

When their shift was over, the men returned to The Totem. Wally checked at the desk to see if Betsy had arrived. She'd left a message for him to call her room. They had time to change from their dress blues back into their summer khakis.

They met up in the lobby. The men had coffee. Betsy got a bottle of water. There was the usual small talk: "How was your flight?"

"Fine, no problems, good weather all the way." Then came the questions. "When is the funeral?"

This is where Tom chimed in. He had gleaned a lot of information while talking to Becca. "This tribe has different ways of handling a death of one of its tribal members. Some elect to have a modern funeral. A few of the older members still like to go the way of their ancestors. Nick's mom has chosen to blend the military funeral, to which Nick is entitled, with the Old Ways."

"Last night Nick's body was brought to the tribal center on the reservation. There is a belief that Nick's soul is on a journey that will take four days to complete. Each of the days has a special tradition to be followed. So even yesterday as we were landing, the tribe was preparing."

"A bonfire was started outside the tribal center. They believe as Nick's spirit completes each day of his journey and he stops to rest for the night, he too builds a bonfire. In this way they can communicate with his spirit. The bonfire will burn continuously until the burial. Also, last night family members began keeping round the clock vigil by Nick's body. That, too, will continue until the funeral. Day one was the day Nick was killed. Today is day two. There will be two more days of traditional activities, and Nick will be buried on the morning of the fifth day."

Wally then picked up the narrative. "Today Tom and I had day duty in the tribal center. Outside was Feast Day. Each family in the tribe contributed food to the table. People were coming and going, visiting Nick in the casket, then going outside and eating. About noon, Nick's mom came in. I don't know if Nick told you, but her name is Minnie. I went out to eat lunch with her. We had a nice visit. She is a very sweet lady, but a very strong lady. I learned that Nick had already told her a lot about you. She is well aware of how much Nick loved you and she is very excited to meet you. She was hoping you and I could stop by at her house after dinner this evening."

Betsy next asked when she would get to see Nick.

Tom again spoke up. "Apparently this is a touchy situation. We outsiders must wait until we are invited to a viewing. It will be a tribal decision, with the wishes of the mother weighing heavily. Perhaps you will learn more tonight."

"Well, I guess, then, the next step will be to go to visit Nick's mom. I have been very excited about meeting her." Betsy gave an almost imperceptible sideways glance at Wally and added, "And, perhaps, a little scared."

"You needn't worry," said Wally, not understanding Betsy's concern. "She is a warm and friendly personality. You will feel very comfortable around her. And I will be there with you. You won't be alone."

"Betsy," Tom said, "we have discovered a wonderful little restaurant. Will you join us for dinner?"

"Do I need to change?"

At that, both men chuckled. "No, this is a very informal place."

As they entered Singin' Sandy's, the chef recognized them. As she worked, she stopped long enough to give them a big smile and a salute. Betsy smiled too and said "I'm liking this place already."

The restaurant was much busier at this time of day. But Sandy was still singing, this time a bit of "Hello Dolly" Betsy suspected that might be for her.

Sandy kept watching them as she worked and they settled in, decided on their orders, then chatted as their meals were being prepared. She was intrigued. Two guys, one very pretty young woman. Was she a girlfriend of one of them? Which one? One man was tall and fair-haired. The other was just as tall with dark wavy hair. Both men were very good-looking, each in his own way. Both were lean and muscular, the epitome of the fighting Marine.

Sandy thought she picked up a spark between the woman and the dark-haired man, but she wasn't sure. The woman seemed to listen a little more intently when he spoke. He, on the other hand, seemed to have a tender, almost protective way of looking at her. Sandy hoped her instincts were correct, because she personally favored the fair-haired guy. Neither was wearing a wedding ring, but that doesn't always mean something. Sandy decided she would like to get to know these people better.

At the table the three were discussing the upcoming visit. Betsy was feeling very anxious about meeting Nick's family. One question she had was about Nick's mother. She asked Wally how Minnie was coping with Nick's death.

Shaking his head, lowering it, and pondering a moment, Wally replied. "Actually, I was surprised when we talked at lunch. She isn't as unhappy as I had expected her to be. She said that because of her strong faith and belief system, she would be OK. But Minnie had many questions about you, Betsy, that I couldn't answer. She really wants to know more about this sweet lady that her son loved so much. Tom, you also met Minnie and Becca. What did you think about how they are doing?"

"Oh, I definitely agree with you, Nick. They are two very strong women. Nick's mom is handling the death of her only son amazingly well. I did mention that to Becca. She also stated that is because of their beliefs. She actually told me quite a bit about the Ojibwa belief system. Even though she is only a senior in high school, she seems unusually mature intellectually."

"Becca told me the Ojibwa people believe they have within them the spirit of the Anishinaabe. It occupies the physical body during their lifetime. They believe in a Creator and that the Creator put us on earth for a reason. They are deeply spiritual and communicate with the Creator for guidance and wisdom. I believe that is where the inner strength that Minnie and Becca possess comes from."

"I don't want to change the subject," Tom continued, "but do you see that man over there reading the newspaper. I keep looking at him. He is a dead ringer for a guy I went to school with. One spring day he and I decided to skip school. Once we made the decision, we were trying to figure out what to do with our stolen day. Tim had this old rusty pickup. He was just driving around when he suddenly pulled over to the side of the road. He jumped out of the truck, went over and picked up a roadkill raccoon and threw it in the truck. He got back in and said 'Let's see how many of these things we can find.' Now we were two guys on a mission. Somewhere along the way we found a cardboard box, so we loaded all the carcasses into that. We intended to dump them all on a friend's porch. But we got a better idea as we were driving by the police station..."

"No!" said Betsy.

"Oh yes, we did. We emptied that box just inside the door of the state police post and then ran like crazy."

"Did you get caught?"

"No, but looking back, it was a miracle we didn't."

Now Betsy had a story to share. "Well, I skipped school once as well. I was sitting in a friend's car at school. There were four of us. Students and teachers were walking to school and we waved at everyone we knew. It was a beautiful May morning just before school let out for the summer. Then someone said 'Let's skip school.' 'Where would we go?' 'To the zoo!'"

"Now isn't that just the dumbest thing? So many people had seen us. Everyone, even teachers, would know. But we never considered that. Two of us had packed lunches that we could share. The other two had money for hot lunch, which we could use for gas. So off we went."

"We pretty much had the zoo to ourselves, except for one strange little man who followed us and peeked around trees and bushes at us. He was so little any one of us could have taken him on, so he didn't worry us much. In fact, at times we would tease him and peek back. Everything about that day was fun."

"We went to the gorilla house. There was a massive gorilla in there all by himself. He was seated in a chair in the far corner, with his back to us. Once a family left, my friend Barbara began making gorilla noises. To our surprise, the gorilla got up, turned and slowly walked over to the edge of the cage right in front of us and watched Barbara. Now she really started to cut up, jumping up and down and rocking from side to side. Amazingly, the gorilla would imitate each move she made. We were all laughing so hard. Then some more people came in and Barbara had to stop for a bit. When she stopped, the gorilla turned and went back to his chair. Once the people left, Barbara tried to reengage him, but he was done."

Wally and Tom were laughing at her story, but Betsy wasn't done. "Next we went to Monkey Island and saw another interesting sight. Someone had thrown a tiny child's red tennis shoe in the enclosure. One monkey had the shoestring in his mouth, and the shoe dangled from that. The other monkeys wanted it. Round and round they went, scrambling up rocks, jumping across rocks, skittering down rocks. One by one, the monkeys got smart and quit chasing him. Eventually there were no more monkeys chasing him. What did the monkey do? He went up to one of the monkeys and swung the tennis shoe back and forth by the shoestring. And the chase was on again. But the chaser soon realized he was not going to be successful. He gave up. The monkey tried hard to interest another monkey in chasing him, but he had no success. What do you think that monkey did next?"

"What?" said both men almost in unison.

"The monkey dropped the tennis shoe and walked away from it. I always thought there was a lesson in there somewhere for humans. What do you think?"

"Maybe we want what the other guy has?" Tom offered.

Wally suggested "Perhaps the more difficult something is to obtain, the more we want it."

Betsy felt those ideas both had merit, and she added, "I often wondered about that. I felt possibly we value things because we have them and nobody else does. Once nobody else wants them, then we no longer want them either. We move on to something new."

"OK Wally, what's your story?"

"I hate to disappoint you, but I was a Boy Scout and tried to live by their strict code. I always tried to do the right thing; never did skip school. Boring, right?"

"Oh no, not at all." Both Betsy and Tom chimed in together.

"Well, I guess I do have a story, too. Not about me, but about two other guys in my class. One day they skipped school and put an entire box of laundry detergent in the city fountain. I guess it made one giant bubble bath."

Tom wanted to talk to the man with the newspaper, so he excused himself. Wally asked Betsy how she was doing. He had noticed her wince a couple of times during dinner, as though she was still having pain issues. But Betsy, not wanting to worry anyone, said she was fine, just a little tired. Wally felt that wasn't exactly true, but had to take her at her word for now. They continued with small talk about the good food, the nice weather.

They did notice Tom was no longer talking to the man and had gone over to the half wall to talk with Sandy as she worked. Soon Tom returned to the table, beaming. "We've been invited to go out for drinks after Sandy closes up tonight."

We'd better get going," Wally said. "Betsy and I are going over to talk with Nick's mom in a few minutes. We can discuss it on the way."

In the car, however, Betsy said she really preferred not to be out late. But they didn't want to disappoint Sandy. It was decided they would go back to Singin' Sandy's for pie and coffee about nine o'clock. If Tom wanted to stay and Sandy would bring him back to the hotel, they could split up then. They dropped Tom off at The Totem and said they would be back to pick him up before nine o'clock. Then they drove to Nick's mom's house. The one thing Betsy said in the car was "I'm glad you are with me, Wally. I don't know if I could do this alone."

Chapter 5

As they entered the reservation, Wally and Betsy were surprised by the level of poverty they were witnessing. Wally had been too distracted to notice it before. The homes were small. Some sported makeshift repairs. Many more needed repairs. Window screens were torn or nonexistent. There were few screen doors. Rusted cars were pushed off to the side, waiting for parts that never could be afforded. Dogs and cats roamed the streets. There was little grass, and what existed generally was not mowed. Broken toys, dirty from road dust were scattered about.

But then there were the children. Oh, the children. Laughing and tumbling, running and playing, giggling and screeching in the darkening light of the day. Beautiful children with coal black hair and eyes, brown skin the color of a permanent tan. They were completely oblivious to the disintegration that surrounded them, secure in the arms of their tribe. Here every playmate was a brother, a sister, a cousin, and every adult was family. This was their world and it was everything to them. Betsy wondered if her baby would be as beautiful as these children. She fervently hoped so.

One thing did puzzle Betsy. All of the children had something black smeared across their foreheads. She asked Wally about it, but he didn't know why either. He did tell her he had noticed it earlier on Annie, Nick's little sister. They entertained the idea that perhaps it was some type of mourning symbol. Yet, the adults did not have their foreheads darkened. Curious!

Minnie's home was slightly better than most. It was similarly small, but neatly painted white. There were a few decorative touches; shutters on the lone front window, a window box with geraniums planted in it. The blue of the shutters brought out the red of the geraniums. There was an air conditioner in a side window, something not noticed in the other homes.

Minnie had mentioned to Wally at lunch that Nick sent home money each month. He wondered if that was how she afforded the modest improvements he saw here.

Somehow Minnie had managed to make the exterior of her home reflect her warm and welcoming personality. When you saw it, you instinctively knew good people lived here.

As they started up the front steps, the door was flung open by a tiny roundish woman with a huge smile and sparkling eyes. It was as if she had been watching for their arrival. Betsy knew immediately this must be Nick's mother. Behind her stood a teenager with an equally large grin; white teeth gleaming in a very pretty face. Peeking out shyly behind Becca, one finger in her mouth, was the little girl named Annie.

Minnie immediately enfolded Betsy in a big hug. What *was* it about this woman? Betsy immediately felt safe and welcomed.

That was followed by a hug from Becca; Annie continuing to glue herself to Becca's leg.

With a sweep of her arm, Becca invited Betsy to sit down. Betsy chose the sofa and Becca sat beside her. Annie, staying close to Becca, chose the third sofa cushion for herself. Wally lowered himself into the rocker, which placed him to Betsy's right side, and Minnie settled into the well-worn easy chair next to Annie. The furniture formed a half-circle in the small living room. On the open side of the circle, against the wall, was a TV on a fold-up table. Other than a lamp on a matching fold-up table between the sofa and the easy chair, there was no more furniture. One large picture hung behind the TV; a collage of family photographs. Although the room was spartan, everything seemed very clean. The floor, some sort of vinyl, was worn but looked to have been freshly scrubbed.

A fluffy grey cat emerged from the hallway to see what the fuss was all about. Surveying the company, she must have decided they weren't worth her attention. She turned disdainfully and quietly padded back down the hall.

Betsy broke the silence by asking about the cat. It was Annie who answered, explaining it was her cat and the cat's name was Frieda. "Frieda, that's an interesting name. Why did you pick that name?"

"I don't know, I just liked it."

"How old is Frieda?"

"Well, she was just a kitten last year, so I guess she is about one now."

"And how old are you?"

"I am 6."

Annie grinned for the first time and Betsy could see a tooth missing in the front." "Oh, you lost a tooth!"

"Yes, the tooth fairy took my tooth and put a nickel under my pillow."

Betsy then asked Annie what she planned to do with her nickel. Annie's earnest reply made everyone chuckle "I'm saving it for college."

"Oh, my!" Betsy exclaimed, "Have you decided what you are going to study in college?"

"I'm going to be a paleontologist."

"Wow!" That's a pretty big word. What does it mean?"

"It means you study dinosaurs. But I already know all about dinosaurs. Would you like to see my dinosaurs?"

At that point Minnie gently broke in, "Another time, Annie. We grownups would like to talk a bit. Why don't you run outside and play."

Annie obediently got up and went to the front door. As she was leaving, she turned, looked at Betsy, gave her a big gap-toothed grin, and then disappeared into the darkness, quietly closing the door behind her.

"That child," Minnie smiled, "she'd talk your arm off once she gets to know you." Continuing, she asked "So how was your flight?"

"Very smooth, thank you."

"You live in San Francisco?"

"Yes, I live with my parents, not too far from the base where Nick was stationed."

"How did you and Nick meet?"

"Well my girlfriend, Bella, was going on a date with a guy named Jerry. They were going to see a movie. It was a movie

Nick wanted to see too, so Bella asked me to come along. The name of the movie was 'The Birds and the Bees', with George Gobel. It was very funny and we laughed all the way through it. At some point Nick reached over and took my hand. I remember electricity just shot all through my body." Then Betsy, remembering who she was talking to, blushed and fell silent.

Minnie noted the blush and its significance, but remained silent. Betsy recovered and continued. "Anyway, Nick called me a few nights later and asked me if I would like to meet him for coffee. We talked for four hours and didn't run out of things to say."

Minnie and Becca both laughed. "That sure sounds just like Nick. He was definitely a talker."

At this point, Becca jumped to her feet, "Goodness—where are my manners! What would you like to drink? I have coffee, lemonade, and pop. And I made you some special cookies." Wally asked for a Coke and Betsy chose lemonade. Betsy offered to help, but Becca simply said "It's all ready. You stay right there and chat with my mom."

During this time, Wally had remained silent, allowing the women time to get to know one another. But now he commented on how lovely the geraniums were out front. "Yes," Minnie agreed, "they were a Mother's Day gift from my girls. They spoil me, I'm afraid."

Becca was back with drinks and cookies—Wally's favorite, chocolate chip. Wally remembered they were Nick's favorite, too, and a wave of sadness washed over him.

Now Betsy asked about the funeral. When would it be and could she attend? Minnie explained that when Chief White Horse came to her and told her of Nick's death, he allowed her to choose the way in which she wished to celebrate Nick's passing.

Celebrate? Betsy thought. What an odd way to describe a funeral. But Minnie continued, telling how she pondered on it. She had seen many different kinds of funerals in her lifetime, both on and off the reservation. But the one type she always felt a connection to was the one sometimes utilized by her tribe for many generations back.

"You see," she explained, "we Ojibwa believe in the power of ancestral spirits. When a tribal member dies, it gives us an opportunity to connect with the spirit world through ceremony and song. Providing spiritual ceremony for the passing of a loved one leads to a positive journey for the deceased and gives comfort to those left behind. You see, we believe Nick's spirit is with us for four days as he travels on a journey down an unknowable path. He is lonely and does not want to leave. We must let him know we love him and will always honor him and show him that we will be OK

"The first day of Nick's passing was pretty much spent in preparation for his arrival from California. We were cooking and baking and cleaning. The men were setting up tables and gathering wood for the bonfire. Once the fire is lit, it must not be allowed to go out. It is tended around the clock. That is why so much wood must be gathered.

"The second day is Feast Day. Now family members take turns staying by the casket. Someone is always there. We do that so no evil spirits can creep in. Evil spirits are especially active at this time. Tomorrow will be my vigil.

"On the third day, which is tomorrow, there will be many ceremonies. There is always singing and dancing during these four days, but tomorrow is special.

"There will be drumming. Drums are special to our people. Their circular shape represents the circle of life. The rhythm represents the rhythm of life.

"There will be hoop dancing. The hoop is another symbol of the never-ending cycle of life.

"Some of the women will don jingle dresses. It is made in this way: several rows of metal cones are sewn on a dress. They will create a jingling sound as the dancers move. When you see them tomorrow, notice how they will move. They will be very light on their feet, barely touching the ground. You will see the dancers turn to the right and turn to the left as they dance, but you will never see them turn completely around. That is forbidden. Also, you will see they do not dance in a straight line forward, but rather in a crooked line like that which a snake would make. The dancers' feet do not cross and they never dance backward. This dance is a healing dance. Often if a child is sick, the performance of this dance will help the child recover. It helps us during our mourning period as well.

"By the way, did you notice the paper snake hanging by the door as you came in? It is made for family members to keep the evil spirits out. Like humans, they are afraid of snakes. This lets the evil spirits know Nick must make his journey alone."

Betsy and Wally had not noticed the snake on the way in, perhaps because their attention had been drawn to the flowers, and then to Minnie as she opened the door. Each made a mental note to look for the snake when they left.

Minnie continued to describe the ceremony. "On the fourth day the family will prepare Nick's body for burial. It will be cleaned. I requested the Old Way of preparing Nick. He will be dressed in special clothing. He will have moccasins placed on his feet. Then his body will be wrapped in birch bark. To us, birch bark is sacred and will protect his body from harm. Food and water will be placed by his body to help his soul travel to the land of everlasting happiness. Others will be making him little birch bark canoes to place in his casket. The canoes might have small gifts of food or other things he enjoyed in life, like his Clark licorice gum. Some might leave tools they believe he might need.

"Early on the morning of the fifth day, Nick will be buried. You are welcome to come and visit Nick's casket at any time. I hope you will also be a part of the ceremonies outside of the tribal center. You were special to Nick and you are special to us."

Betsy and Wally both found Minnie's description of the Ojibwa funeral process fascinating. There was so much more to these people than either had ever realized.

Betsy's next question was a request to attend Nick's funeral. She remembered Tom had said any outsiders would need special permission. "Of course, you can come! You too, Wally. And Tom. White Horse approached me earlier today and we discussed it. He said it would be up to me. I am honored that you came all this way for Nick's funeral. I wouldn't want to disappoint you in the least."

At this point Wally looked at his watch and stood up. "We thank you very much for the hospitality, but I'm afraid we must leave. We promised Tom we would pick him up and take him to

Singin' Sandy's." Chuckling, he added "I think he has a crush on her. You would be welcome to come too, if you wish."

Minnie declined, saying she needed to rest up for her vigil tomorrow. But Becca definitely wanted to go. "I *love* Singin' Sandy's. Can I go, Mom, please?" Wally assured Minnie he could bring her back about ten o'clock.

Annie came bouncing up the steps, eyes sparkling, face ruddy from exuberant play. Her demeanor immediately changed when she saw they were leaving. "Oh," she said, I wanted to show you my dinosaurs." Betsy assured Annie she would be back and she could look at them then. And she gave Annie a hug, which restored the happy look to her face.

Climbing into the car, Wally told Betsy, "It looks like you made a friend."

"Make that two friends—no three. I can tell Mom really likes you." Becca said affectionately.

The two women sat in the back. Wally acted like he was their chauffer. "And where would you two ladies like to go?"

Falling right into the game, Becca said in her most sophisticated voice, "Please take us to The Totem Hotel, Jeeves. We are only stopping there long enough to pick up a friend. Then on to Singin' Sandy's Restaurant where we will partake of a light snack."

"Very well, my ladies."

At the hotel, the "ladies" stayed in the back seat while Wally went to retrieve Tom. When the men got back, the gals were giggling. "What's so funny?" Tom asked.

"Oh, Becca just told the funniest story—tell it again, Becca. You do it so well."

"We were talking about picking wild rice. I was telling Betsy about one of the places where the rice grows. The town is named Pickens. Part of that town noses well out into the river, forcing the river to make a bend around it. There are about six or seven houses on that part of Pickens. We call that little settlement 'Pickens Nose'."

At that, more giggles. Wally thought to himself that Becca was good for Betsy. Her happy personality lifted Betsy's spirits.

As soon as Sandy saw them come in the door, she switched from the song she had been singing to a bit of Conway Twitty's "Hello, Darlin, it's been a long time..." This had them laughing again, with a thumbs up from Tom.

Once seated, Becca heartily recommended the chocolate pie. And that is what she and Betsy ordered. But the men wanted fruit pies; apple for Wally, cherry for Tom. Once Sandy heard Tom's order, she began singing "Can she bake a cherry pie, Billy Boy, Billy Boy. Can she bake a cherry pie charmin' Billy..."

More peals of laughter from the four of them. The restaurant was not terribly busy at that time of night, so Tom went over to the half wall to talk with Sandy. While there, he reached down and Wally saw him withdraw his pack of smokes from his sock. Wally immediately flashed back to John, sitting on the curb. John getting a cigarette from someone. What bothered him about that? What was it? Before he could sort out his thoughts, Tom returned to his pie, saying to Wally that Sandy would get him back to the hotel. Sandy was already beginning her cleanup routine. As they left, Sandy was showing Tom some cleanup tasks he could do.

On their way back to the reservation Becca asked if Betsy could spend the day at the house, since her mom had Vigil. There would be just Becca and Annie at the house. Wally felt that would be a good idea since he and Tom had Military Guard Duty at the tribal center. it was arranged that Wally would drop Betsy off in the morning. The house was within walking distance of the tribal center, so the women could easily go view the festivities during the day.

When Becca was safely inside her home, Betsy slid into the front seat beside Wally. "I'm glad you decided to spend the day with Becca. With both Tom and I on duty I wondered," wry smile, "what I was going to do with you."

Betsy caught the humor and retorted, "Oh, never worry about me. I can always find some sort of mischief to get into."

More seriously, Wally told her "You know, I have enjoyed our time together. You are good company."

"I could say the same about you."

Once at The Totem, Wally found he didn't want the evening to end so soon. "Would you like a Coke, or some more coffee? We could sit in the lobby and talk a bit. Or are you too tired?

"I am tired, but I wouldn't mind talking for a little while." So, Cokes in hand, they found a quiet spot and sat down, each in a comfortable chair.

"I am grateful you talked to my dad. I thought there would be some resistance to the idea of my coming here, but whatever you said must have hit home. He understood this was something I needed to do. He and Mom must have talked as well, because I encountered no resistance there either."

Wally remembered how pleasant Betsy's dad had been. Both being Marines, he felt there was a real connection there.

"I really liked your parents. It is nice to see two people still so much in love after a long marriage."

Betsy agreed "You don't know the half of it! They are always joking around with each other. Then there are the private jokes just between them. Just mention the word 'sand' and they both will laugh. When I ask why that word is so funny, they just pat me on the head and tell me I am too young to know. Come on, I'm twenty years old and I'm still too young to know?" Wally laughed at that.

"He can't keep his hands off her. Hugs. Kisses. They have their separate interests, but they are at their best when they are together. I always thought theirs was the kind of marriage I would have some day." Realizing what she had said, Betsy's voice broke on the last of her sentence and there was a great sadness in her eyes. She started to tear up, but recovered. "Enough about me. Tell me about you."

"You want to hear about my crazy family? I could talk for days about them. It has been a long day for you. I can see how tired you are. How about if we table that discussion for another time. Will you take a rain check?"

"Actually, that sounds great. I didn't realize how tired I was until I sank into this comfortable chair." Betsy agreed. "What time should I be ready in the morning?"

"How about if we meet here in the lobby at six thirty for the hotel breakfast?"

"Perfect. See you in the morning. Have a good evening."

Back in his room Wally was going over their conversation in his head. He realized Betsy had a lot more sadness than she let on.

Just then there was a soft knock at the door. It was Lt. Good. He walked in and his first question was "Where's Tom?"

Wally explained he'd made a friend of the owner of Singin' Sandy's Restaurant and after she closed, she was going to show Tom some of the local sights.

"I hope he conducts himself in the professional manner expected of a Marine on this mission."

"Tom is a very responsible guy, and I can assure you, he would never disappoint you or the Marine Corp. How are things going with White Horse?"

"Chief White Horse has been wonderful. Merging Marine Corp rituals with tribal customs has been easy because he is a gem to work with. He is very smart and solution-minded. You know, I'm only 26 and I've never traveled much, so it has been quite an honor to be given this responsibility. I want everything to go well. There are two things I want to ask you. I need to prepare a short eulogy. Nick was your friend and bunk mate. Can you give me a few things to add to my talk?"

"Well, you might say Nick was a great mentor and friend. He had very strong opinions on how things should be done."

"This is good. I can add these ideas to what I am going to say. Second question Lance Corporal, has anyone told Minnie about the pregnancy?"

Wally explained that no one has said anything yet. "We aren't sure how to approach it, but we are working on it."

"Good. I'll leave that up to you." That said, Lt. Good started for the door. But, with his hand on the door handle, he turned and said "Oh, by the way, I've been in contact with Gunny. I told him how conditions were here on the reservation. He has organized a collection among the men. So far, we have about

$195 that will be shipped here. You and Tom will be welcome to kick in a bit, and I will, too."

"I'll tell Tom and we'll see what we can do." Shortly after that Wally was in bed and out like a light. He never even heard Tom come in.

Chapter 6

The next morning Betsy met the two men in the lobby. At breakfast Betsy was eager to learn more about Tom's evening. Tom didn't have much to say, only that they had a good time and that Sandy was a lot of fun. "Do you think that you will see her again tonight?"

"You bet I will! Wally, do you think you could get me over to the restaurant about nine o'clock? If you can, Sandy will bring me back here. But if you can't, she'll pick me up. Our evening just would get a later start."

Wally agreed to take Tom to the restaurant. He told Tom about the collection Lt. Good had mentioned the night before. All three were happy to contribute what they could.

The men then took Betsy to Minnie's house to meet up with Becca. Betsy said she would walk over to the tribal center to meet them at 4:00 when their shift was done. That way they wouldn't have to drive to pick her up.

As Betsy was ascending the porch stairs, Minnie came out of the house, on the way to her morning vigil. The men offered her a lift. She gave Betsy a quick hug and hopped in the car.

Becca and Annie were at the door welcoming Betsy. Curiously, Annie's forehead was again blackened.

Annie immediately said, "Now can I show you my dinosaurs?" Both women smiled at Annie's eager question.

"Of course you can! I would love to see your dinosaurs." Annie led them back to the bedroom she shared with her sister. There were little plastic dinosaurs on every surface. There were crayon-colored pictures of dinosaurs scotch-taped to the walls. The walls were even painted dinosaur-green. "Oh my—where did you get so many dinosaurs?"

"Nick would find a new one for me and send it." When Betsy heard that, her heart filled with love for Nick. What a great father he would have been.

Annie began picking up her dinosaurs one by one and showing them to Betsy. "This one is a Spinosaurus. He was the biggest dinosaur of all the dinosaurs. This one is Tyrannosaurus Rex. He was very big too. Both of these were very mean." Annie went on and one by one showed Betsy her dinosaurs. She knew each by name and added little comments like "See those sharp teeth? This one was a meat-eater." Her knowledge of the dinosaurs really was impressive. Betsy realized Annie was quite intelligent.

When Annie's little tour was over, she asked if she could go out to play. After she left, Betsy cautiously broached a difficult question. "I am curious about something. I noticed all the children have had their foreheads blackened. Could I ask why? Is it because the tribe is in mourning? Or is it something they always do?"

Becca smiled at the innocence of Betsy about tribal ways. "Mom told you last night of our belief in the spirit world. When someone dies, his or her spirit might be lonely. That spirit might like to take someone along on the journey. Children and babies are especially vulnerable. During the 4 days we blacken our children's foreheads with charcoal so the spirit can't recognize them."

Betsy's reaction was immediate and discernable, as that piece of information sunk in. "What about a woman who is pregnant? Would the child she is carrying be in danger, too?"

Becca automatically began to respond to that question. "Oh yes. It is especially important that any woman with child not be around the deceased until that person is bur...Oh my God, you are talking about yourself, aren't you? You are pregnant? Oh, please, please tell me. It is Nick's baby, isn't it!"

Somehow Becca had made it easy for Betsy to tell her about the baby. She shyly asked Becca if she thought she should tell Minnie; if the news would make her happy or make her sad. She certainly did not want to hurt that dear woman's feelings.

But Becca was positive her mother would be ecstatic over the news. She would have a little of Nick back. And the baby would be Minnie's first grandchild.

Then another thing Becca said began to sink in. "Did you say a pregnant woman cannot be around the deceased?"

"Oh, Betsy! I'm so sorry! Yes, it would be very bad for you to be around Nick's casket at this time. I have known of women who didn't believe and had miscarriages. I know you might not understand our beliefs, but please do take this one seriously. Don't take a chance. Please!

"I have to think about this," Becca continued. "There must be a way you can be a part of Nick's funeral. Let's have some coffee and see what we can come up with."

Betsy knew two things: she had come all that way to say good-bye to the man she loved, and yet she also knew she had a responsibility to honor the beliefs of his tribe. The two things seemed irreconcilable.

It was Becca who came up with a solution. "I know. You can take part in all the festivities around the bonfire. I see no harm in that. You just don't dare go into the tribal center. You won't be able to attend the funeral either. But once Nick is buried the danger has passed. I can take you to his resting place. That is the important part, knowing where Nick's body will be any time you want to come and visit. How does that sound?"

Actually, that sounded very disappointing to Betsy. But she realized that would be the best she could do under the circumstances. To do anything else would cause great stress to Minnie and Becca. She thanked Becca for finding a way she could be there for Nick.

It was agreed Betsy would tell Minnie after dinner that evening. Becca was still apologizing for uninviting Betsy to the funeral, so to assuage her guilt, Betsy explained the funeral was only one of several reasons she had come to Minnesota. Betsy talked to Becca about wanting to meet Nick's family. How she wanted to know all about their family history and their culture. She wanted their baby to know and be proud of it's Native American heritage.

Becca began to fill Betsy in on the Ojibwa people. "If you want to know our history, you certainly came to the right person. My eventual goal is to become a lawyer and then become an advocate for our people. Almost since I first started school, I knew this is what I wanted to do with my life. And for some time, I have been learning as much as I could about our history, particularly all that has happened to us since the Europeans came."

"You amaze me! You have such a good head on your shoulders. Most high school seniors don't know what they are going to do. Not only do you have a goal, it is such a noble goal!"

Becca modestly deflected the praise. "If you only knew how adversarial Washington has been, not just to our people, but to all native peoples, you would understand why we so desperately need knowledgeable people to stand up for us. Maybe someday we can talk about that. But right now, there is so much more I can tell you about our history and our culture. Things you will be able to tell your baby when it is old enough to appreciate them."

The door popped open. There was Annie with her sparkling eyes and big grin. "I'm hungry. Can we go eat now?"

Becca asked Betsy if she was ready for lunch. Betsy agreed and excused herself to go to the bathroom. When she got back, Annie was cleaned up from play and as presentable as any six-year-old could be. Becca grabbed a large covered dish from the refrigerator and they were on their way.

As they walked toward the drumming sound, Annie had some questions: "Will the hoop dancers be there? Or the jingle ladies?" She looked at Betsy and told her how much she loved the jingle ladies. "They seem to float on air. Their feet don't even touch the ground. Someday Mama will make me a jingle dress and I can dance too. I practice all the time, but it is hard." Becca smiled indulgently at her little sister. She was so enthusiastic. Whatever she loved, she loved with all her heart.

The drumming was growing louder as they approached. It was rhythmic and it seemed to be working its way right into

Betsy's soul. Soon she could smell the wood smoke from the bonfire, and it was a good smell. It reminded Betsy of the many camping trips with her grandparents. Good memories. Happy times.

Then the tables came into view, laden once again with food. Becca added her macaroni salad to the other foods on the table. There were quite a few people around the bonfire, others filling their plates with food, or eating, talking, laughing. Most looked over at Betsy. Some faces were friendly, some faces showed curiosity or surprise. A few were unreadable. One woman, about Betsy's age, stared at her most unpleasantly—and continued to stare. It made Betsy feel quite uncomfortable. She realized she was the only white person there.

Becca asked Annie to go see if their mother could leave her vigil to get some lunch. One of the older ladies at the table overheard Becca and volunteered to take Minnie's place so she could eat with her daughters.

Becca, Annie, and Betsy began filling their plates. Soon Minnie joined them. They sat with other ladies, and introductions were made; too many names for Betsy to remember all at once. Becca explained that Betsy was Nick's fiancé. There were many Ohs and Ahs. Betsy suspected they already knew much about her. Apparently, there are few secrets on the reservation. They had many questions: Did she go to school? Did she work? Did she have an apartment? Again, how did she meet Nick?

Normally Betsy wasn't one to talk about herself, but to be polite she answered the questions as they came. After high school she was hired into the county health department as a clerk. And, yes, she loved her job. She didn't have an apartment; they are pretty expensive in San Francisco. She lived with her parents. She met Nick through a blind date about a year ago.

A handsome young man who had been standing over by the other men at the bonfire disengaged himself from the group and sauntered over. "Well, Becca, are you gonna introduce me to this groovy chick?"

With a sigh, Becca complied. "Clay, this is Betsy, Nick's fiancé. Betsy meet Clay, one of Nick's childhood friends." Clay extended his right hand and shook Betsy's hand, enclosing that hand with his left hand. At the same time, he gave her a brilliant smile.

"This guy is used to girls falling all over him," Betsy thought. His cocky attitude was definitely a put-off for her.

"I'll grab some food and be right back." This was Clay's way of inviting himself into the group.

When he got back, he indicated he would like to sit by Betsy; Becca reluctantly moved over. Clay immediately began to dominate the conversation. "I wasn't just one of Nick's friends, I was his best friend. He was one cool cat. He would come up with all these crazy-ass things to do. I remember once when we was gonna build a raft at the pond in the woods. We scrounged up some nails and a hammer and nailed some logs together. We shoved it in the water and hopped aboard. Nick had a pole and began poling out to the middle of the pond. All of a sudden, we realized our ankles was getting wet. Our raft was sinking. Now Nick is poling double-time to get us back to shore. Lesson learned: if you're gonna build a raft, don't pick water-logged logs for your base." Now this actually was funny and the ladies at the table were laughing.

Encouraged by the laughs, Clay continued with another story. "One time, Nick was all excited about a pit he found in the woods. He came and got a bunch of us guys. It was a pretty cool pit. It was knee-deep in leaves; it was October. The coolest part of the pit was the giant tree that had fallen across the whole thing. The trunk was huge. Two of us guys, one at each end, could walk across it easily. When we got to the middle, we would link elbows, pass each other without falling off, and continue walking to the other side.

"We would have wrestling matches there. We wrestled in the pit. The guys who wasn't wrestling sat up on the log. They were the judges. Me and Nick were the best wrestlers. Hardly anyone could beat us."

Betsy had to admit, she was enjoying Clay's stories. Nick had never told her much about his childhood.

Then Minnie joined in. "Clay, do you remember the year you two got bows and arrows for Christmas? You practiced and practiced with that old straw bale."

"Yeah, we got pretty good too. We would compete for the best score. I always won those contests."

Lucinda, another of Minnie's relatives that was seated across the table recalled how the boys were always hanging out at the pool hall. "Yeah, that was one happenin' place. If we wasn't playin' pool, we was at the pinball machines. There was this one guy—dumber 'n a post. But he had a car, so we let him hang with us. We'd hunt up some chicks, pile in that old jalopy, and head to the passion pit for a little back seat bingo."

Before Clay could say any more, Becca was on her feet. "Excuse us, ladies. We need to get back to the house." Minnie, anxious to get back to her vigil, was also ready to leave.

All Clay could add was a quick "Later." and flash another of his rehearsed smiles.

On the way home Becca said "I apologize for that. Honestly, I don't know how Nick ever managed to tolerate that guy. He definitely was *not* Nick's best friend, as he had claimed. Oh, maybe when they were young, they did play together a lot. Maybe then he was Nick's best friend. They had these little plastic army guys and they used to play war. They would build little bunkers in the dirt. Once they found some scrap wood and a cardboard box. They built a fort. It was kinda crazy-looking, but they were proud of it."

"Does Clay always talk like that?"

"I think when he wants to impress the ladies. I do believe he feels they will think he is cool—to use his term. I wouldn't be surprised if he doesn't try to come on to you at some point during your stay here. He views himself as some kind of lady-killer."

"Becca, could I ask you about someone else at lunch? She stood away from everyone else. She was dressed all in black. She was youngish—maybe about my age? She kept staring at me. I got the most unpleasant vibe coming from her. Did you happen to notice her?"

"Long hair worn loose? Dark lipstick and nails?" Betsy nodded. "I didn't notice her, but I'm pretty sure I know who that would be. Her name is Gertrude, but she goes by Tru. But behind her back we called her The Witch. That was probably mean of us, but I kid you not—she was poison. She trapped Nick into taking her out one time after they graduated from hool. I remember Nick coming home and saying he er taking her out again; she was too weird. But she wouldn't give up. She kept bugging him. I've often wondered if that is why he joined the Marines, so he could get away from her. She built up this huge fantasy that when he got out of the Marines, they were going to get married and live happily ever after. She told everybody that. She is one of those people with a toxic personality—always trying to stir up trouble. She seems to thrive on drama. But don't worry about her. Nick couldn't stand her and did everything possible to avoid her."

By then they had reached the house. Annie, as usual, ran off to play with her friends.

"You know," Becca continued, "as I was talking about Clay and how Nick and Clay would play war with those little plastic army men, I had the most interesting thought. Nick loved to play war, especially games where he could be the hero. Do you think the games children choose to play could be a foretelling of their future choices in life? Was Nick—on some level—showing he would someday choose the military? Would a little girl who loves to play school become a teacher one day?"

Betsy thought this over and had to agree this was a possibility. "I had a little desk with some pencils and scissors, and my favorite—a little stapler. I enjoyed doing what I called 'my work' every day. And now my job still involves paperwork."

Becca continued talking about Nick. "Our people are divided into clans. Different clans represent different aspects of our culture. For example, our political leaders come from the loon or crane clan. My clan is warrior, from the Marten clan. Does it seem natural that Nick would play war games as a child and then go on to become a Marine, as did our dad?"

"Becca, if you think about it, you also are choosing to become a warrior for your people."

Becca thought about that idea for a moment, then said "I never thought about it that way, but it makes sense. Righting the wrongs my tribe has experienced is more than just a desire for me, it is my passion."

"Nick told me that you lost your dad at an early age. I'm so sorry about that."

"We believe he died a hero. Did you know he was a medic in the service? He continued to work in the local hospital after his discharge.

"He had a good conduct discharge, by the way. Did Nick tell you that? Anyway, he was on his way home after work late one night when someone ran a stop sign and T-boned another car. One man was thrown from the T-boned car and was lying in the road. My dad went right to him to begin first aid. He was hit and killed by a second car. The driver of that car said he was distracted by the accident and didn't see my dad in the dark.

"After that we moved back here to the reservation. Nick stepped up to the plate and—even though we were very young—became the man of the family. He was more than my big brother. He was my rock." Betsy knew the deep sadness she felt at losing Nick was matched by a sister who has lost her beloved sibling. It was a grief they shared.

"Oh, I forgot, I have made something for you." Becca jumped up and returned immediately with a birch-bark snake. "Please hang this outside your hotel room door tonight and again tomorrow night. Evil spirits are afraid of snakes. That snake will keep you safe."

Betsy was touched by the gesture and the sincerity with [illegible] was given. She had come to love this sweet young [illegible] and she felt loved by her. Now more than ever she wanted to understand the Ojibwa ways. "Becca, I came to be a part of Nick's funeral service. But that wasn't the only reason I came. I wanted to meet his family and I wanted to learn more about the Ojibwa culture. I believe that a part of our ancestors lives on in us and shapes who we are. Part of who Nick was will be in his baby's heritage. I really wanted to understand your tribe's history."

Chapter 7

"I will tell you what I know," Becca responded. "Tomorrow is my day to represent my family at Vigil. But if you could spend the day with Mom, I'm sure she will have much more to tell you."

"I would really like that. Will she have time for me?" Betsy asked.

"She would love to talk with you. But after dinner tomorrow night the family will begin the ceremonial dressing of Nick's body. She will be needed there."

Becca began her account. "Your belief about the fact that Those That Came Before shape who we are parallels our Ojibwa belief. We all have the spirit of *Anishinaabe* within us. In that way, we native peoples are one.

Our ancestors originally lived along the Atlantic coast. But there was much competition among the tribes for resources. Then a prophecy came in the form of a dream. You see, dreams are one way our spirits communicate with us. We take dreams iously. We were told to move to the lands of the setting sun where food grows on water. Today we know the spirits were telling us about the wild rice.

We began moving westward, but the movement was very slow and took many generations. Small settlements were established along the way and some remain to this day. By the time the French fur traders arrived in the Great Lakes region, Ojibwa were already established in Sault Ste. Marie in the Upper Peninsula of Michigan, where they are to this day. That would have been in the 1600's.

The French had trouble pronouncing Ojibwa, and the way they would say it came out more like Chippewa. Chippewa or Ojibwa, we are one. The spirit of *Anishinaabe* is in us all. We just inhabit a physical body during our lifetime. At burial, we sing a traveling song. We believe the spirit is going someplace. We don't know where that spirit is to go, but we believe that story is not over. Our focus is not so much on the afterlife, as your Christian tradition emphasizes. Our focus is on living nobly and well in this life. Does that make sense to you?"

Betsy nodded.

"Some of my tribe eventually made our way to Minnesota." There was pride in Becca's voice as she continued. "We are today the largest tribe in the United States. Our people live on lands in the entire Great Lakes region: Minnesota, North Dakota, Michigan, and Ontario. We have always been hunters. We fish. We still gather wild rice and make maple syrup. Of course, a few things have changed. We don't travel in birch bark canoes or live in teepees anymore."

"Becca, you mentioned the ceremonial dressing tomorrow night. Could you tell me a little about your burial rituals?"

"We believe that when a life ends, it is because that person has accomplished whatever it was that our Great Creator placed him on earth to do. We will miss the person who has passed, but we have satisfaction in knowing our loved one has accomplished his task. Now he enters a new phase of his existence. There is a path he will take that he must take alone. As he goes, he will see the footprints of those who have gone before."

"Oh, Becca, that is so beautiful!"

"I can explain a little of what will happen tomorrow—the fourth day.

"People have been putting tiny birch bark canoes into Nick's casket. Inside the canoes are small food gifts."

"Food gifts?" Betsy interrupted.

"Just little things Nick might need on his journey. We also put birch bark matches in there. Each night as Nick's spirit stops to rest, he builds a bonfire. We, too, gather around our bonfire here. Tobacco is passed from person to person. Some smoke it. Some toss it into the fire. The tobacco helps us to communicate with Nick's spirit. It is also an offering to the spirits to request special care for Nick's spirit. It is a special tobacco made of red osier dogwood, mixed with barberry, tobacco, and other medicinal plants.

"Tomorrow night after our final dinner together, there will be singing. These are special prayers. The smoke of the fire will lift them to *Gichi-Manidoo*.

"You will hear drumming. For us, the drum is special. The circular shape of the drum represents the circle of life.

"There will be hoop dancing. The shape of the hoop is reminder of the circle of life.

"Annie told you earlier about the jingle-dancers. Their dance tomorrow night will be for the protection of our children.

"While this is taking place, my family will be preparing Nick's body for burial. Moccasins will be placed on his feet. His body will be cleansed and wrapped in birch bark. Birch bark is sacred to us. Nick's body will be buried the next morning at dawn.

"After burial, our family will grieve for a year. During that time, we don't join in the dancing or the pow-wow. We don't gather the wild rice or help with the making of the maple syrup. At the end of the year, there will be a feast, followed by drumming, dancing, and singing. This ceremony will be attended by everyone in our tribe.

"We are a proud people; proud of our heritage, proud of who we are. Since the beginning of time our storytellers have told and retold our stories, passing them down through the generations.

"Among my people honor and prestige come from generosity. You have seen all the food on the tables by the bonfire? Each family has contributed. We may not have much, but we share what we have. That is who we are.

"Speaking of food, it is time to go meet Mom. She will be finishing Vigil shortly. Are you ready?"

Becca stepped outside, rang a bell, and Annie appeared almost at once. "That girl is always hungry," she chuckled.

On the way to the bonfire, Betsy had another question. "Earlier, you had mentioned that our government was dishonest with the native peoples in many ways. I really don't know much about that. It isn't something I remember learning in our history books in school. Could you fill me in a little?"

Becca said she would try to find time to tell her about some of the shameful treatment native peoples received from the Federal government before she left to go back to California.

While they waited by the bonfire for Minnie to come out, Clay spotted them and came over, placing himself next to Betsy. "Hello, Doll," he said as he again gave her his best Hollywood Smile. "Where have you been all day?"

Betsy didn't want to be rude, but she definitely didn't want to encourage this guy. Fortunately, Tom, Wally, and Minnie emerged from the Tribal Center together. She waved enthusiastically to alert them as to where she and Becca were in the crowd.

When Clay saw them coming, he apparently decided now was not a good time to further impress Betsy with his charm. "Catch you later," he told her, and headed back over to the circle of men at the bonfire.

As everyone ate, plans were made for the evening. Betsy and Becca would be going back to the house with Minnie and Annie. The men were going back to The Totem. Tom said he had to make a phone call. Betsy said she, too, would like to make a phone call to her folks, so they agreed to pick her up at Minnie's at eight o'clock.

After they left, Minnie asked Betsy if she would like to go see Nick. But Becca immediately stepped in and said, "Not now, Mom. We need to go back to the house. Betsy has something to tell you." Becca gave her mother a look that spoke volumes.

Fortunately, Annie began to prattle on about her day. It began with a jumping contest, followed by crayons and a coloring book, and ended with a loosely-organized soccer game.

Annie ran off to rejoin the game just as soon as they reached the house.

As they settled in, Becca fixed some iced tea for everyone. Betsy asked Minnie how her day went and other small talk while they waited for Becca to return. As she re-entered the room, Becca wasted no time in getting to the news Betsy had to share. "Mom, Betsy has something exciting to tell you." With that, the conversation ball was dropped into Betsy's lap as both women looked at her expectantly.

Betsy had been wrestling for days with how to tell Minnie. She rehearsed several different ways, but never was sure which way was the best way. Now she was very nervous, and what came out of her mouth was not any of the elegant ways she had practiced. Instead; "Umm, I'm not sure how to...I mean, I hope you will be happy with...Ahh, I will understand if you don't..."

Minnie, who by now had a pretty good idea of what the news was, chuckled at Betsy's discomfort and with much amusement said, "Heavens, child, out with it!"

And Betsy blurted out "You're going to be a grandmother. I mean, Nick and I, well, I am going to have a baby. Nick's baby."

Minnie said nothing. She got up, sat down beside Betsy, put her arms around her, and hugged her. This act of kindness was too much for Betsy's rattled nerves. She burst into tears. The emotions of the past few days finally caught up with her. Minnie simply held her and stroked her hair. "Shh, shh."

Finally, Betsy, accepting a tissue from Becca, pulled herself together and said "I'm so sorry. I'm terrible at this. I just didn't know how to tell you. You have just lost your son. You are in mourning. Here I come, this stranger, to tell you I am pregnant. And we weren't even married yet."

Minnie sat back, looked at Betsy, and said, "Hush, Child. There is no need to be ashamed. These things happen. In the old days of my people there was no piece of paper saying two young people were married. There was just a joining of two hearts. Sometimes there was a ceremony. Sometimes not. You and Nick had a joining of the hearts. That is enough. Of course, I am delighted about the baby. I know Nick loved you very much and I can see why. You are a good person, very kind and thoughtful. I know you will be a good mother. How far along are you? How are you feeling? Have you seen a doctor yet?"

"I went to the doctor just before I came out here. He said I was about 3 months along. I had a little trouble at first, but I think I am through it. I'm feeling pretty good now."

"Do your parents know?" Minnie wondered.

"Yes, they know. They asked me what I wanted to do. I told them I wanted to have the baby and raise it. Losing Nick was hard enough. I couldn't bear the thought of losing his baby too. My parents are very supportive and have promised to help me in any way they can."

"You know," Minnie said, "I wondered why you hadn't come to see Nick today. I thought perhaps you had come yesterday and I just didn't know it. But I was still surprised as to why you didn't come today."

Becca chimed in, "That's my fault, Mom. Betsy said something yesterday that caused me to guess she was pregnant. It is a good thing I figured it out because I was able to prevent her from endangering her child. She didn't know about our beliefs. But I have gone over with her all the ceremonies she can be a part of. And I have promised to take her to see the gravesite once Nick is buried."

"Good, Becca. You've done the right thing." Turning to Betsy, Minnie said, "I'm so proud of this girl, of both my daughters, really. Two smart girls. I don't know what I would do without Becca. She is a blessing and I know that someday you will feel the same way about your child.

"In some ways I can understand what you are going through. I was five months along with Annie when my husband was killed. Although my parents had already passed on, I came back to the reservation because I knew I would need a support system. All my family lives here. I am glad your parents will be there for you. If there are problems later in your pregnancy, or even if you just aren't feeling well, it is so necessary that you have someone who understands. And when your time comes, you will be comforted to have someone who loves you there to hold your hand. If you ever need someone to talk to, you know you can call me. You will always be welcome in this house."

"I thank you," Betsy said. "I will want to stay in touch with you. This isn't just my baby. This is your baby too, and I will always want you to be a part of his—or her—life."

Becca queried, "Have you done any thinking about names, Betsy?" "Yes. If it is a boy, I would like to call him Nick. If it is a girl; Nikki. But I want to know if that would be OK with you?"

Minnie was obviously delighted with Betsy's choice of names. "I would be honored to have you use those names. And I love what you said about being a part of the child's life. I would really like that. I'm not sure how we can accomplish that because we live so far from California. But if we want it badly enough, we can make it happen."

"Mom," Becca asked, "one of the reasons Betsy came was so she could learn more about Nick's family. Could she spend the day with you tomorrow? You had such an interesting childhood, and so did Dad. And Aunt Lucinda."

"That would be lovely." Minnie turned to Betsy and added, "You and I haven't had much time together. Will you come tomorrow?"

Betsy was excited about the invitation. "I'm looking forward to it."

Meanwhile, the men were in the car and on their way to pick up Betsy. Wally asked Tom how the phone call to Angie went. Tom said she finally did go see John at Treasure Island. Again, Tom got the impression she really didn't care as much about John as he did about her. Tom suspected she only went out of curiosity, or perhaps so she would look dutiful in Tom's eyes. But Angie did have news. She said John was appointed a lawyer. The lawyer had instructed him not to talk to anyone about what happened. Angie described how she turned on all her charm to try to get him to talk. She said it looked at one point as though he really wanted to tell her, but then he must have decided he couldn't. From then on, he only said he was not allowed to talk about it. Tom said he asked Angie how she was holding up and she said OK For a second time, Angie suggested they should meet up when he got back.

"Hmm. That's interesting," Wally said.

"Yeah. I don't know what to think about her," Tom added.

Back at Minnie's, there was the sound of a car outside. The motor died, car doors slammed, and the men were at the door, ready to pick up Betsy. She excused herself, saying she needed to get in touch with her parents. There were warm and friendly hugs all around and soon they were on their way back to The Totem.

On the way, Betsy saw a large grocery store and asked if they could stop. "I'll only be a minute." She quickly returned, carrying a small plant. The plant had tiny white flowers grouped in round balls which caused them to resemble ping-pong balls. "For Minnie," she explained.

Betsy called her parents from her hotel room. She brought them up to date on all that had happened. They were quite dismayed to learn she had been unable to see Nick, because they knew how important that final good-bye had been to Betsy. "Can't you get Wally to sneak you in sometime?"

"That thought did cross my mind, but I don't want to get Wally in trouble. Anyway, I believe it best to respect tribal beliefs. Nick has the most wonderful family. I don't want to disappoint them." Next came a lot of questions about Nick's family. Betsy told them what she could and explained she would probably learn more tomorrow. They asked when she would be coming home. She would leave after Becca showed her Nick's final resting place.

Before long they were on their way back to Singin' Sandy's once again. When Sandy saw Tom walk through the door, she switched from the song that she had been singing to a variation of "Blue Skies Smiling at Me". She looked at Tom and sang "Blue eyes smiling at me. Nothing but blue eyes do I see..." This caused Tom to laugh out loud and even blush a little. But that was typical of Sandy, who was outrageous in so many ways, from her crazy songs to her beatnik clothes to her wild eyeshadow to the odd bits of feathers and beads in her long brown hair.

As they had their pie and coffee, Betsy filled Tom and Wally in on what she had learned about the Ojibwa people. They were as fascinated as she had been to learn about their history and culture. Tom commented "Here we had such an interesting people living right under our noses and yet we never learned anything about them in school."

By now the restaurant was emptying out of customers. Tom got up and began helping Sandy with her closing routine. After he left the table, Betsy asked Wally "What is going on with those two?"

"Tom is really enjoying being with her. He says she is a lot of fun, and so different from the other girls he has dated. She makes him laugh. Look at them together, like two parts of a well-oiled machine. I think it is time for us to skedaddle on out of here."

Wally's choice of words made Betsy giggle. "Ok, pardner, let's boogie."

When they left Singin' Sandy's, Wally asked Betsy if she was really tired, or if she would like to drive around and see a little of Duluth. Betsy's reply was an enthusiastic "Oh, I'd love to! I've never been here before. Have you?" Wally hadn't.

Tourist attractions had closed hours ago, but they were able to drive along Canal Park and the shores of Lake Superior. The water was dark and beautiful, with lights from the Aerial Lift Bridge glimmering on its surface. Wally parked the car and they walked closer to the water, listening to the waves gently lapping on the shore. There was a slight breeze coming off the lake on the warm summer evening. It was so calm and peaceful there. The moon lit the sky. Wally looked at Betsy in the moonlight. She was going through so much. He wanted to be there for her, to protect her. He felt incredibly close to her at that moment. But he reminded himself her heart belonged to another, and he had to respect that.

On the way back to the hotel, Wally asked, "You haven't said much about your phone call. Is everything ok?"

"It is. I told my folks all about the reservation, and all that I had learned about their funeral customs. They agreed with me that, although it is unfortunate, I can't see Nick one more time, it is best to show respect for tribal customs and beliefs. They were happy that some of the other goals I had for coming here are being realized. They are as excited as I am to learn more about Minnie's childhood. I am going to spend tomorrow with Minnie while Becca is representing the family at Vigil."

"Tom and I will be completing our military vigil tomorrow. All that will be left for us will be the military funeral at dawn the next day. Lt. Good will give us the details tomorrow night. The service will follow at dawn. Then we head back to base. How about you? Will you stay over or are you going home?"

"I told my parents I would be home after the service. I can't attend the burial, but Becca promised to take me to his grave after he is buried so I can say good-bye to him privately."

Wally asked if she would like a ride to the airport. Betsy worried about delaying them, but Wally assured her it was no problem. Betsy said she would pack during the service so she would be ready to go. They agreed to meet for breakfast, wished each other a good night, and parted ways.

Chapter 8

After breakfast the men dropped Betsy off at Minnie's and drove to their station at the tribal center. Minnie again greeted Betsy with a huge smile and a warm hug. Betsy gave her the plant she had purchased the night before. Minnie set it on the little table beside the sofa; the one with the lamp. They settled in with some coffee and cinnamon rolls Becca had made the night before. Betsy began the conversation. "I would love to hear about your childhood, if you care to tell me."

Minnie told how her parents died when she was quite young. Both had T.B. It was not unusual in the tribe in that day. She lived with her aunt for a while, but her aunt already had four children, 3 boys and a girl. Minnie reminded Betsy that she had already met her cousin, Lucinda, earlier.

When some outsiders came to the tribal chief to ask if there were any children they could adopt, the chief thought of her. But before he talked to Minnie's aunt, he checked out the couple very carefully. They had married late in life. They had one daughter, who died at the age of ten from cystic fibrosis. At first, they were in deep mourning. But then they realized they really wanted another child. Too old to have one naturally, too old to adopt one in the usual way, they came to the chief. They hoped he would be able to help. Minnie was eight at the time, a little younger than their daughter had been. They took to her immediately. But all Minnie had ever known was the security of the reservation.

At first it was just a day visit. Then an overnight. Then a weekend. For the first time in her life, Minnie had her own bedroom; a soft bed, crisp sheets. Food was different, but plentiful. In a short time, Minnie was developing favorite foods

The people were kind to her. When she was homesick for the reservation, they would take her back to visit. In time she came to love them and call them Mom and Dad. The visits to the reservation became fewer and fewer, but never stopped completely. Her parents felt it important she always know of her heritage.

She grew up, graduated from high school and began classes at the local community college. It was then that her beloved dad suffered a major heart attack. He was rushed to the hospital. It was touch and go for almost a month, but he didn't make it.

Minnie said she was so distraught she was unable to concentrate on her college classes. She dropped out and got a part-time job in a local department store

The one good thing about the many visits to the hospital during her dad's illness was the nice young man who attended to her father. Even when George was not assigned to him, he would check in on him. Minnie said it made an unbearable situation easier, because she knew her dad was in good hands, even when she couldn't be there.

One day, when she went to visit, her dad was sleeping. George was not on duty, but he had stopped by to check on his favorite patient anyway. He asked Minnie if she would like a coffee in the hospital cafeteria. As they talked that day, Minnie learned about George's history.

He, too, was Native American. He, too, had been adopted early in life. In his case, the family had too many children and not enough food. When a farmer came, offering to take ten-year-old George, they gladly accepted. George never knew for sure, but he suspected some money may have changed hands. He quickly learned why the farmer wanted him. The farmer was a hard worker and expected the same of George.

He had to be up by four thirty to milk the cows. The milk was brought to the basement of the house. There it was placed into milk cans. Later a truck would make a daily stop to pick up the full milk cans and drop off empty ones. Then back out to the barn to slop the hogs and feed the chickens. He next returned to the basement where he was required to shower and change into school clothes. The farmer's wife would not allow him upstairs for breakfast until chores were done and he was cleaned up. Even his shoes had to be changed.

After breakfast a school bus picked him up. He looked forward to school. Compared to his life on the farm, school was easy and, for him, interesting. It was a place where he could excel, unlike the farm where it seemed he could do nothing right.

After school he would change into his work clothes and shoes and go bring in the cows to be milked again. There were between twenty-five and thirty cows. Haul the milk to the basement, separate the cream from the milk, pour it into the cans. Shower. Change back into his school clothes, eat dinner and fall into bed, dead-tired.

In summer there was planting and weeding, a barn to be cleaned, fencing to be mended, and other repairs to be made. George helped with the butchering, the canning, and the preserving in the fall. In the winter there was snow to be shoveled. A lot of repairs to the house, barn, sheds, and equipment were done in the winter.

"Now you would think," Minnie continued, "that George would be very bitter about his treatment during those years. But instead, he took the high road. The work kept him lean and muscular. He learned to be a jack of all trades. He learned how to manage a farm. He learned how to grow, harvest, and preserve food. There wasn't anything that man couldn't fix one way or another. And he was allowed to go to school.

Very young, George was setting goals for himself. When he graduated from high school, he went into the Marines. Perhaps because of his butchering skills, he went into the medic program. That led to a good job in the hospital after he was discharged."

After that coffee in the cafeteria, George and Minnie began dating. George was there for Minnie and her mom when Minnie's dad died. George visited Minnie whenever he could, often repairing things around her mom's house.

In time, they married and lived with Minnie's mom. "Times were good then. I was able to stay home and care for Mom. We raised a garden. We were happy. We continued to live in that house. Nick was born. Then Becca. I was pregnant with Annie when George was killed. I had no way to keep up with the bills. By then Mom was gone. We lost the house and I returned to the reservation."

Betsy listened, entranced. How could one person endure so much tragedy so stoically!

"Well," said Minnie, "now you know the history of your baby's grandparents. It is time to go to lunch. My cousin, Lucinda, has a different childhood story to tell. Sadly, her story is much more typical of the reservation children of my generation. She has agreed to meet us for lunch and tell you about it."

"When I was five," Lucinda began her story, "some people came and took me and my older brothers. They took all the children my age and older. They put us on a school bus and took us away. I was crying. So were many of my friends. We were frightened. They took us to a big building very far from the reservation. There were other children there as well, from other reservations. We were all so scared."

"They separated me from my brothers. Girls went one way. Boys went the other way. The first thing they did was show us how to use the toilet, toilet paper, and to flush. They gave us soap and a washcloth. They showed us how to shower and clean ourselves. A lady watched to make sure we didn't miss anything. This was very embarrassing. Then they handed us a towel to dry off with. We were given new clothes. We girls got white blouses and navy-blue skirts, all exactly the same."

"Then we were taken to a room. There was a very mean lady there. One at a time she would take each of us to a chair and say 'You sit here!' Each chair had the picture of an animal taped to the back of it. My animal was a bear. Each day, she said, we were to come to the same chair. The chairs were grouped around a long wooden table; six chairs to a table, three on each side. The lady told us we were not to talk to one another."

"Then the lady came around to each of us. Jabbing us in the chest, one by one, she gave us new names. Christian names. We were never to use our old names again. The new names were to be ours for the rest of our lives. I would no longer be called by Kiwidinok again."

"She had us stand up, one table at a time. She showed us how to form a line. She had us practice walking around the edge of the room in a line. If anyone got out of line, they got their knuckles rapped with a ruler. She told us once we could walk in a line correctly, she would take us to the lunchroom. Most of us hadn't eaten all day, so we were hungry. We learned very quickly about lines! Before we left the room, the lady told us when we got to the lunchroom we were to listen to her directions. If someone didn't listen, she would take them out of the line and they would go to the end of the line. They would be the last to eat."

"But before the lunchroom, we stopped at the bathroom. We were to use the toilet and wash our hands too. We were so scared of her, we did exactly what we were told to do. She watched to make sure we did."

"In the lunchroom she showed us about trays and silverware. I still remember that first meal. We had soup and milk and pudding. I don't remember ever having chocolate pudding before that day."

"After we ate, we went back to the room with the tables. The lady said this was our classroom and she was our teacher. She told us we would soon be going to a room with beds in it. We would sleep in that room. That room was called the dormitory.

We were to use the toilet and wash our hands. Then we were to get into our beds. Each bed would have the same picture of an animal on it that we had on our chairs. That is how we would know which bed was ours. The lights would be turned out. We were not to cry. We were not to talk. We were to go to sleep. Remember, I was only five years old, still a baby, really. In the morning the lights would come on. A lady would show us how to wash our faces and brush our teeth. We were to use the toilet, wash our hands, and line up at the door. The lady would take us to the lunchroom for breakfast. Then back to the classroom."

"So went our days. We learned to say prayers in the morning, grace before each meal, prayers at bedtime. Christian prayers. We were taught to make our beds each morning. And we learned to read and write in English."

"We were no longer allowed to use our native language or names. But we were stubborn. After the lights went out at night, we would whisper our real names to each other. And we would tell stories in our native language, so we would never forget our heritage."

"This place was called The Christian School. They wanted to take away our language and culture and 'Americanize' us. They wanted to take away our religion. They said we were Heathens. They wanted us to be Christians, which they said was much better than our beliefs." At this, Lucinda smiled. "But they did not succeed."

"It was about a month before I saw my brothers. I missed them so much. But when I saw them, I hardly recognized them. My brothers, like all the boys on the reservation, had long hair. But now all the boys had their hair cut short. It was very shocking to see them like that. The boys had white shirts and navy-blue pants. Like the girls, they were all dressed alike."

"I missed my parents, too. The school was far from the reservation. They had no way to come to see us. This was done on purpose, to lessen their influence on us. At Christmas a bus loaded us up and took us home. But a week later the bus came for us and we had to go back to The Christian School.

The school assumed they could change us. They were wrong. Secretly at night we fought to keep our identity. The school thought their ways were better than our ways. Maybe they were right; maybe they were wrong. But our ways were our ways and right for us.

And that," Lucinda concluded, "is my story."

Betsy was so touched by Lucinda's story she hardly knew what to say. "What a horrible thing to do to a five-year-old child!" she said.

"Whatever doesn't kill you makes you stronger. I am stronger because of that time. I have learned I can get through anything."

Betsy reached across the table and covered Lucinda's worn hands with her own. Looking into Lucinda's eyes, she said "And I am stronger just listening to your story. I will never forget you." In that moment Betsy felt an incredible connection to this remarkable survivor.

Annie was ready to return home so she could go back to play with her friends. She had been remarkably patient while Lucinda told her story, but a six-year-old can only stay still so long. Minnie, Betsy, and Annie started for home.

When they entered the house, Betsy was surprised to see a small kitten. She was playing with a little cardboard box on the floor. It was upside down. She was inside it, peeking out of the corners through the flaps. Occasionally a paw would slip out; a tease for whoever would play with her. Minnie said she was Becca's kitten, one of Frieda's. Her name was Smoke, apt for her fluffy grey fur. She appeared to be about 8 weeks old.

Betsy had another question for Minnie. "Becca was going to tell me about how our government was not fair to the tribes of long ago, but we talked about so many other things, we ran out of time. Do you know much about this?"

Minnie was thoughtful for a short while, then she responded. "Becca is really passionate about this. She could rattle off dates and names of various legislative acts or treaties and how the Federals reneged when the agreements were no longer convenient for them. She could give details about bribes, corruption, and kickbacks. I'm not that up on the details, but I can give you a thumbnail sketch, if you like."

"I would be very interested."

"I think it goes back to this idea of generosity. You saw our feast tables. We may not have much, but we share what we have. When the whites first came to our Great Lakes region, many tribes lived here, including my own. We didn't understand the concept of land ownership or that land could be transferred by a piece of paper. The land was just there, like the air or the water. We shared it.

"At first, land was plentiful and those that came tried to be fair. There actually was an ordinance passed that promised our land would never be taken from us without our consent.

"But when the Europeans needed land, they just took it. Then they would say we couldn't use it. This was very confusing to us. We didn't understand how they could do this. We resisted. There were more and more conflicts.

"We didn't understand how the white man's government worked. How could men so far away make decisions that would affect us? The conflicts put pressure on Congress, so they passed the Indian Removal Act, which took our lands from us.

"That only created a new problem: what to do with the tribes they were displacing. In the 1800's Congress began to create reservations for us.

"Then Congress passed The Homestead Act, promising land to any settlers willing to occupy the vacant land for a few years. Now many settlers were moving to the Great Lakes region. Soon land was scarce. There was much criticism that Congress had been too generous to the tribes and gave us too much land for our reservations.

"Again, the reservations were taken from us and we were given a new system. Each head of household received 160 acres. But many of us had to sell our land because we didn't know how to make a living in the white man's way and we couldn't pay our bills.

"Eventually Congress went back to the reservation system for us, but they were smaller reservations."

Just then the attention of both women was diverted to Smoke, who had spied something interesting on the lamp table and jumped up to investigate. The little kitten stood on the arm of the sofa, looking at the flowers on Minnie's new plant. She looked intently left, right, up, down, as though she was "shopping" for the best flower. She apparently made her decision, for she reached out with both front paws and pulled one flower cluster off and batted it down onto the sofa. From there she batted it to the floor. Then it was game on for the kitten as she enthusiastically batted it all over the floor. Both women were laughing at her antics as she pounced and played.

"Anyway, that is how we wound up on reservations. Throughout our history of dealing with the United States government, there has been a sense of superiority on their part. They feel they know what is best for us. We are the little children who do not know how to manage our lives. We who have survived and flourished on this land since the beginning of time." Minnie shook her head in disgust.

"It might have worked if the Federals had been fair. But they never were. Treaties were made and broken. I think the whites knew they were worthless even as they signed them. For example, one trick they employed was to have just two or three tribal chiefs sign the treaty. How could just two or three chiefs make decisions for land that belonged to all of us? It never belonged to just those few tribes. Additionally, the chiefs did not know how to read the English language. They had to rely on an interpreter, who was employed by the Federals.

"I'll give you just one example; Becca could give you more. In the beginning of the 1800's, the Dakota tribe sold one hundred thousand acres of our land to the Federal government. There were seven tribes represented at that meeting, but only two signed the treaty. The land was valued at two hundred thousand dollars in the treaty. We did not decide this amount, the English did. But when the treaty went before Congress, they decided the land was only worth two thousand dollars. When tribal leaders objected to this change as a violation of the original agreement, even this small amount was withheld until they signed the amendment. Did the tribes receive even that smaller amount? Oh no, there were expenses to be paid out of it first. Today Minneapolis/St Paul sits on that land. That is just one example. Even now, over one hundred years later tribes are owed money never received."

"Oh, my! I had no idea! I can see why Becca is so determined to go into law. She will be a tremendous asset as she fights for fair treatment of her tribe."

"I raised Becca to be a strong and independent woman. I want both my girls to be able to earn a good living. I don't want them trapped in bad marriages or stranded as I was when a beloved spouse dies unexpectedly. I don't want them to ever feel they can't manage on their own. I've seen too many women put up with terrible things; alcoholic husbands, domestic abuse, infidelity, because they cannot see a way out.

"Even now the Federal government traps us on the reservation and keeps us in poverty. We receive a small amount of money each month. We don't have to do anything for that money; it just comes. Some people would say we are lucky. We aren't slaves to a nine-to-five job. But think about it. It is barely enough to live on. Even if we could get a job off the reservation, it is difficult. It is hard to be able to afford a car. Cars we can afford are old and undependable, making us unreliable employees. We have no way to better our circumstances. We as a tribe will always be poor.

"From the time my children, Nick too, were very small, I drummed into them that they needed to break free of this system. Education is the key. Nick chose the military. Becca and Annie will go to college. That is one good thing the government does for us. If our children qualify, they can get an education free or at a reduced rate at certain colleges."

Annie burst into the house, all excited about her latest venture. "Mom, Rolly and I invented a new game. It is so much fun. Rolly had these sticks. We pounded some nails in them and we stuck them in the ground. Then we put a straight stick across the nails. It sorta looks like a capital H. At first, we put it on the bottom nails. Then we jump over it. If we don't knock the stick off, we put it on the next nails higher up. We keep jumping higher and higher until somebody knocks the stick off. Then the other person is the winner. I won four times. Rolly won three. That makes me the winner! Then Rolly's mom called him. They are going to the feast tables. Can we go too? I'm hungry!"

"Betsy, if you are ready, we can go. After the food there will be drumming. The men will have their flutes. You will see hoop dancing and, most important for you, will be the jingle dancers. They will be dancing to protect the children during this vulnerable time. There will be prayers sent up for Nick and for other intentions at the bonfire. People send them up in the smoke. Becca, Annie, and I will be joining my family. We will be preparing Nick's body for burial in the morning. But Wally and Tom will be with you. The celebration will go well into the evening. Tonight, or by morning, Nick's spirit will reach the Land of Never-Ending Happiness. This is why we celebrate."

Just as Minnie had promised, Wally, Tom, and Becca soon joined them, as well as Lucinda and much of her family. There was much activity around the bonfire. Clay was there, and he looked at Betsy several times. But the presence of the men kept him at bay. There were many more people there this evening and the excitement was building.

First came the drums. Rhythmic and loud. The sound was hypnotic. The drummers began chanting along with the beat. Then came the dancers, old and young males in ceremonial dress. The flutes came next with their haunting melodies floating on the air. Now came the drums again, and the hoop dancers. The air was alive with the sounds of the drums; resonating right into Betsy's soul. The drummers were singing in their native tongue. Then the beat became slower, softer, and the singing stopped as the jingle dancers came into the area around the fire. It was just as Annie had described, their feet hardly touching the ground. It was one of the most graceful dances Betsy had ever seen. This dance was performed by the females, both young and old in ceremonial dress. Betsy noticed some of the young ladies were quite beautiful. Even the older ladies with their sun-weathered faces had an extraordinary beauty about them.

Much too soon, the evening was over for Betsy, Tom, and Wally. The celebration would continue into the night, but the men had an appointment with Lt. Good. He would be giving them instruction for the military funeral, which he had been coordinating with local military as well. Betsy could use the time to prepare for her trip home.

Back in the hotel room Lt. Good told the men that he'd met with Chief White Horse and the Commander of the VFW, as well as the local newspaper. A state senator would also be in attendance and giving a short speech.

"Tom, you and Wally will fold the flag after the twenty-one-gun salute. Tom, you will fold and Wally, you hold the other end. After the flag is folded, Wally, you will give me the flag and I will present it to the family. In the morning put on your dress blues. We will meet in the lobby at 0500. We will check out at that time. Any questions?"

Wally wanted to know how they would get to the airport. Lt. Good said he had arranged for a duty driver from the local Marine Corps reserves to take all three of them. Wally asked if Betsy would be able to get a ride with them. He explained how she would go to the cemetery after the service. Could they pick her up at Minnie's house about noon? Lt Good saw no problem with that. "Ok, then. See you in the morning. Have a good night."

After Lt. Good left, Wally called Betsy. He told her he had gotten permission from Lt. Good to transport her to the airport. She would need to get a ticket for the six o'clock flight. They would meet in the lobby at five a.m. and check out, load all the luggage in the car and go to the tribal center. She could either wait in the car until Nick's casket was loaded, or she could walk to Minnie's until after the service. Betsy thanked him, said she would try to get a seat on that flight and call him back.

Then Wally set about packing. Tom wanted to call Sandy, but waited until after the restaurant closed. He too spent his time packing. Betsy called back to say she had booked the six o'clock flight. It was a short call because everyone was busy getting ready for the next and final day.

Tom's call was short. He told Sandy he hoped to see her tomorrow before they left. He talked about how wonderful their time together had been and he wanted very much to stay in touch with her after he got back to base. Although their time together had been short, Wally could tell these two had something special.

Chapter 9

In the morning all four met up, checked out and were at the tribal center by 5:30. Leaving Betsy in the car, the men went inside. Then Lt. Good began meeting up with personnel and dignitaries; organizing the various events that would occur. Family was already arriving. Wally came back to the car briefly and told Betsy he'd checked with Minnie. She was to walk to Minnie's house. He had made arrangements with Becca to pick her up there after the burial.

In no time, Nick's casket was loaded; the American flag was draped over it, with the blue field at the head and over where Nick's left shoulder would be. The procession began its way to the tribal cemetery.

At the cemetery everything was in place. A podium had been set up, chairs were ready for occupants, the rifles to be used in the twenty-one-gun salute were lined up and locked into a V shape, stocks down, barrels up. A lone VFW man stood to the side by the guns. The light of the morning was just beginning to filter through the trees. A gentle breeze whispered through the many bushes scattered there. Birds were singing, promising a beautiful day. Wally could smell the freshly-cut grass and a hint of perfume from one of the shrubs that was in blossom. How peaceful it was here!

Wally realized he needed more moments like this. His life was so busy he never took time to appreciate the natural beauty surrounding him. Glancing up at the sky, the soon-to-emerge sun was lighting up the tops of the clouds in a thin gold line, rays extending outward. It was a spectacular sight. Wally's thoughts briefly wandered back to those few minutes along the shore of Lake Superior with Betsy. Another place filled with beauty and peace.

The family was quickly seated. In lockstep, as directed by their commander, the six VFW pallbearers brought Nick's casket to the gravesite, then took their places near the rifles. Lt. Good stepped up to the podium, introducing Chief White Horse, Senator Stansbury, Minnie, Becca, Annie, himself, and acknowledging the press present and thanking the VFW for their participation. He then turned the podium over to Chief White Horse.

"Our culture is organized into clans. Each clan is made up of family and has a specific function in our tribe. Nick's family was of the Marten clan. That is our warrior clan. It was natural that Nick would choose the military life, as did his father before him and his ancestors before that. Even as a young boy, Nick liked to play games where he portrayed the hero. We Ojibwe believe our Creator put us on this earth for a specific purpose. Although Nick was taken from us early in life, we are comforted by the assurance that whatever his purpose, he had already accomplished it. My condolences to Nick's family. He will be missed by all of us."

Next Lt. Good introduced Senator Stansbury. As he approached the podium, the lightbulbs of the press began flashing. He began by thanking everyone for being there to support the family in their time of sorrow. "It is because of our servicemen that we are a great and powerful nation. Throughout our history, our young men have sacrificed their time, and sadly sometimes their lives. Although they don't ask for special recognition, it is important that we keep them in our thoughts and prayers, and that we never forget the sacrifices they make on a daily basis for us."

At these words, Minnie teared up a little. She was remembering how faithful Nick had been about sending home part of each paycheck. What all had he endured to earn that money? He never would talk about it in his weekly phone calls. All he ever wanted to know was about her and his family and friends on the reservation, but especially her.

Senator Stansbury wrapped up by thanking the family for their sacrifice and reminding the young men present that service to their country could be a noble choice for them as well.

Now Lt. Good took his place behind the podium. "Nick was a Marine's Marine. He was an excellent example for others in the barracks. He was the one with the most squared-away quarters and uniform. His brass was the shiniest. His shoes had the highest shine. He was a top-notch sharpshooter. He mentored many other Marines, helping them to be their best. He was very self-disciplined and he expected the same high standard of others. If another Marine did not meet his standards, he was straightforward about his disappointment. Our motto is 'Semper Fi', always be faithful to the core and each other. He was very well thought-of and he will be greatly missed. Mrs.

Cole, you raised a fine son. I and the Marine Corps are sorry for your loss."

The last person to stand at the podium was the VFW commander, whom Lt. Good introduced as Commander John Neal. "It is an honor to be a part of this detail. I would like to take a moment to read off the names of my squad." After reading off the seven names, he explained the twenty-one-gun salute. This was done in three volleys with the seven guns. "The twenty-one-gun salute has been an accepted practice for a very long time. Originally it was custom during an active battle to have a cease-fire so that the dead and dying could be cleared from the battlefield. The twenty-one-gun salute signaled the conclusion of this operation. I will now give the command for the twenty-one-gun salute." Following the three volleys of fire, he added, "At this point, Stu Neal, from our high-school cadets, will play taps on the bugle."

After taps, Lt. Good gave the signal to Wally and Tom to begin the folding of the flag. With military precision they folded the flag into the traditional triangle, which signified the colonial three-corner hat.

Wally then presented the folded flag to Lt. Good with a crisp salute. He then stepped to Tom's side, executed an about-face, and the two stood at attention.

Lt. Good reverently stepped forward and, bending slightly, presented the flag to Minnie. Lightbulbs flashed as the press recorded this somber moment with their cameras.

As Lt. Good straightened, he could see the tear-streaked faces of Minnie's girls, one on each side of her. Both were looking at their mother with so much love in their eyes. The picture of the three of them, Nick's little family, the mother who lost her husband and now her only son, the girls who lost their beloved brother, their rock, was almost more than he could bear. The presentation of the flag was a very emotional moment. He had to fight to keep his emotions in check. Indeed, it was an emotional moment for many. Behind Minnie many was using Kleenex or handkerchiefs. The entire tribe was saddened by his loss. To them, each member is precious.

Lt. Good stepped back the customary three steps. He stopped and saluted Minnie. He then did an about-face. Three more steps, another about-face, and he was now perfectly aligned with Wally and Tom.

Minnie looked at the three Marines in their dress blues. Behind them the VFW in their khakis. To their right was the senator and his aide. To the left, the young man with his bugle. She then looked down at the flag in her lap. She was touched to the core. This life, so cruelly taken from her, her son who was everything to her, she now realized was important to others as well. People whom she had never met cared about her Nick. It was too much. The emotion she had tried to held back washed over her in a wave of sorrow. Suddenly she felt Becca's arms around her. Reaching for Annie, she found Annie reaching for her at the same time. Pulling her girls close and comforting them comforted her too.

At a signal from Chief White Horse, the assembled mourners sang the traveling song. Then the flutist began. A clear, lovely, melody floated on the air, rising and falling like a gentle breeze. The music grew softer and quieter, until it was no more. The service was over. On cue, the morning sun broke the horizon.

Giving her girls a squeeze of their hands, Minnie rose and went to thank in turn Lt. Good, the senator, and the VFW commander. Each offered a few private words of sympathy.

She also thanked the young bugler and the flutist. There were many sympathetic hugs from friends and family. It was time to leave. Becca drove Minnie and Annie home in the car someone had loaned her for this occasion.

Wally, Tom, and Lt. Good climbed in the car provided by the local Marine base. Their driver took them to Singin' Sandy's for lunch. As the four men entered the restaurant, Sandy glanced over at them. Seeing Lt. Good, Sandy decided now was not a good time to tease Tom with a special song. "Darn," she thought. She had a good one all prepared. She continued to sing, but her song fragments remained generic.

At Minnie's, Becca immediately went to the refrigerator. It was jammed with gifts of food. She pulled it all out and set up a buffet for everyone. No one had eaten breakfast, so lunch would be welcome. Plus, she knew, many people would be stopping by on this day. Sure enough, a knock on the door and there was Lucinda with her little grandson, Rolly. Annie hopped up from beside her mother, took Rolly by the hand and brought him to the kitchen. Soon everyone followed.

As they ate, Minnie outlined what Betsy would see at the gravesite. By the time Betsy got there, Nick's body would be covered with birch bark and the spirit house would be in place over it. "Spirit house?" Betsy did not know about this.

Minnie said "We cover the graves with houses we call Spirit Houses. Nick is by his father. I had intended to be by George and my spirit house was already built and ready to be placed. But when Nick died so unexpectedly, there wasn't time to build one for him, so I gave him my place and my spirit house. I will have a space on the other side of George. I will have another spirit house built for me."

After lunch, Lucinda said she would take care of cleanup. Rolly and Annie helped carry the dirty dishes to the kitchen. Minnie got quick hugs from Becca and Betsy and the two young women left for the cemetery.

Becca parked the car. They began to walk up to the cemetery. Becca was very apprehensive, straining to see if the cemetery workers had done as they were instructed. Informed of the special circumstances, they were to have the grave covered and the spirit house in place. She was relieved to find everything ready for Betsy's visit.

Betsy also was taking in the visual of the cemetery as she walked up the graveled approach. It was surrounded by a rusty iron fence. She realized it must be a very old cemetery. There were many trees, some quite large; another clue that this cemetery had been used for many generations. What must it be like to have a place where all your ancestors are buried? There was a timelessness here. Betsy began to get an even clearer understanding of the continuation of life. We build on those who lived before us. The people that they were and the actions that they took travel down through time to define us, who we are. Without even realizing it, Betsy had placed her hand protectively on her stomach.

As they wove their way around the graves, Betsy could see the spirit houses Minnie had told her about. They had peaked roofs. She estimated the distance from ground to peak to be perhaps four feet. Some houses were long; others shorter. Instead of a door, they just had an opening. All the openings were facing in the same direction. Betsy saw a pack of cigarettes by one; a can of Pepsi by another.

Becca explained how the family would bring little things their loved one had enjoyed in life, so they might have them in their next life.

Becca pointed out Nick's gravesite. It was easy to find because of the brass marker flush with the ground at Nick's father's site. Becca explained the U.S. government had sent that, and that they would send a similar marker for Nick's grave.

As Betsy looked at Nick's spirit house, with the fresh dirt under it, Nick's death became real to her. He really was gone. His body was here, but he was gone. She would never see him again. Not ever. She never would again feel his comforting arms around her; the warmth of his body against hers. This was why she had traveled over two thousand miles. She had to know. In her heart. In her soul. In her very being. Until this very moment there had been some crazy hope. A mistake. Not Nick. Not really Nick. But now she knew. The sorrow was more than she could bear. Tears flooded her eyes. The sorrow bubbled up and out of her, releasing itself in great gasping sobs. She was crying so hard her knees buckled and she sank to the earth. And Becca was there, holding her, crying too, crying for Betsy's sorrow as well as her own.

Then it was quiet. Betsy could hear the gentle breeze in the trees. It tickled a windchime off in the distance, causing it to send forth a pretty little tune of its own invention. Birds were chirping. Just then a chickadee flew down from a nearby tree branch and landed on the peak of Nick's spirit house. It appeared to be quite interested in the two women on the ground. It cocked its head this way and that. It chirped at them.

It hopped a little closer. Becca was thrilled. "Look, Betsy. It is Nick's spirit bird. He is telling us he is OK He is happy. He wants us to be happy, too."

Although Betsy didn't buy into that belief, the thought did bring her some measure of comfort. Perhaps Nick really was in some place much better than this. Perhaps Nick would always be watching over her and their baby. She knew she had to be strong. "OK, little chickadee. No more tears. I will do my best. But you must come to visit me from time to time when I forget to smile."

Almost as if the tiny bird understood, he chirped once more and flew back up to his perch in the tree.

Now that the storm clouds of grief had passed, Becca sensed Betsy might like a few private moments at Nick's gravesite. "I know you would like some time alone here, so I'll wait for you in the car. Stay as long as you wish."

At the car, Becca watched. At first Betsy just stood there, perhaps praying? But then she opened her purse, took out a small notebook and a pen, and began to write. At one point she stopped, looked up at the tree where the chickadee had flown. She took out a Kleenex and wiped her eyes. Then she resumed writing. Finishing, she removed the sheet, folded it, and placed it inside the opening to Nick's spirit house. One more glance back as she descended the hill, and then she reached the car.

At the restaurant, Sandy was busy with her usual morning crowd. Tom walked over to her, but there wasn't much opportunity to talk to her right then. He simply told her he would call once he got back to base. He so wanted to kiss her, but wrong place, wrong time. He did reach across the half wall, and with a twinkle in his eye, chucked her under the chin. Sandy wondered if he really would call, or was she just a fling while he was away from base. She knew how girls were around military bases. As good-looking as Tom was, there would be many temptations for him. She reached across the wall and dropped something into Tom's hand. When he looked, he saw a small silver horseshoe. "For good luck," Sandy said. He smiled and placed it in his wallet for safe keeping.

For the first time in her life, Sandy felt chained to the restaurant. Morning, noon, and night she was always working there: cleaning, cooking, paperwork. She'd inherited the place from her folks. It was all she'd ever known. The restaurant and the regulars who came here were her life. She'd never had much time for a social life. It wasn't until Tom came along that she realized how much she had been missing. And yet, even now, she had no desire to change that. It was Tom. Only Tom. As the men left, Sandy wasn't singing.

When Becca reentered the house, Minnie looked up at her anxiously. Becca gave her a reassuring nod and a smile, signifying everything went well.

Before long there was the sound of a car, a knock at the door and the men were there to pick up Betsy. Lt. Good had met Minnie, but was introduced to Lucinda and the girls. He then stepped over to Minnie. "I have something for you. This is from the men in Nick's barracks." He handed her a card. When she opened it, there was also money in the envelope. Minnie was overwhelmed by this gesture. She knew how small paychecks were. What a wonderful gesture.

Protocol be damned—she got up and hugged a very surprised Lt. Good. "Please thank them all for me. I don't know what to say. Everyone had been so kind and thoughtful."

Lt. Good replied, "The men really cared about Nick and asked if they could do this."

Lt. Good explained that, although it was usual to return a serviceman's belongings to the family, in this case they would need to be held at the base until after the trial. But he assured Minnie they would eventually be returned to her. He would see to it personally.

The duty driver had been waiting in the car and they had a plane to catch. As the others were saying good-bye, Minnie took the opportunity to have a private moment with Wally. Placing his hand between both of hers, she looked him in the eye and said "Watch over Betsy."

Wally simply said, "I will." Hugs, tears, promises to stay in touch, and the travelers were on their way.

Chapter 10

The flight home was uneventful. The men were seated together and Betsy was one row ahead, in front of Lt. Good. Wally would have liked to sit beside her, but asking the lady beside her to sit with Lt. Good just didn't seem like a good idea. The guys took advantage of the opportunity, once again, to get a little extra sleep.

Betsy appreciated the quiet time and used it to do a lot of thinking. She reviewed everything that had happened in Minnesota, the people she'd met and come to love, the things she'd learned. She was ever so glad she had gone. Now it was time to begin thinking about the future; hers and her baby's. Occasionally her mind would slip back to that final night at the park on Lake Superior with Wally. So calm. So peaceful. So safe.

Betsy was met at the airport by her parents. She introduced Lt. Good and Tom and reintroduced Wally. Handshakes all around. Wally joked "See? I told you I would get her back to you all in one piece." Mr. Miller smiled at this.

As they were parting, Betsy turned to Wally and teasingly said "Call me. You never did tell me the story about your crazy family."

Wally laughed and promised he would. Holding up three fingers, he added, "Scout's honor."

Wally and Tom got back to base in the wee hours of the morning. They were permitted to sleep late. An announcement came over the loudspeaker to see Gunny after noon chow. At lunch they were peppered with many questions from the men in the barracks. There was much curiosity about the reservation and the burial customs there. The two put off answering questions because of the meeting with Gunny, but promised to go over everything later.

Gunny commended them on the manner in which they conducted themselves during the trip. He'd received a glowing report from Lt. Good. He added that, although he would like to hear the whole story, he was positive everyone in the barracks would like to hear it too. He'd asked Lt. Good, and wanted Wally and Tom as well, to meet in the barracks classroom at 0800 tomorrow to go over everything. That way everyone could hear it at the same time.

At this point, Gunny dismissed Tom. Gunny then informed Wally that soon he would be interviewed by both the trial counsel and John's defense counsel, and perhaps others. There even may be more than one interview by these men. The court martial would be in four weeks.

Wally no sooner got back to his bunk when tomorrow's meeting in the classroom was announced. Even the captain would be coming. He slumped onto his bunk, thinking over everything. He stretched out, tired yet keyed up. So many thoughts were running through his head. He glanced over at Nick's locker. It had been taped. The message on the tape read "Do not break this seal." There was a new lock on it that looked pretty substantial. Bulletproof? He looked at his watch. An entire hour had slipped away since talking with Gunny.

Tom came up and sat on the edge of Wally's bunk. He'd just called Angie to get updates on John. Angie planned on seeing John tomorrow night. She suggested she and Tom meet up at Fisherman's Wharf for dinner and she could update him then. Wally asked, "So, are you going to go?"

"Oh yeah—should be an interesting evening, Tom replied.

"Well, be sure to fill me in on the details."

Captain Morgan began the meeting with the usual, "Good morning. Just like you I am here because we all are interested in the story of Nick's funeral and burial. But before I turn the mic over to Lt. Good, you know I like to start any meeting with a little light-hearted humor. A ninety-year-old man went to his doctor and said 'Doctor, I must be in pretty good shape. My eighteen-year-old wife is expecting a baby.' The doctor said, 'Let me tell you a story. A man went hunting, but instead of a gun, he accidently picked up his umbrella. When a bear charged him, he pointed his umbrella at the bear, shot and killed him on the spot.' 'That's not possible' said the old man. 'Somebody else must have shot the bear.' The doctor said, 'My point exactly.' "

Amid laughter, the Captain brought Lt. Good to the podium. Lt. Good thanked the Captain and began. "I would like Tom and Wally to come up here as well. We will talk about all that took place, but to save time, please hold your questions until the end of our account."

"As you know, we were entering a particularly difficult situation. We did not know how we would be received. Nick was a member of the Ojibwe tribe in Duluth, Minnesota. My task was to coordinate the military funeral with tribal custom. I worked with the tribal chief whose name was White Horse. Most funerals in this day on the reservation are quite traditional, pretty much the same as any of you might have attended. But Nick's mother wanted to have an Ojibwa funeral that honored the Old Ways. She also wanted some Marine presence because Nick was so proud of being a Marine. My account will explain what Chief White Horse and I worked out. Nick's body was accompanied to the reservation by two Marines, as is our custom. In this case the two Marines were Tom and Wally. Once there, we were assisted by both local Marines and the local VFW. They provided cars for us."

"According to ancient tradition, Nick's body was held at the tribal center for three days, and buried before dawn on the fourth day. That really was Day Five, as the first day was spent in transit."

"Tom and Wally stood watch by the casket from 0800 to 1600 each day. Other shifts were provided by local Marines, so that Nick's body was never left unguarded."

"During this time, the tribe conducted various ceremonies, according to their traditions. On the fifth day local military transported the casket to the cemetery. There were short eulogies by chief White Horse, a state senator, and myself. The VFW signaled the usual twenty-one-gun salute. The VFW also found a high school student to play taps. Wally and Tom folded the flag and I presented it to Nick's mother. Chief White Horse ended the service with music from a flute. It was a very moving service. Wally and Tom, do you have anything to add? "Both men shook their heads, so Lt. Good opened the floor up to questions.

The first question was about why so many days. Tom answered that one. "Tribal belief is that at death the soul begins a journey that will conclude on either the fourth evening or during the night. Burial follows that. Each day there were specific rituals took place outside the tribal center. A different one each day. It was very interesting."

"What kind of rituals?"

"A bonfire was started on the first day of Nick's death. It was kept going by family until Nick was buried. There was drumming, dancing, singing. Lots of potluck food. Various members of Nick's family also took turns standing vigil by Nick's body inside the tribal center. People would come and pay their respects and leave little gifts in Nick's casket."

"What is a reservation like?"

Wally took that one. "I was surprised by the level of poverty there. Many live on small checks from the government. It is barely enough to get by. There doesn't seem to be much work there. Some, like Nick, leave the reservation for a better life. By the way, your gift of money to Nick's family was much appreciated"

"What about John? What happened out there?"

At that point Lt. Good stepped in. "No one is allowed to talk about that at this time. It is important that you men do not talk about it as well. We don't want a lot of misinformation flying around that might taint John's trial. We want him to have a fair trial. We can tell you he is incarcerated at Treasure Island.

He has been appointed a defense attorney. The court martial is in four weeks."

The Captain added, "Each of you may be summoned for questioning at some time. You may know something relevant to the case and not even realize it. In the meantime, if there is something you know that you believe either the prosecution or the defense should be aware of, please contact Gunny and no one but Gunny. Are there any more questions? No? I would like to thank Lt. Good, Tom, and Wally for doing an outstanding job. Dismissed."

As Wally and Tom were walking out, they talked about the meeting. They both felt good about the special praise they had received from the Captain and Lt. Good. They talked a bit about the people they had met and the things they had learned. Both agreed these were memories that would last a lifetime. When Wally mentioned Singin' Sandy's, Tom said he was really missing Sandy. He said he had never met anyone he enjoyed being with so much.

Life resumed its normal rhythm after that. Tom went back to his guard duties at the front gate. Wally started his duty-driver responsibilities once again.

One day, Wally was summoned to Gunny's office. As he walked, he saw Gunny with a bigger-than-life black man; a private. He seemed to take up the entire office. He towered over Gunny, and was even taller than Wally. There were a few black men in the barracks, but this man was darker-skinned than any of them. Despite his intimidating size, he had a very friendly smile on his face.

Gunny introduced him as Allouishus Jackson, but quickly added that he goes by AJ. Gunny said AJ would be his new bunkmate and that Wally should take him to Supply and then show him around.

Wally and AJ went downstairs. On their way to Supply, Wally pointed out various rooms in the basement. "Here is where you work out. You can get your uniforms pressed here. It is free, but after two or three times, you have to send them to the dry cleaners. You have to pay for that. This room is called the Marines Club. You can go in there and have a beer, snacks, stuff like that. On the weekends they have dances in here. It is pretty small. Not many of the gate girls will come here. Most prefer the Enlisted Men's Club, which is larger."

"What are gate girls?"

"Oh, when there is a dance, girls will gather at the front gate. They can't come in unless someone signs them in. Whoever signs a girl in is responsible for that girl while she is on base. The guys like to joke that it is a girl whose ass you can bounce a quarter off of."

At Supply, Sgt. McClellan issued bedding, including a mattress, which AJ hoisted onto his shoulder.

The men went up the stairs leading back to the first floor. On the first floor Wally pointed out the Day Room, visible through a pair of double doors. AJ could see pool tables in there. On the far side of the Day Room was the Mess Hall.

They continued on up the stairs to the second floor. Wally pointed out the classroom on the right. Now they were in the squad bay. Walking across the bay to the far end, they reached Wally's bunk area. Wally pointed out two more areas. "Through that door is the bathroom and showers. And that second door is the NCO room."

Wally helped AJ get his mattress onto the top bunk, not that he needed much help. Not only was the man tall; he was exceedingly muscular. Wally pointed out the two lockers, formerly Nick's and now unsealed and emptied, that now would be AJ's. He told AJ there would be an announcement over the loudspeaker when it was chow time.

As AJ was beginning to make up his bunk, Wally showed him a few things that were inside his pillowcase. One was a white cartridge belt, to be worn when on gate duty. The other was a white helmet liner, also to be worn on gate duty.

"There is a bulletin board on the first floor by Gunny's office. Those are the doors we come in and go out by, so it is convenient. You check there to see if you have gate duty. If you do, you go out with the other Marines who will have duty and get your uniform inspected. That is done out back and before morning chow."

"AJ, I will warn you, you are going to hear talk about my former bunkmate, Nick Cole. He was killed while on duty at the back gate. We are not allowed to talk about the circumstances until after the trial. Just so you know. Nick was a really good guy. He helped me get squared away when I first came here. And I would be happy to do the same for you, if you would like. Do you have any questions so far?"

"Yeah, I do. When do we get liberty?"

"Good question. You have twenty-four hours on followed by twenty-four hours off duty. But every other weekend you have to work. This might mean you will work two days in a row that weekend."

"I don't understand. I have to work for twenty-four hours?"

"You don't work twenty-four hours; you are on duty for twenty-four hours. You actually only work eight hours; four hours at a time. You will have to check the bulletin board for your on-duty hours."

Wally asked AJ where he was from. "Detroit. How about you?"

"Hey, I'm from a little town outside Detroit called Rochester."

"Once you get unpacked, I'll walk you across the street to the police station. Our shower is under repair, so we have to shower over there."

"Police station?"

"We are military police. Across the street they are civilian police. There are thousands of civilians that work here at the shipyard. Catch you later."

Wally walked down the squad bay aisle. He saw Teddy by his bunk. "Hey, Teddy, how're things at the Red Garter?"

"Hard to say. Payday is a few days away, but the last time I was there Maria was breaking in a new gal. I've had better luck at the Enlisted Men's Club. Met a beautiful German girl. She's only been in country for two years. She stays at the YWCA. I told her about you, if you want to get fixed up."

"Teddy, let's go to chow and talk about it. Let me go get my new bunkmate and see if he wants to eat."

The men went to the first-floor mess hall. They each grabbed a tray, chose what they wanted to eat, and looked around for a place to sit. Teddy found room for three at one of the long tables and they sat down. Wally introduced AJ to the other guys seated there. Soon AJ was conversing freely with them. There were the usual questions about where each was from, etc. AJ had questions for them and he learned a lot about military life as they ate. AJ had a gift for gab and made new friends easily.

One day the loudspeaker summoned Wally to Gunny's office. There Gunny introduced him to Lt. Sanchez, whom he said was John's defense counsel. Gunny then left the two men alone, closing the door behind him.

Lt. Sanchez told Wally to take a seat. He also sat down in a nearby chair.

"Sir, how's John doing?" Wally asked.

"As well as can be expected, under the circumstances."

Lt. Sanchez continued. "I'm sure what happened must have been quite a shock to you. I understand you and Nick were very good friends. This is a small base and we both know the brotherhood between Marines is very strong. I would like for you to take me back through that night, remembering every little detail, to the best of your ability. Can you do that for me?" Wally recounted all that he could remember.

"Let's go back to the beginning of your account. Why were you on your way to the back gate?"

"Sir, the Corporal sent me. This was just a random check to make sure the men that were posted were doing their job."

"Is it true that you did not get along with John?"

This question shocked Wally so much, he jumped up. "Sir, I don't know what you are talking about, Lt. Sanchez. John was a good guy. He got along with everybody, including me. We all liked him."

Lt. Sanchez chuckled. "Sit down, Wally. I threw that question out to try to rattle you. I want to use you as a witness, but I needed to know how you felt about John; if you had any bias. I can see now that you don't."

"I want you to think back to that night. You stated earlier that it was a very quiet night. Do you recall any other vehicles on the road? Did anybody pass you?"

"Sir, no one was out at that hour."

"Did you see any other people in the area?"

"Sir, it was very foggy, but I don't think so."

"Wally, didn't you just post guard an hour before your return?"

"Yes sir, I did."

"How many times do you come around during a shift?"

"Sir, it is random."

"Let me get this straight. It is a four-hour shift. You posted the guards in question one hour before. Correct?"

"Yes, sir."

"When you posted the guard, who was with you?"

"Sir, Corporal Keno, the two men being replaced, as well as Nick and John."

"What are the names of the two men coming off duty?"

"Sir, PFC Bill Summerfield, and Private Ben Copeland. They got in the back of the duty truck and I dropped them off at the barracks." Sanchez wrote those two names down.

"Did you notice any problems between Nick and John at that time?"

"No, sir."

"Have you ever known either John or Nick to have a disagreement?"

"No, sir."

"Have you ever known Nick to have a disagreement with anyone in the barracks?"

"Well, sir, he had a big mouth. He was gung ho about the Marines. He did let people know if they were making our unit look bad."

"Did you ever see Nick get into any kind of argument or fight?"

"No, sir. If I may, Nick helped me out tremendously and I respected him."

"Ok, let's go on. Have you ever known John to lose his temper?"

"No, sir. If I may, he was a very easy-going guy. I never knew of anyone at the barracks to get into a fight with either John or Nick."

"PFC Wally, what do you think happened that night out there?"

Wally paused, giving the question some thought. "Sir, I honestly don't know, but there have been a few other things that happened out there. I know because I stood duty at the back gate for the first year I was at Hunter's Point. They were high-jinks, usually played on a newbie. Like taking the fire extinguisher and squirting foam on someone's leg."

"Are you saying pranks?"

"Yes, sir."

"Have you ever heard of someone playing fast draw?"

"Yes, sir."

"Have you ever played fast draw?"

"No sir, but I've heard it did happen a few times."

"Now, Wally, this is very important. It could help John's defense. Who did you hear had played fast draw?"

"I'd have to think about it. Right now, I couldn't say, sir."

Lt. Sanchez removed a large photo from his briefcase and showed it to Wally. "This was taken that night. Can you point out what we see here?" Wally pointed out the guard house. He pointed to another building, which was a bathroom. He explained the bathroom roof extended outward on one side to shelter people waiting for the bus that would take them off base.

"Where was John, when you first saw him?" Wally pointed to a spot in the middle of the outgoing lane.

The next photo was of the interior of the guard house. Wally turned his head away from that photo. Seeing Nick on the floor once again gave him a sick feeling in the pit of his stomach.

"Is this the way that you found Nick?"

"Sir, no, he was seated, leaning up against the wall. When I went to shake his shoulder, and I touched him, he slid to the sideways position you see here in this photo."

Pointing to the gun on the floor beside Nick, Lt. Sanchez asked if that is where the gun was originally.

"Sir I'm not sure. It may have moved slightly when Nick's body slid over. I, however, did not touch it. I left it for others to pick up."

There were many more questions and many more photos to try to explain. The session with Lt. Sanchez went on for most of the afternoon. As Wally was leaving the office, he was reminded not to say anything to anyone about what had been covered regarding the upcoming trial.

Chapter 11

When Wally got back to his bunk, AJ was there. "Teddy is going to take me to the Red Garter. He said to see if you and Tom would like to come along. He's got a car." That sounded like a perfect way to spend a Friday night to Wally. He had liberty and he just got paid. The two men went to hunt up Tom.

They found Tom at his bunk, freshly showered and getting dressed. "No, I can't go with you guys. Wish I could. Got that dinner with Angie. She wanted to go to Fisherman's Wharf, but that was a little above my pay scale. She was disappointed, but then suggested a bar around the corner from her apartment called the Hideaway. Ever hear of it?" Negative. Wishing him a good evening, they left to go hunt up Teddy.

They found Teddy with his buddy, Domer. Teddy had a card-board hand-made license plate tucked under his arm. Someone asked about it. "Oh, you know. I screwed up and lost my liberty again. They knew I have a car in the lot. So, to keep me from leaving base, they removed my license plate. Not gonna stop me. I just made me a new one."

Now Teddy could best be described as a good ole' boy from the South. Vero Beach, Florida, to be exact. He had that "whatever works" mentality, a hilarious sense of humor, and the occasional tendency to skirt the law; common traits among a certain breed of Southerner. He was also wild about the ladies; the wilder the ladies, the better.

When they got to the car, Teddy whipped out a key and unlocked a padlock on the driver's side door handle. "What's the matter, Teddy. Door lock won't work?"

"Oh, the damn door won't stay shut. So, I installed this. Keeps the door from flying open when I am driving. Hop in boys, while I put this license plate on."

Once inside the car, Teddy rolled the window down, reached out, and put the padlock back on, securing the door. The motor stumbled and sputtered a bit, but eventually caught and they were off.

AJ asked about the Red Garter. Nathan explained it was a bar in downtown San Francisco. It was a favorite hangout for the guys. It was a place of new friends, loud music, and fast women. "Think I'm gonna like it," he laughed.

At the bar the men took two tables and slid them together. Teddy was up and bouncing about from table to table. He seemed to know a lot of the men in there. Soon he was back with a couple of guys in tow. He introduced them as Bently and Nathan.

Maria came over to introduce the buxom new waitress. "Guys, this is Jennifer. She'll be taking your orders. Take it easy on her, she's new. Teddy, keep your hands off her. Separate checks, as usual?" The men all ordered the same thing, Hamm beer; beer happening to be the cheapest thing on the menu. Teddy did ask Jennifer if she had a boyfriend.

"I have an ex." Jennifer asked if anyone wanted something to eat, but no one added to their order.

The conversation began to flow. Wally stated that it was good to be back at the base after the trip to Minnesota. He asked what had been happening since he was gone. Domer said he'd heard the Marines were going to lose two more guys. Their two years were up. Teddy added that one of them had gotten his girl pregnant. Bently spoke up. "Yeah, I heard that too. What's he going to do; take her to his new duty station?"

Teddy said "No. He's not taking her to a new duty station. He's getting out."

"Is he taking her with him?"

Teddy again. "No, He's gonna leave her here for you guys. Who wants to be the dad?" Someone volunteered AJ.

"No way, man." Then everybody laughed.

"Naw, we're just messing with you."

"Hey, AJ, have you been approached yet?"

"Approached? I don't understand."

Domer again. "There are a lot of gays here in San Francisco. It is perfectly legal for them to come up and proposition you. It might make you want to take that mother****** down. Just so you know, they are protected here. You touch one and you go to jail."

"No kidding?"

"Seriously. Just walk away."

Someone piped up, "Domer never walks away. He loves the attention."

Domer said "Screw you! If my dick's diving into someone tonight, it won't be some gay guy."

The banter continued. "Oh yeah? When's the last time you got a piece of ass?"

"I dunno, when's the last time your sister was in town?"

The fun ceased when Jennifer came to the table asking if anyone was ready for another beer. While the others were placing their orders, AJ whispered to Wally, "Do you think someone is going to get into a fight here?"

Wally whispered back, "If you're going to dish it out, you'd better be able to take it."

Teddy said "Hey. If you've got a girl and you are wanting to get into her pants, I might be able to help you out. On base."

"Oh yeah? Where? I sure can't come up with anything!"

"Are you talking about the balcony at the flicks?"

"Much better than that."

"The baseball diamond? I heard somebody struck out there."

"Way better." But Teddy wasn't giving it up. "You got a girl that's hot to trot and you seriously need a place, I've got a good one. It's clean, it's private, and it's handy."

All conversation abruptly ended and all heads swiveled to the door as two good-looking ladies stepped into the bar. "Well," said Teddy. "Look who's here. Hey, Lorraine, bring your friend and come on over. We've got two extra chairs just for you."

Lorraine came over and introduced her friend as Debbie.

Teddy jumped up and pulled out two chairs, seating Debbie, the prettier of the two, by himself and Lorraine by Domer. The guys introduced themselves and Jennifer appeared at their table, prepared to take new orders.

"So, Ranie, did you drive, or walk?" Teddy asked.

"We walked. We figured someone would give us a ride home later."

"Where do you live, Debbie?" Teddy wanted to know.

"I moved in with Rainie after Patty left."

"Oh? Where did Patty go?"

"She met some guy and moved in with him."

"Damn, I liked her. Gonna miss her around here."

Conversation was beginning to split into smaller groups. Teddy was busy getting to know Debbie. Lorraine was talking with Domer and the rest were bantering back and forth, but keeping it clean for the ladies.

Lola walked in. Teddy waved her over, instructing Nathan to pull up a chair at his end of the table. "I think you know everyone here except AJ (AJ waved) and Debbie (another wave)."

One more beer and everybody was ready for a game. Bently suggested "Rumble" and explained how it works. "You tap your hands on the table, like this. Then with your right hand you make a gesture. You invent your own. No two at the table can use the same gesture. It can be an OK sign, or a thumbs down, or something else. Mine is the thumbs up. OK, everybody show your gesture. Now, I'll start the game. Everybody tap." He gave his sign, the thumbs up, and Domer's sign, two fingers down, like a baseball catcher might signal to the pitcher. "Now," Bently said, "Domer has to give his sign and follow it with somebody else's." The game continued, with the tempo of the tapping ever increasing, until somebody didn't realize his sign had been given. It was AJ. Everybody laughed and as a penalty AJ had to take a swallow of his beer. Then the game resumed.

Before long, people were getting up to use the head. The game died down, people were shifting seats, and conversation became more one on one.

Eventually Lorraine and Debbie decided to call it a night, taking Domer and Bently with them. Shortly after that, Lola took her cue and invited Nathan to go with her. Teddy, always the instigator, had made arrangements with Maria and Jennifer to go out with them after closing. Since it would be late, Teddy asked AJ if he would like to stick around and they would get him back to base. Or Teddy gave him the option of taking the jitney. AJ didn't know about the jitney, so Teddy explained it could get him back to base. He told him where to catch it, and that it only cost him a quarter to ride. AJ opted for the jitney.

As AJ was getting into the jitney, the driver took one look at the size of him and joked "Hey, Big Guy, I should charge you double." AJ sat down with the other military on board, all in civilian clothes after a night on the town. Everyone waited for the jitney to fill up. He didn't realize it, but he was the only Marine. The others were Navy. On the trip back, they were joking about the gate house guards, not realizing AJ was now one of them. AJ was uncomfortable about the conversation, but had to admit the jitney was a very convenient service.

Wally and Teddy had taken their drinks over to the pinball machines. By the time they had played two games, the raucous atmosphere of the bar had become much more subdued as the Friday night crowd thinned out. Soon the bar was empty and the girls were ready to go.

Outside, Teddy flipped Wally the keys. "You drive."

"Where?"

"I don't give a shit. Just drive." Teddy and Maria hopped into the back seat and lost no time getting down to business.

Wally put the key in the ignition and tried to start the car. He pumped the accelerator several times. Old Semi-Faithful sputtered and wheezed, but eventually she started.

Teddy came up for air long enough to gasp out "Golden Gate Bridge. Far side. Parking lot by fort."

To shut out the somewhat disturbing noises emanating from the back seat, Wally suggested to Jennifer she find some music on the radio. She giggled, slid over to the center of the seat and reached forward to turn the dial on the radio. Somehow her ample breast brushed against Wally's arm. A thrill shot through Wally's body. Now he was acutely aware of her warm thigh against his leg. Soon her hand rested on his thigh, then it was going up and down his thigh, slowly, caressingly. He could hardly concentrate on his driving.

A parking spot was easy to find in the deserted lot. Teddy hopped out, opened the trunk, tucked a blanket under his arm, and disappeared into the darkness, Maria in tow. In no time, Wally and Jennifer were steaming up the windows as well. Fifteen minutes later, just as things were getting interesting, Teddy and Maria were back. The men dropped the ladies off, returned to the barracks, fell into bed, and were soon dead asleep.

That same evening, Angie was having her much-anticipated date with Tom at the Hideaway Bar. When he'd asked how he would recognize her, she told him to look for a tall blond—long hair—in a red dress.

When Tom saw her, he could see she hadn't been exaggerating. She was everything she had described, and yet somehow all that she had done to enhance her appearance had only served to cheapen it. Her height was due to stiletto heels so tall he wondered how she could stand up in them. Her hair was long and blond, yes, but with dark roots. Too much rouge, too much eye makeup, lips as red as a monkey's ass. Her eyebrows had been shaved off and replaced with drawn-on, highly-arched eyebrows, a la Marlene Dietrich. The red dress had the sparkle of a New Year's Eve party garment, and was barely there. It was designed to show off cleavage, and Angie had plenty of cleavage to show. It was short, barely covering the essentials. A hemline like that might be attractive on a gal with good legs. But Angie's were pudgy, a fact she tried to disguise with black fishnet stockings. Everything about Angie screamed "I'm available," and despite her flaws every male's jaw dropped open when she walked into the bar. She obviously was relishing the attention.

Tom stood up and waved. She saw him and wobbled over. As she drew closer, her smile widened. She was liking what she saw.

Tom, however, was noticing she was probably older than his first impression. The heavy makeup was an attempt to conceal a puffy and aging face. He could see where someone like John, a farm boy from the Midwest, might be smitten by someone like Angie. But what could she possibly see in him? His sweet nature? His large package? A steady paycheck? Would any of that inspire loyalty in Angie? He doubted it.

Tonight, dressed as she was, Tom guessed that she was already moving on, and he wondered if he was her next target.

Still, he wanted all the news about John that he could pry out of her. He had the impression from previous phone calls that she was deliberately withholding information so that she could wrangle a date with him. Well, she got her way.

Dinner was simple; pizza and beer. Conversation was light. Every time Tom brought up John, she would divert to a different topic. She was openly flirting with him, batting her eyes, playing with her hair, talking a little too loudly, laughing a bit too much, touching his arm. At one point she withdrew a cigarette from her purse, tapped the end of it on the table, stuck it in her mouth, and asked for a light. As Tom held the lighter to the tip, she took his hand in both of hers, as if to steady it. She then leaned back, arching her back slightly, a movement which pushed her breasts forward, straining the fabric of her dress. She drew in on her cigarette and then expelled the smoke upward and out of the side of her lips in a manner she supposed would appear sexy.

Three beers later, she suggested they go to her apartment to talk about John. She claimed it was just too noisy there in the bar. "It is just around the corner. We can walk there. We'll have a drink and I can tell you all I know about what happened."

Angie's apartment was upstairs, small, and cramped. She sat Tom down on one end of the stained and grungy sofa and asked him what he would like to drink. He said another beer would be fine, but she claimed to be fresh out of beer. She could fix him a mixed drink, she said, a rum and Coke. Tom, who was already feeling the effects of more beer than he was used to, said to go easy on the rum. Instead she went heavy on his rum and light on hers.

Bringing the drinks, she sat down next to him on the sofa. Now she did begin to open up about John. Tom asked her how they met. "It was at a dance on base. I needed someone to sign me in and he was available. He was so shy and somehow that appealed to me. He was sweet. He'd show up with a single rose or a little piece of jewelry for me. You know, little things a girl likes. Yeah, I'm gonna miss all that."

"Miss all that? Do you think he'll go to prison?"

"Who knows. All I know is I'm moving on. Anyone that would shoot somebody like that gives me the creeps."

"But you did go see him?" Tom asked.

"Yeah. I knew you wanted me to, so I went. 'Bout froze my ass off. Do you have any idea how cold and damp it is out there on that island? John said he couldn't stay warm no matter how many clothes he put on. The chill just goes right through you. All that grey cement. Man, that place is drearier than Sally Stanford's brothel on the night before payday."

"So, did he tell you what happened out there?"

"His lawyer told him not to talk about it. But I put on an act that should've won me an academy award. I was sooo disappointed. I'd come all that way, blah blah blah… well, I laid it on pretty thick. The schmuck was so eager to please me, he gave in. Ready for another drink?"

When Angie came back with the drinks (Tom's again heavy on the rum), she was off on a tangent about how she was going to redecorate her apartment. Try as he could to bring her back to John, he couldn't break in. He sipped his rum and Coke. He was definitely feeling the effects of too much alcohol. He was slouching lower and lower on the sofa. Suddenly feeling very warm, he slurringly asked Angie would she mind if he loosened his shirt.

"Not at all. Here, let me help you." Kneeling between his knees, she had his shirt unbuttoned speedier than a Marine leaving base on a liberty weekend. He was starting to feel a different kind of warm. Her perfume, wafting up to his nostrils, was intoxicating. He found himself aroused by the feel of her breasts against his thighs. His blurred thinking remembered how this had always been a teenage fantasy of his. Reaching down, he pulled her up and on top of him. She was kissing him passionately; wriggling against his firm cock. She felt wonderful to him.

Suddenly she stood, pulling him up onto his feet. Taking Tom's hand, she led him into the bedroom. Then came the pants dance as they struggled with zippers, belts, buttons, hose, and anything else that could stand in the way of total skin against skin.

The last thing Tom remembered doing before they tumbled into bed, was placing his wallet on the bedside stand. Angie straddled him and with a practiced hand soon had him inside her. Tom groaned. She felt so good. He grabbed her ass. She was rocking back and forth, the bed squeaking loudly, making music of its own. Tom wanted more. Without disengaging, he picked her up and rolled her onto her back. He began thrusting harder and harder. She moaned in delight. All of a sudden, and without warning Mount Vesuvius erupted.

After, Angie laughed. "Look at the size of that wet spot on the bed! It's been quite a while for you, hasn't it, honey. Let me go get a towel. You stay right there." Tom was in no condition to move even if he wanted to. She returned with a towel, which she placed over the wet spot. She produced a pack of cigarettes and they talked as they smoked.

Tom told her he had never experienced anything like that. "You were incredible. I can still feel the pulsing of my cock inside you."

Angie was happy as well. "You were wonderful. When I was on top of you, I wanted you so badly. And when you took charge, you curled my toes. It was so good. You were probably too busy to notice, but my nipples were as hard as rocks. In fact, just talking about it is making them hard again."

Maybe it was the alcohol, or maybe it was the conversation, but Tom was horny again. He rolled over on top of Angie. "I'm ready to go again. Are you"

"Oh my god, yes! I think I can never get enough of you."

After that second marathon session, Tom was exhausted, but it would probably take a week to wipe the smile off his face. Angie didn't want him to leave. "Stay the night. I'll wake you in time to make roll call." It didn't take much persuading and soon he was in a deep sleep.

Angie kept her word and had him up in plenty of time to make it to base. She offered him coffee, but he had neither the time nor the stomach to accept it. He dressed quickly, grabbed his wallet off the nightstand, and started for the door. As he was leaving, Angie gave Mr. Happy a pat and asked if he was ready again. Tom had one hell of a headache and was in no mood for Angie's games. "I'll call you," he said, and left.

In the cab on the way back to base, he felt terrible. He was trying to figure out why he was in such a funk. He remembered a cartoon he'd once seen. A little female mouse was caught in a trap. All the male mice were lined up, ready to take advantage of the situation. He felt like he was the trapped mouse. On the other hand, maybe Angie was in the trap and he was one of the mice in line. It was very confusing to him. He should have felt good. Instead, he felt sick. He realized Angie had never told him about John. Damn her!

Roll call, a quick shower, and Tom was soon immersed in his military duties once again. Even though he was hung over, his work was a necessary distraction from having to think about what he'd done. Somewhere deep inside him, he knew he had made a huge mistake. It wasn't Angie he'd wanted; it was Sandy. Steady, reliable, crazy, quirky, sweet Sandy.

He was feeling unbearable guilt, yet his sensible side told him that was ridiculous; there was no stated commitment on either side. But deep down, Tom knew there was a commitment in his heart, and it had been there almost from the start. That was why he was feeling so low. He had betrayed his own love for Sandy. He needed time to think, to figure out how to climb out of this black hole; what to do to assuage the despair in his soul.

Unbeknownst to Tom, Wally was going through some of the same emotional turmoil. Making out with Jennifer the night before had seemed so right then and so wrong now. Wally, too, was trying to sort out how you can love one girl, yet be so easily tempted by another. He was feeling disappointed in himself, as though he had violated some personal code of ethics, he didn't even realize he had.

Some part of him was worried Betsy would find out somehow. Although he knew it a paranoid notion, he wondered how many friends her father might still have on base. Or Teddy might say something. Or AJ. Innocently. Why did he care if Betsy found out? Why did it matter to him? What if she did find out? She wouldn't care. Or would she?

It was a couple of days before Tom's and Wally's schedules meshed and they had a chance to talk. Wally was anxious to hear any news about John that Tom may have gleaned from Angie.

It was known all over the barracks that Angie was an easy score, so Wally was expecting an elated Tom. He was alarmed to see how gloomy, dispirited, and deeply depressed his friend was. Tom's whole demeanor had changed. His face was slack and expressionless. His eyes were dulled, his voice hollow. Concerned, Wally suggested they find a quiet place to talk, enticing Tom by saying he needed some advice. They found a quiet spot in the barracks rec room.

Even though he was anxious to know what had happened with Tom, Wally felt it safest to begin with his own problem. He outlined what had happened on his double-date with Teddy and the inner conflict he now felt.

Sometimes seeing a problem through someone else's eyes can clarify one's own difficulties. Tom realized he and Wally were experiencing the same crisis of conscience.

He then told Wally all that had happened with Angie, how terrible he felt about it, and how he had discovered the reason he was feeling so badly was a profound sense that he had betrayed Sandy. He'd not realized it fully before, but now he knew he was in love with Sandy. It was clear to him that Angie had tricked him, strung him along, and tried to trap him into a relationship with her. He felt like such a fool.

The worst part was not knowing what to do about it. Part of him wanted to confess everything to Sandy and hope she could forgive him. But he also knew how hurt she would be, and he didn't want to hurt her. He didn't want to take a chance on losing her either

Just as Tom now understood the reason for his despair, his tale illuminated Wally's dilemma; he was in love with Betsy. The difference between their two situations was that, in Tom's case, there was a good chance that Sandy loved him too. In his own case, Wally felt he was in love with someone who could never love him back. Yet he couldn't ever see himself moving on.

Counseling Tom, Wally told him he needed to just put the past behind him. What was done could not be undone. A bell once rung cannot be unrung. But it could be a lesson learned. He needed to call Sandy. Let her know she is the only one for him.

Wanting to encourage his friend as well, Tom told Wally he might be mistaken about how Betsy felt. Tom told him how Sandy had picked up a vibe that first night when the three of them went to her restaurant.

Wally started thinking about little things Betsy had said. He remembered how happy she was that he went with her the first night she went to meet Minnie. Then there was their last night together on the shores of Lake Superior. For the first time he was hopeful. Maybe they did have a future together. But he was stymied as to how to go about contacting her now that the funeral was over. No doubt, she was still in mourning.

Betsy solved that problem herself by calling the next day. She wanted to invite him to dinner on his next day off. She said her mom really wanted him to come. Mom was all excited about fixing him a special meal as a way of thanking him for all he had done for Betsy.

Again, the loudspeaker summoned Wally to Gunny's office. This time it was the trial counsel, Lt. Pulaski. Again, Wally was asked to revisit that terrible night at the back gate. His questions for Wally were pretty much the same as he had already discussed with Lt. Sanchez. It was obvious the prosecutor had done his homework. He seemed to know every detail of Wally's statements taken that night, as well as the statements of others. His questions were relentless, but not confrontational. Wally never felt uncomfortable with him. The court martial was drawing closer; two and a half weeks.

Tom had received a call from Angie. She'd invited him for a home-cooked meal. He begged off, citing an erratic schedule. She asked him when he could come over. He said he wasn't sure. Angie reluctantly accepted this explanation. He again promised to call. He had no intention of keeping that promise. He also was pretty certain she wouldn't give up. He was correct. She kept calling.

He and Wally devised a plan about how to deal with Angie. They would foist her off on some other guy; the hard part was who? Everyone already knew about Angie. That only left one guy, the newbie, AJ. Tom would invite Angie to the upcoming dance, then pull the old switcheroo. At the last minute, he would have AJ sign her in, saying Tom couldn't make it - bad cold or something. They discussed the plan with AJ and he was all for it. Problem solved, hopefully.

Tom had followed through on their other plan. He'd called Sandy and let her know how much he had enjoyed their time together and how much he was missing her. Sandy was echoing the same sentiments. As they talked, Tom became more and more convinced this was going to work out some day, some way. Long distance phone calls can take quite a chunk out of a serviceman's slender paycheck, so Tom said he would write faithfully. He could use the extra money to start saving for a plane ticket for her to come out and visit. Sandy said she would work on training someone to take over the restaurant while she was gone. At the close of their phone call, Tom was jubilant.

The night of the dance The Plan worked perfectly. AJ was happy to finally have a date. Angie's initial disappointment evaporated when she saw the tall, handsome marine. It didn't hurt that AJ had a great personality, either. Angie wore the same red sparkly dress she had worn on the date with Tom. Between the dress and her seductive dancing, she was drawing many admiring glances from the males in the room. She had moves better than most women AJ had dated. In the slow dances she locked eyes with him and gave AJ the feeling her performance was only for him. "Damn," AJ thought. "This is one fine woman."

From time to time other men would come up to ask Angie to dance. But all she would say was "I'd jump over the head of every man in this room to get to AJ. He's my man."

About three-quarters of the way through the evening AJ saw Teddy. He recalled what Teddy had said about a private place. Saying he had to use the head, he got Angie a drink and worked his way over through the dancers to The Man with The Plan.

Teddy told him the room was currently in use, but he would be next in line. "It'll cost you ten bucks."

"Ten bucks!!!"

"I got expenses, you know. You won't believe what it cost me to get a copy of that key."

"OK, Teddy, ten bucks it is."

"Keep watching." Glancing at his watch, Teddy said "I figure the room will be available in about fifteen minutes."

AJ returned to Angie and told her there was a good chance he could find them a private spot nearby in a few minutes. How would she feel about that? She said "Honey Bun, if you don't find something soon, I'm gonna do you right here on the dance floor."

AJ laughed and said, "Mmmm, Baby."

Although time seemed to drag, Teddy's estimate was pretty accurate. AJ saw a man come up and drop something into Teddy's hand. To AJ's surprise, it was an officer. Teddy looked at AJ and gave an almost imperceptible jerk of his head in a "come here" gesture.

Key, directions, Angie in hand, AJ soon found his way to their temporary Pleasure Palace. Although it was a dental office, it smelled more like a cheap hotel room after a long Friday night.

AJ and Angie managed to utilize every square inch of that space, from the door to the counter to the treatment chair. Angie was hotter than a mouthful of wasabi. The treatment chair proved to be a comedy of errors. Angie got her stiletto heel caught in the spit bowl. AJ almost knocked himself out when his head hit the overhead light. In one of their more energetic moments, someone stepped on the pedal that raised and lowered the chair, resulting in an almost near-miss. When it was over, AJ remembered thinking it was the best ten dollars he'd ever spent. And the best ten minutes.

The next morning an announcement came over the PA, "In the barracks, in the barracks. It has come to my attention there were some unauthorized trips to the dentist last night. I know seeing the dentist can put a smile on your face, but from now on visits will be confined to regular hours." Although Gunny's topic was serious, there was amusement in his voice.

Saturday night Wally took the bus to Betsy's house for dinner. She and an orange cat greeted him at the door. Betsy had a hug to welcome him. The cat, named Punkin, rubbed against his leg.

As he walked in, there was a tantalizing aroma coming from the kitchen. Wally remembered a saying, "Home cookin' makes you good lookin'." How he missed a good home-cooked meal. Betsy's mom, Laura, poked her head out of the kitchen doorway. Her face was ruddy from the heat of the stove. Wally thought she was absolutely beautiful. Betsy's dad, Joe, was right behind her. Both were wearing aprons. They waved a greeting and retreated to the kitchen to finish their cooking. Wally could hear them in the kitchen, happily chattering away as they worked.

Betsy settled Wally on the sofa in the living room and asked what he would like to drink. He chose coffee. While she went to fix his coffee, Wally looked around the room. The carpeting and draperies at the large picture window were a deep green. Under the draperies were white semi-sheers. The sofa, love-seat, and chair were white as well. There was a rocking chair, two end tables with lamps, and a coffee table, all were oak. On the coffee table was a white pitcher filled with artificial tulips. Behind the sofa was a very large framed needlework picture of colorful tulips as well. By the front door was a high fi system with a record player. The overall effect of the room was tasteful and serene.

When Betsy returned with the coffee, he asked about the needlework picture. "Yes, my mom made that. She would work on it in the evening as we watched TV. It took her almost a year to complete. She also crocheted the doilies." Wally looked at the doilies under the lamps and pitcher. "Mom is very creative; her hands are always busy with something. Our beds are covered with her quilts. But I think her favorite pastime is working in the kitchen. She loves to cook and has been very excited about your visit."

Right on cue, the dinner bell rang, summoning Wally and Betsy to the dining room table. It was beautifully set with their "company" china, silver-plate silverware, and goblets for water and red wine.

In from the kitchen came a beef roast, mashed potatoes, gravy, several dishes of vegetables, and homemade rolls. Wally thought he'd died and gone to heaven. Everyone joined hands and Joe said grace. The food was passed around and soon everyone was happily eating.

Wally wanted to know what Joe did after he got out of the service. Joe said he went to work for his uncle, who owned an insurance agency. He and Laura lived very frugally. He worked hard at making money; she worked just as hard at maximizing it. She raised a garden and canned. She became the Coupon Queen. She sewed a lot of her own clothes and Betsy's. By the time his uncle was ready to retire, they had saved enough to buy the agency.

They continued their frugal lifestyle, and one day they were able to afford to buy a house. Betsy came along. Joe taught himself how to do many of the repairs on the house and their car. Eventually they saved enough to start investing in real estate. Joe said with pride that now they were quite comfortable financially. He added modestly he never could have done it "without this wonderful woman at my side, helping me every step of the way." He reached over and gave Laura a sideways hug.

Joe asked about Wally's family. "I grew up in a small town outside of Detroit. My dad is the supervisor for a local car dealership that sells Studebakers. My mom is a housewife busy raising my younger brothers and sister. I have three brothers and a sister. My sister is the youngest. I am the oldest."

Betsy prompted, "You said your family was crazy?"

Wally laughed and continued. "My mom is a very social lady. If she sat down with you, within five minutes she would know your whole life's history and you would know hers. She loves people and has a heart as big as Texas. If someone needs a place to stay, she'd insist on dragging them to our house. If someone needs a meal, there is always a pot on the stove and leftovers in the refrigerator. Our house is the gathering place for family, friends, delivery men, and any stranger Mom happens to meet. It is a chaotic crazy place, with people coming and going; the telephone constantly ringing. Half the time the caller would ask for a name we didn't recognize. We would holler out the name and, sure enough, someone sitting at the kitchen table would get up to take the call. My brothers used to joke, 'How do you sleep four in a bed? You wait until the company goes home'." Everyone laughed.

"Mom always made do with what she had. We drank out of glasses and ate off dishes pulled from boxes of Duz detergent. My dad used to joke that once you pulled a serving bowl out of one of those boxes, there wasn't much detergent in there. And she was a fanatic about green stamps."

Laura laughed and held up her spoon. "Me, too. Every time I went to the A&P, I would get those green stamps and paste them in the little book they gave me. When I had enough books, and it took quite a few, I would send away for things. This silverware was purchased with green stamps."

It was time for dessert. Wally and Betsy helped clear the table, while Laura cut up the warm apple pie and Joe dished up the ice cream to go with it.

As they ate, they talked about the upcoming court martial. Joe said he had heard John's counsel waived his right to a pretrial hearing. They discussed why counsel might do that. The consensus was that it might mean whatever happened out there could have a simple explanation. Joe added that John's counsel had asked for a single judge instead of a tribunal. Could that also mean they were expecting a quick and easy resolution? Joe also said the judge would decide John's guilt or innocence. Counsel had waived right to the five, or six, man jury, as well. Interesting!

Betsy said Minnie and Becca were coming in for the court martial. She had invited them to stay at their house. Joe insisted on buying their plane tickets. Betsy asked Wally if he would be willing to help her show them around San Francisco. He said it would be his pleasure any time he wasn't on duty.

"Speaking of San Francisco," Joe said, "I was driving by the RKO theater downtown and was surprised to see, instead of the title of what was currently playing, there was a plea to save Caryl Chessman posted up on their marquis.

Laura spoke up. "I disagree. The man deserves to be executed for what he did."

Wally hadn't heard of Caryl Chessman. Apologetically, he inquired about who that was. It was hard to keep up with current events on base when schedules can be so erratic.

Joe explained "In 1948, he was known as the Red-Light Bandit. He'd put a red light atop his car to give the impression that he was a policeman. This was in the Los Angeles area. He would drive to lover's lane type places and target the young people parked there. He was convicted of robbery, kidnapping, and rape, and sentenced to death. Some people think he should not be put to death because he never actually killed anyone. Now, because of him, there is a movement afoot to banish the death penalty in California."

"Enough of the heavy stuff," said Laura. "Betsy, why don't you take Wally out on the porch for a while. Your father and I can handle the dishes."

Out on the porch, Betsy was encouraging Wally to tell more about some of the people that visited his house.

He promised he would tell a story or two, but first he wanted to know about her. How was she feeling?

"Well, this is something new for me. I'm not sure how I am supposed to be feeling but, truthfully, I feel great. I have so much energy, I surprise myself. But enough about me. I want to hear more of your stories."

"Well, one I could tell you about had the nickname 'Flipper'. Flipper was born without arms. All he had were hands at the ends of his shoulders. My sister always wondered how he could zip up his pants, among other things. He really was pretty clever. He found ways to circumvent his lacks. For example, he bowled with his feet. He got pretty chummy with another of the regulars at our house. Her name was Bunny. One day he and Bunny went for a little stroll down the street to where there was a patch of woods. He really got teased about that, 'Flipper, did you go for a hop?'

'I never laid a hand on her, I swear'.

"And then there was Earl. Earl was a man in his early fifties. One day my mom fixed him a tuna fish sandwich for lunch. After he ate, he went out to the picnic table under the scrub tree in the yard. He crossed his arms on the table, laid his head down, and took a nap in the warm sunshine. When it was time for supper, Earl was still zonked out at the picnic table. Mom sent one of the boys out to wake him. Whoever she sent came back and said he couldn't wake Earl up. Mom went out and couldn't wake him. Earl had passed away. The next time I came home, I was in the service by then, everyone was sitting at a brand-new picnic table. I asked why they bought a new table when the old one was still sitting over there under the scrub tree. In reverent tones they pointed to the old one and said, 'That's the Earl Memorial Picnic Table now.' However, the Earl Memorial Picnic Table was not going to waste. That was where all the spare car parts were stored. From that day forward no one would eat one of Mom's famous tuna fish sandwiches."

Wally concluded, "Well, Betsy, this has been fun, but I really need to get going."

Betsy had one more question. She teasingly asked him: "Was *anything* normal at your house? What about a pet? Did you have a pet?"

"I did. We had a dog. It was a stray my mom found one day. It only had three legs. My sister wanted to call it Piano Stool, but that was awkward to say, so we named it Tripod."

Betsy was laughing so hard. "Wally, I never know when you are serious and when you are joking. What funny stories!"

Wally grinned. He poked his head in the door to say good-bye to Laura and Joe. Laura was knitting something and Joe had been reading her excerpts from the newspaper. They had been listening to Betsy's occasional bursts of laughter out on the porch, and were happy to hear her joyful again. Wally thanked them for such a delicious meal and said he'd had a wonderful time. They said they hoped he could come again soon.

Wally gave Betsy a quick hug and started down the porch stairs. At the bottom he turned to look at her one more time. She was at the top of the steps, illuminated by the moonlight. She looked so lovely. Maybe it was his imagination, but he thought he could see the beginnings of a baby bump. He wished it was his baby. Even though it wasn't, he realized if he was given a chance, he would love it as his own. He smiled and waved to Betsy. She smiled and waved back. As he walked down the street, he was reminded of a refrain from a current song, "After all is said and done, I know you are the only one."

Chapter 12

The opening day of the court martial arrived. Wally, being a material witness, was not allowed to be in the courtroom. His military duties would have kept him away most days anyway. Joe and Betsy were working as well. He was happy to have a pipeline in the form of Minnie, Becca, and Laura. Wally would call each evening to get updates. By the time he could call, Betsy would be home from work and had already talked to the attendees. Although he was hearing the news secondhand, he didn't mind. It was one more excuse to talk to Betsy.

It was the first trial Becca had ever seen, and her enthusiasm amused Betsy no end. Becca had phenomenal recall; even picked up on things Minnie and Laura missed. Not only that, she was critiquing the two counsels, saying things like "He should have asked this question or that question." Or, "I would have explored that topic a little more."

The first day, as in most trials, began with opening statements; trial counsel, Lt. Pulaski, outlined his case first. He intended to prove the shooting was an intentional act, that the shooting was perpetrated by PFC John Anthony Lewis, that the shooting resulted in the death of PFC Nicholas Alexander Cole. Defense counsel, Lt. Sanchez, of course, had a different take: "Two young people, late at night, nothing to do. They decided to see who could draw and point their gun the fastest. It was an accident, a tragic accident. Clear and simple."

Wally was the first witness to be called by Lt. Pulaski. He was sworn in. Questioning had him revisiting that fateful night once again. Despite the pea-soup fog, how the bright lighting at the back gate permitted, at close range, clear visibility.

Yes, when he came upon John, he was still holding a .45. Yes, John was disobeying an order to put the gun down. Photos were shown and Wally was asked to identify positions of the guard house, the lights, John.

A description of how he found Nick. More photos were submitted of Nick inside the guard house. Yes, Nick's .45 was unholstered and beside his right knee. No, he did not touch that gun.

More questioning about why Wally returned so soon after posting. Did he suspect a problem? No, it was just procedure to do random checks.

The questioning became more personal. Yes, Nick was his bunkmate and best friend. Yes, Nick could sometimes anger other men in the barracks. Yes, he had witnessed Nick taunting some of the men. No, it wasn't personal. It was always about dress or conduct. Nick always wanted others to be their best. Yes, he had seen Nick taunt opposing players on the baseball diamond. Yes, he could rattle them enough to cause them to make mistakes.

Having established the fact that Nick had a tongue so sharp that he could anger others, Lt. Pulaski closed his questioning and yielded the floor to the defense.

Lt. Sanchez asked how long Wally had been a duty driver. One year. How long had that included the back gate? One year. "As you would approach the back gate, what would you normally see?"

"Sir, in good weather I would see two gate guards outside. One would be watching the incoming lane, here." Wally pointed to the appropriate photo. "The other would be on the far side of the guard house. His back would be to the other guard. But if it was inclement weather, they both could be inside the guard house, back to back, watching the incoming and outgoing lanes."

"What was the weather like on the night in question?"

The answer was "Sir, very foggy, cold, and damp."

"Would you consider that to be inclement weather?"

"Sir, I would."

"Would it be the kind of weather where you would expect to find both guards in the guard house?"

"Yes, sir, I would."

"What did you see as you approached the back gate that night?"

"Sir, I saw a single guard outside the guard house. At first it was hard to make out who it was because of the fog. But as I drove closer, I could see it was John."

"Wally, in the photo your duty truck is parked at an angle in front of the gate. Is that a normal way to park the duty vehicle?"

"Sir, I saw John had his .45 unholstered and in his hand. I had the impression there might be some sort of problem. I positioned the truck between me and any danger there might have been."

"What did you do next?"

"Sir, I unholstered my .45 and asked John what was going on."

"And what was his response?"

"Sir, he did not answer. I wasn't sure why. So, I asked again. But even while I was asking, I was looking around, trying to assess the situation."

"What was your observation?"

"Sir, even though the fog was very thick, the area around the guard house is brightly lit. I could see no potential danger. It was then that I noticed that John was behaving differently than I would have expected."

"Describe what John was doing that caused you to think that."

"Sir, he was walking in a small circle, in baby steps. I had the impression he was not even aware that I was there. Especially when he didn't answer me the second time."

"What did you do next?"

"Sir, I looked on the other side of the guard house, where the outgoing lane is, for Nick. Next, I looked in the guard house, but I didn't see him there either. I knew he should be in one of those two places. So, I asked John where Nick was."

"Did John answer your question?"

"Sir, he told me Nick was in the guard house. I didn't believe him because I couldn't see him through the glass sliding doors."

"But you did enter the guard house?"

"Sir, I did enter the guard house. I thought the two guards were trying to play some kind of trick on me, especially since John was acting so strangely."

"What did you see when you entered the guard house?"

"Sir, I saw Nick sitting on the floor with his back to the wall. His eyes were open and he was staring straight ahead."

"What did you do next?"

"Sir, I thought Nick was playing a trick on me. I told him the joke was over. When he didn't respond, I moved closer. I expected he would grab my ankle or something. But he didn't move at all. I began to wonder if he was OK. I reached down to shake him. When I touched his shoulder, he slid sideways. It was then I realized he had been shot."

"Did you see Nick's .45?"

"Sir, it was unholstered and by his right knee."

"At what point did you notice Nick's gun?"

"Sir, after Nick slid sideways."

"Not before?"

"No, sir."

"Did you move or touch that gun?"

"Sir, no. I left the gun as I saw it."

"Did you notice anything else out of the ordinary at that time?"

"Sir, Nick should have been wearing his white helmet liner. But it was laying on the floor near the gun."

"Once you realized Nick had been shot, what did you do?"

"Sir, my first thought was that the only other person with a gun besides myself was John. I felt I had to get that gun away from him. Twice I asked him to drop his gun. Twice he did not do so. But after the second time John did ask if Nick was dead. It was the first indication I had that John had any idea what was going on."

"Could you expand on your statement that John did not seem to know what was going on until he asked about Nick?"

"Sir, other than telling me where Nick was, he did not react to anything I said. He seemed to me to be completely unaware of my presence. But when he asked about Nick, I knew he had some awareness."

"You say some awareness. Please explain."

"Sir, even as John asked about Nick, he wasn't using his normal voice. His voice was kind of strained and hollow-sounding. It was like he was having trouble forming words."

Lt Sanchez had Wally go over how he got John to drop the gun, how he retrieved it, and how he put it in the guard house and called for help.

The next question for Wally was if he had ever seen Nick taunt John.

"No, sir. Never."

"No further questions."

On redirect Lt. Pulaski asked, "Wally, have you had training in psychology?"

"No, sir."

"Do you feel qualified to ascertain whether John is actually, to use your words, unaware of your presence, or is so angry he doesn't want to speak to anyone until he can cool down?"

"Sir, I base my observation on the fact that John was quite meek when I asked him to go sit on the curb and watch for the ambulance. I saw no anger in him."

"No further questions."

Once Wally was dismissed, he left the courtroom and returned to his military duties. From now on he would have to rely on others for any information about the trial.

That evening Wally called the Millers. It was Betsy who answered. Wally wondered if she had been sitting by the phone, as she had picked up immediately after the first ring. "Wally, you were wonderful on the stand. I was so proud of you. I especially liked how you put that Lt. Pulaski in his place when he asked about whether you had training in psychology."

"I didn't mean to embarrass him, but I guess his question did backfire on him. What worried me, however, was how Minnie was holding up. We had to go through some pretty tough stuff in my testimony. How did she do?"

"Mom said at one point she looked over and Becca was holding Minnie's hand very tightly. Mom said she reached over and took Minnie's other hand. The three of them got through the rough parts by supporting each other."

"So, what happened after I left?"

"The judge called it for the day. They will resume tomorrow. But I wanted to tell you about the opening statements, before you got called into the courtroom. Lt. Pulaski said he is going to prove intent to shoot. Lt. Sanchez is claiming it was an accidental shooting after Nick and John were playing a game of fast draw."

"Well, Betsy, I guess we will all have to wait and see."

"Oh, Wally, I wanted to ask you something. Tomorrow night after supper I am going to take Minnie and Becca to see some of the sights in town. The stuff going on in the trial has to be very hard on them. I want to give them a little distraction. Do you have time off where you could come too?"

"If you could pick me up at 5:00, we can go to Chinatown. I know of a good restaurant there. I think Minnie and Becca would love it. How does that sound?"

Betsy liked that idea. Wally rang off, saying "Since you have guests, I'd better let you go. Thanks for filling me in. Say hello to Minnie and Becca and your folks for me. I'll see you tomorrow."

"I'm looking forward to it."

Wally was waiting at the front gate when Betsy pulled up. Becca and Minnie were eager to talk about the day's happenings at court.

Becca said the prosecution brought in the man in charge of the investigation into the circumstances of Nick's death. His name was Lt. La Croix. He was from the Criminal Investigation Division. "CID," Becca said, proud to be able to use some military lingo.

"He testified about the bullet. Ballistics testing showed it came from John's .45. It was the only bullet fired from that gun. It was irrefutably the bullet that killed Nick. Mom, will you be all right if I talk about this next part?"

"It's ok, honey. But thank you for asking."

"It just nicked the lowest part of his heart. Lt. La Croix said Nick died almost immediately, probably even before he hit the floor. He talked about trajectory. He said Nick was shot when he was in a standing position. Nick and John were three and a half to four feet apart when John fired."

Becca said Lt. Pulaski had several questions about the position of Nick's gun. Lt. La Croix said it was in an unnatural position. He said if Nick had been holding it when he was shot, the handle should have been quite close to Nick's right hand. Instead, it was by his right knee. It was Lt. La Croix's professional opinion that the gun had been placed there after Nick fell.

The prosecutor next asked Lt. La Croix if there was a round in the chamber of Nick's .45. Lt. La Croix said it appeared that although there was a clip in the .45, Nick never got a chance to rack his gun and put a round in the chamber.

Both Minnie and Becca said after the CID expert finished testifying for the prosecution, they had no doubt John had shot Nick and it was no accident. They believed Lt. Pulaski's version of events; that John staged the scene. After he shot Nick, he took Nick's gun and placed it by his side to make his fast draw story look believable. But he was careless and there were things he overlooked.

Becca then talked about what happened when John's counsel got up to question Lt. La Croix. "He really didn't question the ballistics or the distance Nick and John were apart. He asked LaCroix if Nick's .45 had been tested for fingerprints. Yes. Were John's fingerprints on that weapon. No. There were other fingerprints on the .45, but none were John's. He asked questions about the helmet liner. Yes, it was lying on the floor. He had La Croix point it out in a photo. He asked La Croix how he thought it wound up on the floor. La Croix said probably the impact of the bullet on Nick's body flung him back into the window. The liners have no chin strap, so either the impact of the bullet or perhaps Nick's head hitting the window could have dislodged the helmet liner from Nick's head and caused it to fall to the floor."

Wally said, "That makes sense. It could get knocked off easily under the right circumstances."

Becca continued her account of the day's trial, telling how Lt. Sanchez asked if the liner had fallen right side up or upside down. "La Croix said upside down. Lt. Sanchez asked the same question in a different way. I thought that was pretty clever of Lt. Sanchez, to come back at that critical point from a different angle. He asked if the rounded part was the part touching the floor. Lt. La Croix said it was. Lt. Sanchez asked if there was blood on the rounded part. La Croix said there was. Lt Sanchez asked Lt. La Croix if, in his professional opinion, that blood indicated the helmet had been moved from where it originally fell. La Croix seemed a little startled, like this wasn't something he had considered. Don't you think so, Mom?" Minnie nodded. Becca said he agreed it was possible.

"Sanchez then started questioning La Croix about the position of Nick's .45. If the impact of the bullet was forceful enough to dislodge the helmet liner, could it also have dislodged the gun from Nick's hand. La Croix said that was possible. Could the force have been great enough to cause the gun to fly from Nick's hand, perhaps hit the wall, and bounce back to where it landed by Nick's knee? That, too, was possible La Croix admitted. Sanchez asked how far the wall would have been from Nick's hand before he was shot. La Croix said maybe a foot at best."

Wally agreed, "Yes, the guard house is not very wide. I will show it to you if I can get permission to let you tour the base."

Becca went on, "Sanchez continued questioning about the helmet liner. He pointed out how close the liner was to the gun. He asked if the helmet could have hit the .45 if, perhaps, someone accidently kicked it, and, in that circumstance, could have moved the gun from its original position? La Croix said that was not very likely. But Sanchez again asked if that could have happened. La Croix reluctantly agreed it was a possibility. Wouldn't the blood on the bottom of the helmet indicate the helmet liner had been somehow moved from its original position to blood that only could have pooled in the minutes after Nick fell? To me," Becca said, "Lt. La Croix didn't seem too happy about those questions, but he had to admit it could have happened that way.

"Then Lt. Sanchez goes again to the position of the .45. He asked Lt. La Croix if the .45 also had blood on the side touching the floor. Yes, said La Croix, it did. Did it not seem likely, then, that the gun was also moved from its original position? The answer was yes." Minnie and Becca agreed that Lt. La Croix seemed to act defeated when he left the courtroom.

The women said now they did begin to question whether John's version might have been the truth. Becca said she had a lot of admiration for Lt. Sanchez. At first it looked like an open and shut case against John. Now they were no longer sure. Lt. Sanchez was fighting hard for his client. Both were eagerly looking forward to the next day's proceedings.

By now they had reached Chinatown and had been taking in the sights as they talked. They marveled at the quaint little shops, the interesting signs, the open-air markets, the people on the streets going about their everyday activities, laughing, talking, shopping. The ever-curious Becca asked how long Chinatown had been in existence.

Betsy had taken the time to prepare for their visit to Chinatown. She began with a little of the history of the Chinese people in the United States. They began coming in 1815. Two men and one woman were the first to arrive. Soon the trickle increased to a couple hundred each year. Then China had a serious economic downturn. And immigration to America exploded. One year 20,000 Chinese entered the country."

"Wow!" Becca said. "When was that?"

"Well, that would have been in the 1850's. You can't blame them. Things were tough in China, and we had a gold rush going on here in California. They came with visions of striking it rich, like many Americans who came to search for gold. They quickly learned mining for gold was not going to be the way to wealth. Many Chinese found other work. Americans realized they were good workers and cheap to hire. In the 1860's it was the Chinese who helped build the Transcontinental Railroad.

"But then things got tough here. The United States went into an economic depression. Jobs dried up. There was resentment directed toward the Chinese. To ease tensions, Washington banned all new immigration from China. Some of those already here settled in this area we now call Chinatown. That would have been about 1900."

Becca, always sympathetic toward the underdog, was shocked. "You mean no Chinese can come to the United States anymore?"

"The government partially lifted the immigration ban after China became an ally during World War II. They now allow about 100 into the country each year."

Betsy had parked in the lot for Mr. Lee's restaurant. Entering, Minnie and Becca gasped at how unusual and elegant the interior of the restaurant was. The carpet was a red plush flecked with gold. One wall was painted red, with a gigantic overlay of a magnificent golden dragon. Illumination was provided by many red and gold Chinese lanterns hanging down. The restaurant was filled almost to capacity with Chinese families.

Becca was seated by a large picture window. Minnie was beside her and Betsy and Wally were across from them. No sooner was Betsy seated, than she got up and went to talk to the women behind the counter. Soon she was back. She asked Becca, Minnie, and Wally to follow her.

She led them back to the kitchen, where they could watch the food being prepared. One woman was mixing dough. A second was rolling out the dough, and cutting it into very long, wide noodles. To Minnie they had the shape of lasagna noodles, only they were wider, a little thicker, longer, and totally flat. A third woman was dropping the noodles into a big vat of chicken broth. It was very interesting to see.

Soon after they returned to their table, they were served big bowls of the noodles and broth. Although silverware was provided, Wally elected to use chopsticks. Becca, always up for an adventure, wanted to try chopsticks too.

Although Wally was skilled with chopsticks, Becca was a novice. Much to her amusement, the slippery noodles would slide out of the chopsticks before she could ever get a bite of them. Giggling, she tried over and over. She was not one to give up. Soon she had everyone at the table laughing at her struggles. Other patrons in the restaurant were looking over to see what was so amusing and enjoying the hilarity at that table. Even those walking by outside on the street were discretely smiling. One wizened old gentleman did an about-face and came right up to the outside of the window. With a huge grin, he was cheering Becca on. He was obviously having as much fun as Becca. She loved it.

Minnie was curious about the dragon on the wall. When she got the opportunity, she asked their waitress about it. Ai-Yun explained why the dragon is so special to the Chinese people. China's first Emperor was said to have come from a constellation in the sky known as the dragon. He was like a god to his people. Ai-Yun told them that in the Chinese horoscope, the Year of the Dragon only comes once every twelve years. People born in the Year of the Dragon are said to be very powerful.

Becca asked if the color red had special significance. She had noticed many of the signs and storefronts in Chinatown were painted red, as well as the décor in the restaurant. Ai-Yun said red was considered by the Chinese to be a very lucky color.

When they left the restaurant the ladies behind the counter were smiling and waving at Becca. Wally teased her, saying he was sure they would be talking about her noodle episode for a very long time. Becca replied that she would never forget this place. "What fun!"

Next on Betsy's itinerary was the world-famous Golden Gate Bridge. Becca was in awe. "I've seen pictures of this, but wow! I can't wait to tell my friends back home. I've always wondered, why do they call it the Golden Gate Bridge?"

"It is built right where the Pacific Ocean meets the San Francisco Bay. It spans the gateway to San Francisco. Before it was built, people used to have to take a ferry to get across the Bay."

"Why didn't they build a regular bridge, like the ones in Minnesota?"

The engineers had three problems to overcome. One was that this bridge would be built on an earthquake-prone site. The less contact with the ground, the better. The second problem was the strong winds that sweep in from the Pacific Ocean. They needed a design that could sway with the wind, just as a willow can withstand strong winds better than can an oak. The third was cost. This design was much cheaper, but safer in every way."

Next Betsy took her guests to the Golden Gate Park. They were astonished by the variety of things housed within its massive acreage. Betsy said that when the 1906 earthquake hit, it left many people homeless. The United States Army built four encampments for temporary housing. One of the encampments was just for the Chinese. There were barracks, a mess hall, latrines, bathhouses, laundries, even play areas for the children. Residents were charged $2 a month.

Betsy drove around, showing her passengers some of the work done during the Great Depression by the W.P.A. There were thirteen miles of roads, a path along the water, a building for fly fisherman, and several ponds for them. They built horseshoe pits, an archery range, planted a lot of trees, and constructed several buildings. Later a polo field was added. There was a semi-circular outdoor space for concerts. Minnie's favorite was the Japanese Tea Garden, which she found to be very tranquil. Betsy said there is a rumor that the idea of the fortune cookie began there. All agreed it was an awesome park.

Betsy said there was a lot more she wanted them to see before they went back to Minnesota, but it was getting late and they would have to table it for another day.

Chapter 13

The next evening was a work day for Wally. When he got a break, he called to find out about the trial. Betsy answered promptly, but she put Becca on the phone to tell about the trial.

Becca said the prosecutor put a civilian on the stand. Wally smiled at how fast Becca was picking up the lingo of the court. This was a man who managed a gun range where people could go and work on their accuracy. About six months ago, John began coming frequently to practice with a .45. Lt. Pulaski submitted into evidence a log of all the times John had been there.

Then it was Lt. Sanchez's turn to question the man. Becca said the man's name was Pete Andrew. "Sanchez asked if other Marines also visited his gun range. Mr. Andrew said yes. He asked if some of those Marines came as frequently as John. Some did. Lt. Sanchez asked why they might do that. Mr. Andrew said they wanted to do better in the accuracy test that the Marine Corp would give them. Lt. Sanchez asked if the gun range supplied weapons to practice with. Mr. Andrew said sometimes. Some people would bring their own weapons, and others would use range guns. Lt. Sanchez asked if John would bring his own .45, or would he use a range gun. John would use a range gun. Mr. Andrew showed in his log where he had kept records of that. Lt. Sanchez produced a .45 and asked if this was the type John used at the range. It was. Did John ever use any other gun at the range? Sometimes a rifle. The defense counsel then asked Mr. Andrew to demonstrate and explain for the court how one would load the .45. This type of .45 had a cylinder and Mr. Andrew showed how to load it, explaining each step. Then Lt. Sanchez produced a gun similar to the one John had that fateful night. He again asked Mr. Andrew how to load that gun. Mr. Andrew showed how to insert the loaded clip, then rack the carriage to place one bullet in the chamber, again explaining each step."

Becca was really impressed with Lt. Sanchez. She believed the prosecution intended to prove John was practicing at the gun range so he could be accurate when he shot Nick. But by bringing out the fact that he was practicing with a .45 that was loaded differently, Lt. Sanchez's argument that it was an accidental shooting was made more believable. Also, the questioning brought to light a different reason for going to the range; to do well on the Marine Corps accuracy test.

After a break, Lt. Pulaski called as witnesses for the prosecution three men from the barracks. Each testified about how Nick had come down hard on them at one time or another. Lt. Pulaski had each describe in detail what was said and how it affected them. All three said it made them angry.

Lt. Sanchez got each to admit the criticism Nick leveled at them was never personal. It was always about the appearance of some part of their uniform or some behavior that was unworthy of a Marine. Sanchez asked if the barbs Nick used were justified or deserved. Each admitted there was basis for Nick's criticism. One added, however, that he didn't feel it was Nick's place to criticize him because they were of the same rank.

Becca said that was pretty much all that was covered in the trial of that day. She then put Betsy on the phone. After each catching up on how their day went, Betsy wanted to know if Wally was still planning on going with them after work the next day. He said he could hardly wait. Plans were made to rendezvous at the front gate at 5:00, as usual.

Again, Wally was at the gate when Betsy arrived. He no sooner got into the car than an eager Becca was bombarding him with the trial proceedings of the day.

She said that the prosecution had presented all of its witnesses. The defense began calling up its witnesses.

"The first was Dr. Corbin. Dr. Corbin was the psychiatrist who had interviewed John the day after the shooting. He said John was devastated by what had happened. He was deeply remorseful. In his professional opinion," he said, "John was suffering from shell shock and needed help. Sanchez asked if John was on any medication. Dr. Corbin said it was offered, but John refused it." Becca added "At the time, I didn't understand why he would ask a question like that. It seemed out of place."

Lt. Pulaski asked a few questions about Dr. Corbin's credentials and experience with shell shock. "But it seemed to me," Becca stated, "the more questions Lt. Pulaski asked, the more certain it seemed Dr. Corbin was well-qualified to give the diagnosis of shell shock.

"Lt. Sanchez then had John's girlfriend come up on the stand. Her name is Angie. He asked her about John's personality. She told the court John was quiet and sweet. She said he didn't have a mean bone in his body. Lt. Sanchez asked if she went to see him on Treasure Island. She had. Was there any change in his personality? She said definitely. That was her exact word. Definitely. She said he was distant and dreamy. She would have to ask him questions more than once. It was like he couldn't stay focused. She said it was like trying to talk to someone who just wanted to go to sleep and be left alone."

Becca said through all the witnesses that had been on the stand, John just sat with his head down. He didn't look at a witness or talk to his counsel. But when Angie got on the stand, he looked at her through her entire testimony. He didn't smile. He didn't frown. He didn't react to anything she said. He just looked at her like one might watch an insect crawling along in the dirt. Just kind of disengaged.

"Anyway," Becca said as she continued her account, "Lt. Pulaski asked how long John had dated her. She said about six months. Was John ever sharp with her? Never. Did she ever see him get mad at anybody? No. How well did John know Nick? Angie didn't know because John never mentioned him. Are you still John's girlfriend?" Becca said at this question Angie looked at John. Then she licked her lips and answered that she had broken up with him. Lt. Pulaski asked when they broke up. She said after he went to Treasure Island. Lt. Pulaski wanted to know if she was thinking of breaking up before the shooting." Becca quoted her, "'Oh, no. We were talking about getting married. He was going to buy me a big diamond engagement ring.'" Becca said with some disgust, "Angie emphasized the word 'big'. I really didn't like her very much!"

Becca talked awhile about Lt. Pulaski. She had the impression the prosecutor was digging for a reason John might have purposely shot Nick; a mean remark about Angie, perhaps. If so, he didn't succeed.

"Lt. Sanchez next had the Corporal of the Guard take the stand. I assumed it was because he was with you, Wally, when John and Nick were posted that night. Sanchez questioned him about the mood of the men being posted. Corporal Keno said they were in good spirits. He wanted to know if there was any evidence of alcohol."

Minnie broke into Becca's account to add that she felt the Corporal bristled at that question because he retorted that he never would have posted them if he thought they were unfit for service. "No," he said, "there was no indication of trouble ahead. Zero." Corporal Keno was quite firm about that.

Becca continued, telling how both Gunny and Captain Morgan also testified, saying John was an average Marine. Always did his job. Not outstanding, but steady and never a problem. Sanchez also submitted an affidavit from John's boot camp sergeant that said pretty much the same thing. The sergeant commented on how even-tempered John was. Nothing rattled him.

The prosecutor did not question these witnesses.

Becca then said the next witness after Captain Morgan really did not want to testify. His name was Manny Wirth. He also pulled guard duty at the back gate during the midnight shift sometimes. He said the night shift was really boring. Hardly anyone came by that late at night, so guys would come up with things to do to pass the time. One was the fast draw competition. Manny Wirth had personally played that game. Lt. Sanchez submitted a list of Marines who lived in the barracks who had also played that game.

Pulaski had no questions of that witness either.

The last witness for the defense was John, himself. Becca said he was a pretty sad sight. He shuffled up to the witness stand with his head down. He seemed to have trouble understanding the questions, and had to have some questions repeated. He was slow to answer, like he was gathering up his thoughts before speaking. His voice was hollow and so soft you could barely hear him. The judge kept having to ask him to speak up.

His lawyer asked him to tell what happened that night. John apologized, saying his memory of that night was blurry.

He said he remembered the duty truck leaving. He remembered Nick wanting him to play fast draw, but he didn't want to do it. Lt. Sanchez asked him why not and he said he didn't want to get into trouble. Guards weren't supposed to play fast draw. But Nick wouldn't leave him alone. Nick kept asking and asking. Finally, he gave in, but said he would only draw one time.

He remembered the two of them standing in the guard house at the ready. Nick said "Go". The next thing he remembered was a loud noise and Nick was sliding down the wall. John said at first, he just stood there. He didn't understand what had happened. Then he realized Nick had been shot. He was in a panic. He ran outside. But he said it was like everything was in slow motion, like when you are trying to run under water. His arms felt heavy. His legs felt heavy. He couldn't hear. He couldn't think. He didn't know what to do. He remembered being very scared. Then the duty driver arrived and took over. His memory was what he described as all jumbled after that.

Becca said she thought she would hate the man who shot her brother, but instead at this point she felt really sorry for him. Minnie said she did as well.

But Becca had more to tell. "Now it was the prosecution's turn to try to tear John's testimony apart. He asked John how you play fast draw. John showed him. Had he ever played it before? No. Lt. Pulaski produced a .45 like the one John used at the guard house. Using an empty clip, he had John load it into the .45. He asked John if the weapon was ready to fire. John said no. Why not? There is no bullet in the chamber. Pulaski asked John to show him how to get the .45 ready to fire. John racked the gun and explained that brought a bullet up into the chamber. Then it was ready to fire. Pulaski asked if it was standard procedure to have a bullet in the chamber. John said no. Pulaski asked how come there was a bullet in the chamber that night. John looked confused and said he didn't know. Pulaski asked him if he could have put a bullet in the chamber accidently. John said no. Pulaski tried to badger him into saying he somehow put a bullet into the chamber, but John insisted he didn't do it and he didn't know how it got there." Becca said it seemed to her that John honestly didn't know.

At this point Wally had to break off the conversation briefly. Some guy had been hammering on the door because Wally had been on the phone for so long. Wally opened the door to tell the guy he was just about done. But as he did, the other booth door opened, freeing up the other pay phone. Problem solved.

So, Becca could continue. She said "The last part of the questions for John by the prosecution had to do with gloves.

Lt. Pulaski wanted to know if either John or Nick wore gloves at any time that evening. The answer was no.

"After a long break, both lawyers presented their summaries. The prosecution went first.

"Lt Pulaski began by ticking off the facts. John shot Nick. That fact was not disputed. Nick was killed by a single bullet. Ballistics proved that bullet came from John's gun.

"Next the prosecutor moved into probable conclusions. He said they had learned that Nick knew how to rattle people, how to make them angry. He said we may never learn what Nick said to anger John, but emphasized that he said something. Maybe about his girlfriend. Maybe it was something else."

Wally interrupted Becca's account, "I bet you it was something about Angie. John was crazy about her."

"Well, Pulaski said we may never learn what was said. But he went on building his case. John planned the murder carefully. He began going to the gun range. He wanted to be deadly accurate. He didn't want to wound Nick. He wanted to kill him. He also planned a cover story. He'd heard in the barracks of guys playing fast draw. John testified Nick proposed the game. But did he? Only two people know the truth, and one of them is dead.

"Next John staged the scene to make it look like Nick had pulled his gun. John removed Nick's .45 from its holster. Why was there blood on the bottom of the gun? When John would have placed in weapon on the floor, blood would not have pooled yet. Perhaps the defense is correct here. Someone may have kicked the helmet liner, the liner hit the gun, knocking both into the pooling blood. Who could have kicked it? Not Pfc Walter Allen. He testified under oath he did not touch anything other than to feel for Nick's pulse. Not the CID personnel. They are highly trained in how to process a crime scene. Most likely it was John as he hurriedly tried to stage the scene. True, his prints were not on the weapon. He wore gloves, then quickly hid them somewhere, intending to dispose of them later. The last part of the plan was to act, yes *act*, dazed and confused. That would give him time to answer whatever questions that came his way.

"Lt. Pulaski summarized his case by saying this clearly was premeditated murder, the deliberate taking of a life. He said," and Becca commented how she really liked this part, "We know the who. We know the when. We know the where. We know the how. We may never know the why. But we can use logic. The facts support provocation of some sort. I submit to the court that PFC John Anthony Lewis planned, prepared, and executed his plan to murder PFC Nicholas Alexander Cole, then staged the scene to make it look like an accident. I rest my case."

Becca then gave the account of how the defense summarized their case.

"Lt. Sanchez said in his opening statement that the prosecutor's case was weaker than the marine corps baseball team's bullpen." Becca added that people in the court, especially the Marines chuckled at this remark. "Anyway, he said this was a case of an accidental shooting, pure and simple. He said, "Here we have a fine Marine. Not an outstanding Marine, but not the worst. Average, but working to be better. That was why he went to the gun range. That was why he was reluctant to play fast draw. He didn't want anything to tarnish his record. John wasn't the type to risk that. For some Marines, their reputation is all they have. John was such a Marine. His captain and his gunny both said as much. John was a very even-tempered man. Slow to anger. He had no problems withstanding the taunts of boot camp, and he could easily have withstood the taunts of someone like Nick.

"How did John's .45 get loaded? We may never know. Life has unknowables.

"Why were John's prints not on Nick's .45? The prosecution claims John had a glove. Yet they were not able to produce a glove. Why were John's prints not on Nick's .45? Sanchez said, 'I submit it was because John never touched Nick's .45. Nick's .45 was on the floor because Nick dropped it. This means he had it in his hand at the time when he was shot. Why would he have it in his hand? Because he was playing a game of fast draw, just as John said. Tragically, this game ended with the death of a fellow Marine. Tragic, yes, but accidental.' And with that Lt. Sanchez rested."

Becca said the judge would render his verdict tomorrow at 10:00 a.m.

Becca then turned the phone over to Betsy. The first thing Wally said was how remarkable Becca's memory was. "That girl is going to go far. I'm so glad you brought her here for the trial."

"It has worked out even better than I thought. I think seeing the trial has really cemented Becca's desire to follow through with her plans. And it has provided a wonderful opportunity for the two grandmothers to form a bond as well."

Betsy and Wally did some planning for the next few days. It would be liberty weekend for Wally. He would ask Gunny for the morning off so he could attend the court martial. He would meet Laura, Minnie, and Becca at the courtroom. He knew Betsy had to work.

After court, Wally wanted to show Minnie and Becca, and Laura around the base. He'd gotten permission to do that as well. He knew they would find it interesting. Then all would go back to Betsy's for dinner. Betsy felt it would be more convenient for him to stay at her house, if he could.

Then on Saturday Betsy, her two guests, and Wally, would do some more sight-seeing in San Francisco. Saturday evening, Betsy's dad had planned a cookout. Her mom was inviting in family and friends and they intended to have a nice going-away party for Minnie and Becca.

Sunday morning it would be time for them to catch their flight back to Minnesota. Betsy would drive them to the airport. She was hoping Wally could come along as well.

Wally said "Of course, I would like that."

The conversation again was brief, so Betsy could get back to her guests.

The next morning Wally walked to the front gate to sign Laura's car in. He put his overnight case in the trunk and got in the car. Laura drove herself, Becca, and Minnie to the makeshift courtroom in a little-used room at the Officer's Club. They parked and walked toward the entrance. As they walked, a grey bus pulled up and stopped. They watched as two MP's marched John into the courtroom.

Inside the courtroom, they found 4 folding chairs where they could sit together. There was a smattering of other onlookers in the courtroom, mostly Marines. Perhaps more Marines would have attended but work kept them away. The case had high interest in the barracks. There was a low buzz of conversation as everyone waited for the judge.

Becca asked if anyone knew why Lady Justice wore a blindfold. Answering her own question, she said it was because justice should be rendered without regard to wealth, power, or status.

Promptly at 10:00 a.m., the bailiff announced "All rise, all rise. Court is in session."

The judge began with the fact that the defendant was charged with negligent homicide. He then stated that the prosecution has the burden to prove the charges beyond a reasonable doubt. "I have listened to the testimony and reviewed the evidence." He listed the various points each lawyer had presented. He then said "The prosecution failed to carry its burden to establish beyond a reasonable doubt that PFC John Anthony Lewis knew there was a round chambered. Therefore, I find PFC John Anthony Lewis not guilty. The defendant is free to go. I hereby order the defendant released from custody." A subdued but collective gasp could be heard among those who had come to hear the conclusion of the trial.

The gavel came down. The bailiff announced "Court is dismissed."

John's gear was already packed. His superior officers had decided he would be transferred to Camp Pendleton immediately, if the verdict was favorable. He remained behind just long enough to fill out some paperwork, but he would walk out of court a free man.

Chapter 14

The first stop for the four of them in Wally's tour of the base was The Base Canteen Restaurant. Minnie commented on how it looked to her like a 50's diner, with the chrome and Formica tables and chairs, the aqua and black color scheme. It even had a jukebox.

As they ate lunch, they discussed how they felt about the judge's ruling. Both Minnie and Becca agreed with the judge. True, they had lost a loved one at the hands of that man, but they actually felt sympathy for a young Marine who killed a man, albeit accidentally. It was something he would have to live with for the rest of his life.

Next, Becca and Minnie wanted to see the back gate that Nick had been guarding that fateful night. Minnie commented on how small that gate house was. Everyone was silent for a couple of minutes. Wally broke the silence by drawing their attention away from the gate house to the new stadium being built. Construction was visible from the back gate. It was to be called Candlestick Park, after the many Candlestick birds that frequented the area. Wally thought the strong winds that came in off the Bay would make it a challenging location to play baseball.

Wally wanted them to see the huge ships mothballed at the piers. "Mothballed?" Becca asked, curious. "What a funny term." Wally explained that when the ships were not in service, essential parts were carefully covered to protect them from salt water and weather, but in such a way that they could be quickly and easily put back into service on short notice.

Wally pointed out the dry docks where they bring ships in. "Why are they called dry docks?" Becca wanted to know

"They shore up, prop up, the ship under water. They pump all the water out of the area where it is sitting so they can work on the bottom of the ship."

Next on the tour was the area where the submarines were berthed. All that could be seen were the tops of the subs.

"Do you see that building over there; the one that has no windows? Can you guess what happens in there?"

Imaginative Becca hazarded a guess, "A top-secret lab?"

"Actually, it is the radiological defense laboratory." Becca wanted to know what they do there. All Wally could say was that the most secret of all operations goes on inside those walls.

Wally's next stop on his tour of the base was the baseball diamond where Nick had played.

Last stop was in front of the barracks. Wally told them about the various parts of the barracks interior, adding all Marines are housed there. The barracks, he said, is like a little city within the base, which is like a larger city. There is a police department, water department, fire department, motor pool, even a railroad.

As they were preparing to leave, their attention was diverted to some unusual activity happening at the front of the barracks. Marines began filing out and lining up. At a signal from Gunny, fifty Marines saluted Minnie and Becca in their car. The three women in the car were surprised and very touched by the thoughtfulness of these men. Wally, of course, already knew. With a big smile, he saluted back.

Again, as they passed through the front gate, the guards saluted.

Becca had really hoped they could again visit the back gate. She wanted to fix in her mind some of the things that came out in the trial. But cognizant of how difficult that part of Wally's tour was for her mom, she didn't ask. She was pretty sure the one visit would suffice.

On the way back to their home in Half Moon Bay, Becca wanted to know why Marines were stationed on a Naval base. Wally said the Marines Corps began in a tavern on November 10, 1775. At that time, it was designed to be support on land and sea. Navy was not designed to be on land, and Army was not designed to be at sea. Eventually the Marine Corps progressed to the point where they are on land, sea, and air. "Here on this base, Marines are the ones who guard the base, and at sea they guard the brigs on the big ships. But guard is only one specialty of Marines. A Marine can be a rifleman, work in intelligence, be a cook, a pilot, or many other specialties."

"Pilots?"

"Marines have helicopters. They need trained crew."

"Oh, I didn't know that."

The next day, Betsy, Wally, Minnie, and Becca set off for San Francisco. The first point on Betsy's tour was the famous

Lombard Street. As they zig-zagged their way down the steep hill, Wally commented that it was more crooked than his crazy friend, Teddy. "He's so crooked, when he dies, they will have to screw him into the ground."

Minnie commented on what a clever solution for getting up and down such a steep incline. Betsy assured her, she had very good brakes.

Next stop on the tour was Pier 39. On their way Wally asked Minnie if they had ever eaten lobster. Clams? Shrimp? Seafood? They had not. The foursome parked and as they walked, they passed a lobster vendor. Becca commented on how tiny their eyes are. As they continued walking, there were so many interesting things to see for two inlanders like Minnie and Becca. There were seagulls overhead, seals and otters swimming in the ocean. A little boy sitting in front of his parent's booth was selling slices of bread for five cents. They bought one and Becca delighted in tearing off little bits to feed the birds.

At lunchtime the group decided to purchase one lobster so everyone could say they ate lobster at Pier 39. Betsy said the seafood was very fresh here. The fishermen would bring it in and sell it to the vendors right from their boats. Minnie was especially interested in the process of selecting the lobster, then the cooking of it. Both Coles had fun cracking the claws and pulling out the lobster meat. Minnie giggled when they were handed bibs to put on. But she soon found cracking the claws could be a messy business. They all agreed, dipped in butter, lobster was delicious. Trying to be easy on Wally's budget, everyone chose the clam chowder to round out the meal.

Sitting outside as they ate, they enjoyed watching the people, obviously of many nations, walking, shopping, eating, biking, and photographing the sights on the Pier. Steam was rising from the cooking lobsters. The smell of many foods cooking permeated the air. Gulls screamed overhead. People talking and laughing and enjoying the day. The warm sun. The gentle breeze coming off the Bay. Minnie and Becca were thoroughly enjoying Pier 39.

After their visit to Fisherman's Wharf, Betsy announced no visit to San Francisco would be complete without a ride on a cable car. Becca was very excited about this; she had seen pictures of the cable cars, now she would actually ride one!

They would catch the cable car at Market Street. Wally gave them instructions on how to catch a cable car. "Run and jump on the side of it. If you want, you can work your way inside of it, and if you sit sideways, you can sit and look out at the scenery. You need to hang on tightly because we will be going up a hill. The conductor rings a bell when he starts up. Usually he will stop at intersections. People will jump on and off there."

While they waited, Becca noticed some type of vehicle going up and down on Market street. "Is that a cable car?"

"No, that is a streetcar. Do you see the arm connected to the wires that run over top of the street car? Those wires are what powers the streetcar. When the cable car gets here, you won't see those overhead wires. The cable car is pulled up the hill by a cable buried under the street. The conductor has a simple control that he pulls toward him to stop and pushes forward to go. The cable cars began in the late 1800's. Originally steam engines powered the cables. The cars don't go very fast, maybe ten miles per hour at most.

They took the cable car all the way up to the top of the hill. Now came the fun. People got off and helped turn the cable car around on the turntable. Then back down the hill they went. It was time to go home.

By the time Betsy reached her house, the going-away party was already getting started. People were arriving with covered dishes. Some were family. Some were neighbors. Some were Betsy's friends. Laura's sister, Nan, was in the kitchen getting everyone drinks. Laura was organizing the buffet. To Wally's surprise and Minnie and Becca's delight, Tom came. Betsy had the four of them in tow and was taking them around to introduce them to everyone. She was especially excited to introduce them to her Grandma Sophia and her Uncle Roger, who had come all the way down from Eureka, California.

Grandma Sophia was a round little Italian lady with twinkling brown eyes and a lovely smile. She had lots of white hair piled high in a coil on the top of her head. There was something about her eyes that intrigued Wally. He had the feeling she didn't miss much.

Uncle Roger was one of those bigger-than-life types; tall, robust, a big booming voice, he could dominate a room just by being in it. Betsy said Roger was a commercial fisherman. That was how he earned his living.

Joe was on the back patio warming up the grill. After introductions were completed and Betsy was busy helping in the kitchen, Wally and Tom went out to join the Grill Master. They were soon joined by Roger.

Eventually conversation got around to the incident at the back gate. Joe asked, "What do you think actually happened that night, Wally?"

"I really don't know what to think. Just because the prosecution didn't prove their case doesn't mean John didn't deliberately kill Nick. I didn't know John that well, hell, nobody did. But to me he just didn't seem like the type. I never saw him get angry. And I don't know if he would have been clever enough to pull off something like that." A thought slipped into Wally's mind. John smoking. Why did that memory bother him? But Joe was asking another question and the thought slipped away.

"Did they ever suspect you, Wally?"

This question surprised Wally. He'd never considered that, but he realized it was a legitimate question. All he could say was that the CID never even brought it up.

Conversation around the grill turned lighter after that. Roger had a funny story to tell. Actually, every time Roger was around, he had a funny story to tell. Tall tales, every one.

Roger said his buddy was sitting in his boat with a bucket-full of fish. DNR came up and said those were an illegal catch. "Oh, no," his buddy said. "These are my pet fish. Once a week I bring them out and let them swim in the lake with their friends." With that, he dumped the fish into the lake. "They'll be back in about ten minutes."

The DNR guy laughed at this story and looking at his watch, said, "I've got to see this."

Ten minutes came and went. Then fifteen, twenty, thirty. "OK, that's long enough. I'm going to write you up for possession of illegal fish."

Roger said his buddy looked at the DNR guy and said "What fish?"

The guys all laughed at that story.

Laura poked her head out of the door. "How's the grilling coming? Everything else is ready."

"We are good to go. I'll bring it in."

Time to eat. There were grilled hamburgers, hot dogs. Laura made some fried chicken. There was potato salad, macaroni salad, several bean dishes, coleslaw, and many desserts.

As they ate, Wally got a chance to talk to Tom. He'd been so busy with the trial and Nick's family; he hadn't had time to catch up with Tom's news. Wally asked him how things were going with Sandy. Tom was beaming and eager to tell Wally; Sandy was definitely coming out to San Francisco in early January. Betsy was sitting next to Wally and when she heard the news, she offered to let Sandy stay at her house. Tom thanked her and said he would check with Sandy and then let her know.

The next morning Betsy needed to get her guests to the airport. As planned, Wally came too. As Minnie and Becca were getting ready to board, Betsy pressed a small wrapped gift into Minnie's hand, "A dinosaur for Annie," she said. Tears, hugs, promises to stay in touch and Minnie and Becca were on their way back to the reservation.

The trip back to the base, where Betsy would drop Wally off, was a chance for the two of them to talk privately. Betsy admitted that when she heard some of the testimony at the trial, it really made her think about Nick. He had many good qualities. He was smart. He was ambitious. He loved her, no question about that. Nick had very high standards for himself. That was good. But she had witnessed some of the same type of rebuke others had spoken of in the courtroom. Nick could be very harsh when people didn't do what he thought they should. He had never been critical of her, but she was beginning to question the wisdom of a lifetime with someone like that. What if he began to be upset with her; her cooking, her housekeeping, money she spent on something, how she spent her time. Betsy even thought about the baby. Babies can be smelly, messy, cry for seemingly no reason, have tantrums, be stubborn. Could Nick have handled that? She wondered.

As Betsy talked, Wally also began to think of these things. On one hand, he wanted to defend his friend. But knowing Nick as he did, he could see Betsy might have had reason to worry.

"I can see what you are saying, Betsy. I wish I had answers for you, but I don't. I know Nick was a good friend to me. We never had a cross word. I know Nick was a devoted son and a caring brother. But you are right. A husband and wife, that is a different kind of relationship. I know the ability to accept that one's partner isn't perfect and loving them anyway is an important part of a happy marriage. I remember my minister telling our Sunday School class, when I was a teenager, that someday we guys would meet a girl so sweet we would just want to eat her. After we marry that girl the day would come when we would wish we had. Yes, I think if a marriage is to be a success, you have to realize things won't always be sugar, and spice, and that would be OK I believe you are that type of person, Betsy. But like you, I do wonder if Nick had that ability."

"I've been thinking a lot about this, Wally. If I'd known then what I know now, I don't think I would have considered marrying Nick. But good has come out of this; he brought me two remarkable friends in Minnie and Becca. They will always have a special place in my heart."

Wally thought to himself, "That is so like Betsy, she always seems to see the positive."

With promises to stay in touch, Betsy dropped Wally off at the base.

Staying in touch happened sooner than either expected. The Marine Corps 185th Birthday Ball was coming up on November 10th. Wally had really wanted to ask Betsy to go, but he didn't know how she would feel about it. After their conversation in the car, he decided to ask. The worst she could say was no. But to his surprise, she was delighted and readily agreed.

He met her at the front gate and signed her in. She'd chosen to wear a high-waisted gown that artfully concealed her expanding waistline. He teased her about being his special gate girl. She laughed. But the truth was, even with the baby bump she was, to him, the most beautiful woman in the room. Holding her in his arms was a dream come true, a dream he didn't ever want to end. But too soon the Ball was over and it was time for her to leave.

Before she left, Betsy asked Wally what he was doing for Thanksgiving. If he didn't have to work, she hoped he could come for dinner. If he could stay an extra day or two, she could show him around Half-Moon Bay. His heart skipped a beat. He told Betsy as soon as he knew his work schedule, he would call.

Back in the barracks that night, Wally was asking AJ who the woman was that he took to the ball. AJ said it was a German lady who lived at the "Y". Teddy had introduced them. AJ said her name was Gerta. Wally asked what happened to Angie. "Angie was a little too clingy for my tastes. Besides, it is a little embarrassing when your girl is the dirty joke of the barracks. But don't worry about her. She's already found someone else. That woman can find guys faster than flies can find a shit pile."

Wally was able to get Thanksgiving and one extra day off. He arrived just in time for dinner. Another much-appreciated home-cooked meal. Turkey, dressing, potatoes and gravy, sweet potato, corn, green beans, salad, and, of course, pumpkin pie for dessert. This time Wally and Betsy shooed her parents out of the kitchen and insisted they could handle clean-up. Wally washed dishes while Betsy put away leftovers. Soon she was drying and putting away the clean dishes. In no time the kitchen was clean. Punkin provided them with some special amusement. After his generous meal of leftovers, the cat's little belly was all puffed out. Next thing they knew, he was draped over the top of the TV, paws hanging down over the screen, sound asleep. "Ahhh," said Joe. "The traditional after-Thanksgiving meal nap."

Betsy and Wally decided they would prefer a traditional after Thanksgiving dinner walk. Since there had never been a traditional after Thanksgiving dinner walk before, they joked about starting this new tradition. It was officially titled the First Annual After Thanksgiving Dinner Traditional Walk.

As they walked the quiet streets of Betsy's neighborhood, they talked about everything and nothing. They did a little window peeking into the homes with brightly-lit front windows. Several were filled with people gathered together on this special holiday. They looked at architecture and landscaping; talking about what they liked and didn't like. Nothing special. Just two friends, easy in each other's company.

When they returned to the house, Laura suggested a game of cards. A fun game, a light snack, and it was time to retire. Laura joked "I guess you know by now where your room is, Wally." It made him happy to feel so included in this family.

The next morning Betsy fixed a special breakfast that included Bulldog[2] gravy over biscuits. As she cooked, Chubby Checker came on the radio, singing "The Twist". Much to Wally and Betsy's amusement, Laura began doing a modified version of the dance. Then Betsy jumped in to join her. Laura laughed and said "Honey, with that tummy you better be careful." But that remark encouraged Betsy to get sillier, just to tease her mom. But after a minute, she did sit down.

After breakfast Betsy took Wally for a stroll on one of the beaches. The surf was pounding in. Betsy explained this was a popular spot for surfers. At times the waves would reach almost fifty feet high. She pointed to the bluffs rising high on one side. She told Wally he would have to come back sometime when he could spend the night. She wanted to take him to the bluff at sunset. She said it was a spectacular sight. Before they returned to the house, Betsy took Wally to her favorite spot downtown, The Sweet Shop. They discovered they were both dedicated ice cream connoisseurs. Betsy claimed that at one time or another she had tried everything on the menu, and it all was good. She ordered a hot fudge sundae. Wally had a banana split.

Back at the house, Laura had leftovers set out for a light meal. They giggled with their own first private joke; they had just eaten a backwards dinner—dessert first.

It was time for Wally to catch his bus back. But Betsy didn't want their time together to end. She insisted on driving him back to the base. Wally again thanked Betsy's parents for their

---

[2] The bulldog is the official mascot of the Marine Corps.

hospitality. A hug for Laura. A handshake for Joe and the two were on their way.

On the way back, Betsy had the radio on. They sang along to "It's Now or Never" and "Sugar, Sugar". Too soon they'd reached the base. Wally reached over and making a fist, affectionately laid it alongside Betsy's cheek. In his best John Wayne imitation, he said "See ya around, kid." Then seriously, he thanked her for a wonderful couple of days and promised to call soon.

But it was Betsy who called next. She had news from Becca. Did he remember Clay? Wally did. Did he remember Tru? He couldn't place her, but when Betsy said "Dressed in black, black lipstick and nails, stood off by herself," he did remember. Betsy said the two of them were now an item. They had moved in together.

"That seems like an odd pairing to me," Wally said.

"Oh, I agree. I hope it works out for them, but I just don't see it."

Wally called a few weeks later to ask Betsy if she would like to see a movie. Elmer Gantry was playing on base. She was excited about it. She'd heard it was a very good movie.

After the movie they stopped by the px for Cokes. Betsy asked if he would like to come for Christmas dinner. She said she would love it if he could stay an extra day or two. Wally said he would let her know as soon as he could. As Betsy was leaving, he gave her a hug and thanked her for coming. They both agreed it was a great movie.

Betsy called again in a few days. Something funny had happened at work that day and she couldn't wait to share it with him. She said at her end of the building there was one bathroom for staff. At the other end of the building was a public restroom with several stalls. Every day one guy would take his newspaper and disappear into the staff bathroom for a full half hour. It made everyone mad because now they had to take time away from their work to go all the way to the other end of the building. So, they decided to teach this guy a lesson. That morning after he took his newspaper and went into the bathroom, they quietly took every chair out of the staff lounge and piled them up outside that bathroom door. They didn't just pile them, they tangled them. The door opened outward, so he couldn't get out. And they left him there. Wally agreed, that was a very funny story.

Wally didn't want to go to Christmas dinner at the Millers empty-handed, but he hadn't a clue as to what to take. He looked in the px, but nothing seemed right. He took the bus downtown and somehow wound up in a furniture store. He explained his problem and his limited budget to the kind saleslady. She had several suggestions. He settled on a small marble bowl that could be used to display fruit. Since Betsy had enjoyed Elmer Gantry so much, he thought she might enjoy a play. He bought tickets to "A Raisin in the Sun".

The gifts were a success. Laura raved over the bowl and promptly put it atop the refrigerator. Betsy was very excited about the play. The Millers gave Wally a sweater and Betsy gave him a matching shirt.

On the way to the play Betsy was telling Wally some of the backstory to "A Raisin in the Sun". The title came from a line in a poem about a deferred dream drying up like a raisin in the sun, and since the play was about deferred dreams, it seemed an appropriate title to the author.

"Did you ever have a dream about your future, Betsy?"

"I guess my only ambition ever was to have a happy marriage, like my parents. I'd like children, take vacations, do things with friends. You know, not a big dream, just a nice life. How about you, Wally?"

"Well, this may seem odd to you, but that is my dream too. My family life was always so torn up and chaotic, so stability is very important to me. My dream is to have a good-enough job that my wife could stay home and take care of the children. But I would be OK with a wife that worked, if that is what she wanted. I would want her to do what makes her happy."

Wally's answer surprised Betsy. She thought his dream would be much grander. And yet, it made sense to her; the desire to provide for your family and for yourself something basic that you needed as a child but never had. The more Betsy learned about Wally, the more she liked him. He was considerate, well-mannered, dependable, steady. He had a silly side and often made her laugh. She liked that, too. It occurred to her they'd never had a disagreement. They both had a sense of fairness, that give-and-take that makes a relationship work seamlessly.

After the play they talked about Sandy's upcoming visit. Tom had told Wally he'd found a place for Sandy to stay there on base. It was with a friend's wife in married housing. She was alone while her husband was out to sea and would welcome the company. Because Betsy was still working, and because of the distance to Half-Moon Bay, Tom just thought this arrangement would work out better. He did greatly appreciate Betsy's offer and he hoped the four of them could get together during her visit.

Wally said Tom was on cloud nine. Sandy would be staying for two full weeks. He wanted to take her to the coffee houses in North Beach. He wanted her to meet the people there; the people he thought were so much like her. They were kindred spirits. He was hoping she could see the potential in opening her style of restaurant there. He was convinced she could make a success of it. He had plans that they could make a life there together. That was what he wanted. All he had to do was convince Sandy.

Chapter 15

Tom's plans were going exceedingly well. When he wasn't working, he was with Sandy. He was in heaven. They traveled by bus to San Francisco where he showed her the sights, but especially North Beach.

She loved the coffee houses. Sandy would examine the menu and have ideas on how to expand or improve it. She was especially impressed with the coffee house that had couches, books, and board games for the patrons. There was the same homey, friendly vibe that her place in Minnesota had. She was surprised to find that in such a big city. At night there would be readings by would-be poets and writers. After the readings, there would be interesting and thought-provoking discussions. The proximity to the university was a plus, as well. Sandy could definitely see potential here.

She and Tom scoured the newspaper real estate ads looking for restaurants for sale, and what the approximate cost would be. They even looked into apartment rentals to see what the cost of living would be in Long Beach.

They began talking about Sandy selling her restaurant and starting another there in Long Beach. Both were very excited about their plans. Everything seemed doable.

Then it all came crashing down.

Tom and Sandy were on a bus, headed back to base after another great day at North Beach. The bus stopped and Angie got on. Tom saw her right away and cringed. He fervently hoped she wouldn't see him. But the bus wasn't crowded and she did see him. Her eyes flicked from Tom to Sandy. Tom didn't like the smile that slowly spread across her lips.

As luck would have it, the seat in front of them was empty and Angie sat down. She turned around and gave Tom a friendly smile and said hello. "And who is this lovely lady you are with?"

Tom reluctantly introduced her to Sandy. He was very nervous about where this was going to go. But surprisingly, Angie was very pleasant, inquiring of Sandy where she was from, how long would she be staying, how was she liking San Francisco. She hardly even looked at Tom. He began to relax a little.

Angie's stop was coming up. She stood to exit, but then she stopped. She said to Sandy, "Be careful of this one, honey. He's a love 'em and leave 'em kind of rat. Once he was mine. Now all I have left of him is this. She pulled a silver chain out from beneath her shirt. Dangling at the end of it was a silver horseshoe.

Sandy gasped. It was the horseshoe she had given Tom that last day in Minnesota. Tom gasped, too. "H...h...how did you get that?"

Angie smiled, and her smile had revenge written all over it. "Don't you remember? You gave it to me on our last night together. I guess it was my kiss-off gift." With that, she turned and got off the bus.

Tom had a flashback to that night. When Sandy gave him that horseshoe, he'd put it in his wallet. He forgot it was there. He remembered putting the wallet on the bedside table at Angie's. He remembered grabbing it on his way out of the door the next morning. Angie must have gone through his wallet during the night when he was asleep.

He looked over at Sandy. She had tears in her eyes. A few were starting down her cheeks. She didn't bother to wipe them. She said nothing. She stared straight ahead. Tom's heart sank. His mind was racing. Should he hold her? Should he say something? What? What words could possibly make this right! Worse, he was getting stares from those passengers close enough to Angie to be able to hear what she said. The stares were not friendly. Tom realized the bus was no place to talk to Sandy. He chose to remain silent until they were off the bus.

At the first possible moment after exiting the bus, Tom tried to talk to Sandy. But she said nothing. She just kept walking toward married housing. Tom tried to tell her how sorry he was. How it was only one time. How Angie got him drunk. The more he tried to explain, the worse it sounded, even to his ears.

And Sandy just kept walking. She said not a word. The tears had dried. Her face was stony.

By now, Tom was frantic for her to listen. He grabbed her arms, forcing her to look at him. She didn't resist him. He told her it happened right after he got back. It was one night only. But that one experience made him feel so badly. It was because of that night that he realized how much he loved her. She was all he ever wanted. For ever and ever. He never gave

Angie that horseshoe. She stole it out of his wallet. He begged her to believe him.

Sandy just stood there, staring right through him, quietly waiting for him to finish. He hugged her to him. It was like hugging a piece of wood. When he let her go, the girl of his dreams turned and walked out of his life.

Wally had been getting frequent updates from Tom. He was happy for his friend. Tom's plans for Sandy's and his future together were unfolding beautifully. Tom had been ecstatic. But not now. This night Wally was amazed to find a totally shattered Tom.

Again, seeking out a quiet place to talk, Tom told him everything. Wally was shocked that Angie could be so spiteful. Maybe that is every man's nightmare, that some indiscretion from the past will come to light just when everything is going so well. And ruin it irrevocably.

Working out a plan had lifted Tom's spirits before. They simply had to get through to Sandy and explain. If she wouldn't listen to Tom, maybe she would listen to Wally. Or maybe Betsy; woman to woman. But somehow, they would fix this. They had to. Tom and Sandy were meant to be together.

Plan One: Call Sandy. Tom said he already tried. No answer.

Plan Two: Call again tomorrow. Tom agreed to let Wally know how the call went as soon as their schedules meshed again. In the meantime, Wally would not say anything to Betsy. He would not involve her in such a private matter unless it became necessary.

Tom caught up with Wally the next day. He did try to call Sandy again. But it was Cara, his friend's wife who answered the phone. She said Sandy was gone. All she knew was that when Sandy got in last night, she asked for a ride to the airport, right then. All she would say was that she and Tom were through and she wanted to go home. She seemed very upset. Cara tried to get her to talk about whatever happened, but all Sandy would say was that it was a private matter. Cara had to respect her wishes. Cara seemed to Tom to be quite bewildered by the whole matter. She had really come to like Sandy. The two were becoming fast friends. Cara had enjoyed her company and knew how deeply she loved Tom.

Tom told her what had happened between them was his fault entirely, and that he intended to fix it. Tom thanked her for all she had done. Cara asked if Tom could let her know once they got things worked out. He said he would.

Plan Three: Wally would try. Sandy did listen to him. Wally told her what a mess Tom was after that night with Angie. Wally said, "He wanted to tell you, Sandy. He felt terrible. He realized how much he loved you and he knew he had betrayed that love. But I talked him out of it. I told him how much it would hurt you, and he didn't ever want to hurt you. I never in a million years thought you would find out. I'm sorry. I feel like I made a bad situation worse. Tom is a good guy, Sandy. I know Tom has learned his lesson and that he would never do something like that again. But if you knew Angie, you would know she is not a nice person. She tricked him into coming to her place by saying she had news of John. As for the horseshoe, he did not give it to her. He treasured it. He never would have done that. She stole it."

Sandy's answer was that she'd believed Tom was the most upright guy she'd ever met. She thought when he left Minnesota, he was hers alone. He didn't actually say it, but he certainly gave that impression. Wally could hear the bitterness in her voice. Tom kept his word and wrote faithfully, letters full of love. Those letters made her happy. Her time in San Francisco was wonderful. So, the fact that he had been with another woman after Minnesota blindsided her. Fidelity was very important to Sandy. She said she would never have done that to him. It destroyed her trust in Tom. How could she ever believe him again? She'd been willing to give up everything to be with him in San Francisco. Now she felt like such a fool. She'd been played by a player.

Wally pleaded with her to give Tom another chance. But Sandy told him she was really hurting. She promised to think about what Wally had told her, but right now she wasn't ready to renew any relationship with Tom. Sandy thanked Wally for the phone call and hung up.

Plan Five: Wally got permission to tell Betsy about Tom's dilemma. He asked Betsy if she had any ideas. Betsy asked for Sandy's phone number and said she would try to talk to her.

But Betsy had an idea of how to interject something new into the talk with Sandy. She called Angie and arranged a meeting with her. Somewhere in their discussion, Betsy convinced Angie to give her the horseshoe. Angie did admit to her she took it from Tom's wallet; he never gave it to her as a gift.

Then she called Sandy. She said she'd had a long talk with Angie. Angie admitted she stole the horseshoe. She gave it back to Betsy. "Angie also admitted that she kept giving Tom extra alcohol because she wanted to get him very drunk. She took full blame for all that happened. She was mad at Tom for not continuing to date her after that night, and when she saw a chance to get even, she took it. She never meant to hurt you, Sandy. She never knew Tom was in love with someone else, or she never would have done that."

Betsy continued. "I know this is a lot for you to absorb right now. To prove I am telling you the truth, I am sending the horseshoe back to you. Further, Tom is going to call you once a week. Even if you can't bring yourself to pick up the phone, you will know he is thinking of you and only you. But he is praying that someday you will find it in your heart to pick up that phone. Don't give up on him, Sandy. You are so lucky to have someone who loves you that much. I only wish I had someone like that in my life."

Sandy said, "You do have someone, only he doesn't know how to tell you, Betsy. Tom told me all about it. But don't let on that I told you. I don't know how you feel about Wally, but I know how he feels about you. I promise I will think about all you have told me. Maybe there is a way we can work things out. Thank you for calling. When is the baby due?"

"About two more months."

"Well, I wish you all the best. Thanks again for the call. I can tell you are a very caring person."

Betsy reported back to Wally all that she had talked about with Sandy. The next week when Tom called, Sandy picked up the phone.

Chapter 16

Not long after that, Betsy called Wally. "When is your next liberty?" Wally told her. "Would you like to spend it with a woman who is beginning to look like she is carrying a pumpkin?" Wally laughed. It seemed to him he was spending every liberty with the Millers. Not that he minded. Quite the opposite. He wished he had more time to spend with Betsy. He couldn't get enough of her. When he wasn't with her, he was thinking of her. "Do you think you could stretch it into three days? Betsy told him what she had in mind. Grandma Sophia had wanted her to come up to Eureka. And Grandma Sophia had specifically asked if she could bring Wally with her. That would be one day up, one day there, and one day back. Wally said he would see what he could do.

He was waiting at the front gate when Betsy pulled up. Betsy grinned, "When Grandma Sophia invites you, it is an offer you can't refuse." Wally laughed.

They enjoyed the spectacular views of Highway 101 as they drove along the Pacific Ocean toward Eureka. After a while they stopped to stretch their legs. They parked and strolled to the end of a pier where they saw two men fishing. Betsy asked what they were fishing for. "Sharks," was the reply. The man pointed to a bucket which contained two small sharks. Wally was surprised. He didn't realize sharks could be that small. Even though they were small, fish that size would warrant bragging rights back in Michigan.

Grandma Sophia greeted them at the door with hugs. Immediately she was fussing over Betsy's baby bump. This would be her first great-grandchild, and she was very excited about it.

Wally was sniffing the air. Something was cooking in the kitchen and it smelled wonderful. Soon Grandma Sophia was dragging them into the kitchen. She was in the middle of cooking dinner. There was a pot of homemade spaghetti sauce simmering on the stove.

"Wash your hands, you two. I'm a-gonna teach you how to make the meatballs. OK now. Oil your hands. Use this spoon. Scoop out the meat, this much." She measured about two tablespoonfuls. "Now roll it around firmly." Wally proudly showed her his first meatball. "No, no, honey. Not firm enough." She showed Betsy as well. "See those little cracks? We don't want those. Keep rolling. Nice and firm. That way they won't fall apart when you put them in the sauce." Finally, Wally's meatball met with her approval. "We Italians put the love into the food we prepare. That's what makes it taste so good. Now do another. Do you need more oil on your hands? When the meat begins to stick to your hands, you need more oil." Little by little, under Grandma Sophia's careful scrutiny and encouragement, their meatballs were measuring up to her exacting standards.

Soon she had Betsy frying the meatballs. Keeping a close eye on Betsy's skillet, Grandma Sophia was bustling around the kitchen, pulling bowls from the cupboard and vegetables from the refrigerator. "Here, Wally, you chop for the salad." Handing him a knife and a chopping board, Grandma Sophia set him to work. Still keeping an eye on Betsy's frying pan, and now on Wally as well, she was busy preparing the garlic bread and mixing the homemade dressing for the salad.

In no time dinner was ready, and right on cue, the front door flew open and Uncle Roger burst in. "I'm ho-ome!" He called in his booming voice.

Wally had to admit, Grandma Sophia's spaghetti was indeed the best he'd ever tasted. As they ate, Uncle Roger had another fishing tale to tell. His stories always started the same way: "I had this buddy..."

"I had this buddy. He was out fishing in his boat one day. He wasn't having much luck. Then he saw a snake swimming very close to his boat. The snake had a frog in its mouth. My buddy realized that frog would make excellent bait. Reaching down, he grabbed the snake right behind its head and hauled it up out of the water. He wrestled that frog out of the snake's mouth. Then he realized he was holding a poisonous snake. He didn't know how to let it go without it sinking its fangs into his hand. There it was, jaws wide open, just waiting to strike. My buddy had an idea. Reaching into his tackle box, he withdrew a bottle of Jack Daniels whiskey and poured a little into the snake's mouth. Immediately he could feel the snake relax in his hand. He gently placed the snake back in the water, and the snake slowly swam away. He baited his hook with the frog and before long he had caught one of the biggest fish ever. Just when he was wishing he had another frog, he looked down, and here came that snake again. This time in his mouth he had two frogs!" Everyone at the table laughed at Uncle Roger's funny story.

Uncle Roger asked Wally if he did much fishing back in Michigan. Wally said he had done a little shoreline fishing. Once he got to go out in a canoe with a friend. Wally said he was pretty excited about that. He believed you could do better out in the lake. Less fishing pressure. It was a nice summer day and it felt good to be out. As they paddled out to his friend's fishing spot, they passed other fishermen going in. "Any luck?" "Naw, fish aren't biting today." Boat after boat said the same thing.

Sure enough, they didn't have any luck either. It was starting to get dark and they were headed back toward shore. As they paddled, they saw an old man off in the distance who had been fishing on the shore. He was packing up and preparing to leave. He had a stringer full of fish! They paddled as fast as they could, hoping to catch up to the old man. They wanted to find out how he caught all those fish. But he was gone by the time they got close enough to talk to him. Wally never learned his secrets.

Uncle Roger agreed that there are secrets. Water temperature, bait type, hook size, bobbin placement; there are many factors to consider. It might take a lifetime to learn them all, unless you have someone willing to share their knowledge and experience.

After dinner, Uncle Roger asked Wally if he had ever split wood. Wally admitted he had not. "Well, come on then. We'll work off some of the calories we gained from Grandma Sophia's excellent meal. "I'm gonna turn you into a woodsman."

In the far back yard, a lot of split wood was already racked and ready for Grandma Sophia's wood stove. One wide piece of log was standing on end and braced on all sides. Selecting a cut piece of log from a pile, Uncle Roger stood it up on the even surface of the braced log. Then he called Wally over to examine the log. "You always look at your log. The log will tell you where to place your wedge. See this crack here? That is where we will start. I'll start it, and then you can take over."

Using the back of the long-handled sledge hammer, Uncle Roger pounded the metal wedge into the crack until it was secure. Then he handed the sledge hammer to Wally and let him pound the wedge into the log. Gradually the wedge went deeper. As it did, the log crackled and groaned and complained. Finally, the top of the wedge was flush with the top of the log Wally was trying to split. He could pound it no further, but it still hadn't split in two.

Uncle Roger then laid the log on its side and showed Wally how to attack the crack from the side with a second wedge. Finally, the log split in two. But Uncle Roger wasn't done with that log. Putting one half aside, he showed Wally how to examine the other half for the best place to start the next split. After a while, the wood-splitting was proceeding smoothly and Wally was thoroughly enjoying the process.

Meanwhile, the two women were in the kitchen, cleaning up after the meal. From time to time one or the other of them would look out of the kitchen window to see how the wood-splitting was going. As they worked, they talked.

Grandma Sophia was never one to mince words. If she gave advice, which was often, you'd better listen. She was a very wise woman and never off the mark. Now she had something to say about Wally. She'd seen how Wally looked at Betsy. And she'd noticed how Betsy looked at Wally. Grandma Sophia grabbed both Betsy's hands. "Look me in the eye and listen. You've got a good man there, Betsy. Don't let him get away."

"Oh, Grandma. I don't know what to do. Look at me! My big belly. And it's only going to get worse. I love my baby. But at the same time, I feel so ugly. I don't see how any man would be interested in me, let alone someone as wonderful as Wally. What's worse, it isn't even his baby. What man could ever accept that!"

"Any man worth his salt, honey. And unless I've got him pegged all wrong, Wally will love you and love that baby. Has he said anything to you?"

"Not a word, Grandma."

"Have you said anything to him?"

"No."

"He probably doesn't know how to approach you. You are going to have to let him know how you feel."

"How, Grandma? What if we are wrong? What if I make a move and he thinks I am being desperate? Or being disloyal to Nick. You know, Nick was his best friend."

"I will leave that up to you. The right moment will come along. Your heart will prompt you. But let me ask you this. Your mom tells me you two have been spending a lot of time together lately. He even took you to the Ball. Has he been dating anyone else lately?"

"Well, no. Not that I know of."

"He is choosing to spend his free time with you?"

"Now that you mention it, yes, that is probably true."

Grandma put her arm around Betsy as they again looked out the kitchen window at the men working out back. "I think that should tell you how he feels. Now what are you going to do about it?"

"You know I always listen to your advice, Grandma. And I am listening now. I will see what I can do. I promise."

They finished cleaning the kitchen and took coffee into the living room. "Grandma, how did you meet Grandpa? You never told me that story."

Grandma Sophia chuckled as the memory came flooding back. "My neighbor was having a corn shuckin' and a sing. Have you ever been to a shuckin'?" Betsy hadn't. "Well, you harvest all your field corn, you know, the corn you feed the animals. You let it dry. It all has to be shucked. So, you gather it up into a big pile. Then you invite all the young folks in to shuck the corn. If a young feller is lucky enough to find a red ear of corn—of course the farmer plants a few of these in the pile to make it fun—then he gets to kiss the gal of his choice on the cheek. Now, your grandpa was up visiting a cousin, so they both came to the shuckin'. When he got a red ear, he chose me to kiss. After the shuckin', we ate. He sat by me. He sat by me during the sing, too. My, he had a wonderful voice! That was the start.

"After that, it seemed like he was up visiting that cousin a lot. He would come a'courting. We'd sit on the front porch swing and talk. One day he asked my father for my hand. That was that. More coffee?"

Betsy shook her head. "Tell me more."

"I do have a funny story about one of his visits. As you know, your grandpa was quite the opportunist. One time when he was up, he ran across a farmer with 10 cows to sell, and the price was good. So, your grandpa bought them. Now he had to figure out how to get those cows down to his father's farm. He'd come up by train and it was a forty-mile trip back. So, do you know how he did it?"

Betsy got a huge grin on her face and shook her head. "Grandma, I can't imagine!"

"Well, Betsy, he walked them home. He mapped out 10 miles a day, then put them up with some farmer for the night. He would trade lodging and a meal for their milk. It took him four days, but he got them home, safe as could be."

Betsy laughed. "That sure sounds like Grandpa!"

Soon the men were back in. Uncle Roger never just entered a room. He always came charging in, full of vitality, bigger than life itself. Grandma Sophia jumped up and came back with two cups of coffee. Somehow, she had Wally's perfectly correct, cream and honey. How did she know! Grandma Sophia was the most observant person Betsy had ever known.

Wally told Betsy what fun he'd had out there splitting wood. Uncle Roger said he'd had to pry Wally away from the wood pile. He didn't want to quit. Betsy joked, "Oh yeah, you were out there having fun while we ladies were slaving away in the kitchen."

Uncle Roger chimed in, "Just wait until tomorrow. You may think the Marine Corps toughened you up, Wally, but you are going to be really sore in the morning." Everyone thought that was pretty funny.

Betsy asked Uncle Roger if he'd made any new box kites lately. Grandma Sophia said, "Oh, yes. He's always out in his shop working on a new one."

Betsy explained to Wally that was one of Uncle Roger's hobbies. He'd begun making them as a boy and just never stopped.

Wally asked what he did with them once they were finished. "Oh, some I fly. Mostly I give them away. As I go down to the shore to get in my boat, there's usually a kid or two hanging around the shore. I give them a kite and show them how to fly it. Then I get in my boat to go out for my day's fishing. But not before I tell them I'll be looking for that kite once I get out there."

Betsy commented on how nice her grandmother's hair looked. "Thank you. I went to the beauty shop this morning. Wendy styled it for me. She had an interesting story to tell. She had a friend; this was when she was young. Anyway, she had this friend who wanted her to come and visit. Since they lived in the country, she would stay the night. At bedtime they brought her a pillow and blanket to sleep on the sofa. It was summer and the front window was open. Wendy remembers a gentle breeze blowing in. It was very pleasant there in the living room. In the morning at breakfast the family asked her how she slept. She said the sofa was very comfortable. She said the only thing that would awaken her was the rocker on the front porch. Whoever was rocking in it was making it squeak. The family looked at one another knowingly. The mother said Wendy wasn't the first to report that squeaking rocker. She explained that before they bought the house, the previous owner died in that rocker. For ever after, it would sometimes squeak in the night. The family was convinced that rocker was haunted."

Uncle Roger said "Oh, baloney. Probably just a gust of wind would push the rocker and make it squeak.

Wally had a story to tell. He said he had a great aunt, sister to his grandmother. Her name was Aunt Pearl, and she was a God-fearing woman; not the type to ever make up a story. She was married to a very cranky older man named Carl. One night when she was a new bride, Carl wanted to go see a farmer. He had some business to conduct with that man. He parked his Model T on the side of the gravel road, leaving Aunt Pearl in the pitch-black while he went into the farmer's house. After a while, Aunt Pearl could hear a team of horses coming from behind her. She could hear their hoofs striking the ground. She could hear the rattle of the wheels of whatever they were pulling. She could tell from the sound they were coming fast. She was worried the driver might not see the car in the darkness. She turned around to see how close they were, but she couldn't see anything. The sounds grew closer and closer. She was getting scared. She kept looking back, but saw nothing. Now they were right behind her. Still, she couldn't see them. Then, to her astonishment, the sounds came right around her, on her left. Yet she never saw a thing. They came around, passed her, and continued on their way, yet she never saw them. In a panic, she ran to the house, pounding on the door and screaming for Carl. She said he was very annoyed at her for disrupting his business with the farmer. Wally said, "I don't know what happened out there that night, but I know my Aunt Pearl was the most unflappable person I've ever known. Till the day she died she swore that was the scariest thing that had ever happened to her."

Soon it was time for bed. Grandma Sophia and Uncle Roger retired to their respective rooms. Betsy got the guest room.

Wally was on the sofa in the living room. He went to sleep dreaming of squeaky rockers.

After breakfast, everyone went their separate ways. Grandma was going to her weekly Bingo with her friends. Uncle Roger went out on his boat. Betsy and Wally began their excursion to see the giant redwoods that grew in that area.

First on their itinerary was a visit to the Chandelier Tree. The signs said the tree was over 400 years old, 21 feet across and 276 feet high. The two young people gazed in awe at the mammoth size of this redwood. "Oh, Wally! Isn't this magnificent?"

All Wally could say was, "Wow!"

There was a tunnel cut through the center. It was 6 feet wide, barely wide enough for a car to pass through. Betsy was nervous about driving her car through. She asked Wally if he would like to do it. Carefully he inched his way through the tunnel. Now they had a story to tell their friends; they had driven through the Chandelier Tree.

From there, they visited the Humboldt Redwoods State Park, home to the 31 mile long Avenue of the Giants. It was a beautiful drive, with the branches of the trees forming a canopy overhead. Sunlight filtered through, creating ever-changing dappled patterns on the dashboard of the car. Music was playing softly on the radio. Betsy was wearing some kind of perfume that smelled wonderful to Wally. He thought this was one of those moments that would be fixed in his memory forever. His heart was overflowing with happiness.

As they traveled through on the Avenue of the Giants, there were little towns sprinkled along the way. Betsy and Wally had a great time exploring all the gift shops each town had to offer. There were funny sayings on signs, bumper stickers, mugs, and t-shirts. They took turns reading their favorites to each other. At one, Betsy found a little snow globe depicting the Chandelier Tree for Grandma Sophia to add to her collection. At another Wally found a mug for Uncle Roger. It showed a giant redwood. The inscription read "Stand tall and be proud of who you are." They also purchased a little book about the history of the redwoods.

They stopped for lunch at a little town called Pepperwood, just because they liked the name. Over coffee, Betsy read a little of the book to Wally. Originally loggers were very excited about all the wood they could harvest from the giant redwoods, and began cutting them down. A man named John Muir saw how special these coastal redwoods were. Some were estimated to be over 2000 years old. "That is before Jesus even walked the earth!" Betsy said with wonder in her voice. John Muir fought to preserve those trees for over four decades, preserving them for the generations to come.

It was time to return to Eureka. It had been a wonderful day. Betsy and Wally chatted all the way back about the things they had seen and done, things neither had ever seen before. Somehow, the pleasure of seeing something so spectacular as those ancient redwoods is magnified tenfold when you are sharing that experience with someone special.

The aroma of pot roast permeated the air of Grandma Sophia's home. It was a welcome smell for two hungry people. Wally loved being in Grandma Sophia's warm, sunlit kitchen, with its cheerful colors, decorative touches, and the incredible smells. He spied a witch hanging by the window. It seemed incongruous there, and he asked about it. "If you hang a witch in your kitchen, you will never burn food." Grandma Sophia smiled. "It's an Old-World superstition."

After dinner, Betsy and Wally insisted on being the clean-up crew and chased Grandma Sophia and Uncle Roger out of the kitchen and into their comfortable chairs in the living room.

Later all four were assembled in the living room and the conversation turned to politics over pie and coffee. Uncle Roger said he was sure their governor, Pat Brown, would probably be the best nominee for the Democratic Party presidential race that was coming up.

Grandma Sophia said all the ladies at Bingo were talking about a young senator named John F. Kennedy. Uncle Roger said he didn't think Kennedy had much of a chance. He was way too young. He didn't have enough experience. Plus, he was Catholic. Uncle Roger didn't think the voters would elect a Catholic to such a high office as the presidency. Down at the Coffee Bean, where Uncle Roger often stopped for breakfast, the guys said most folks thought if a Catholic was elected, the Pope would soon be running the country.

Grandma Sophia was speculating on who the Republican Party might nominate to run. It was her opinion that it would be Richard Nixon. She thought he might be a formidable candidate for the Democrats to beat. Everyone was looking forward to the party conventions in the summer.

Betsy chimed in. "Yes. The conventions are so exciting! We stay up all night, if necessary, counting the delegate votes. Of course, once one candidate has enough votes, we will try to get some shuteye. But oh, the drama, as the delegate counts mount for one candidate or another. I can just imagine the wheeling and dealing that is going on behind closed doors to get those delegate votes."

Uncle Roger said he'd heard that once the parties had settled on their candidates, they might actually debate on television. That would help the voters decide who they felt would make the best choice for president. That, too, would be very exciting. It had never been done.

Wally was feeling very left out of the conversation. It was hard to keep up with current events when you lived on base and had an irregular work schedule. Still, he was finding the conversation interesting and quietly resolved to try harder to catch the news when he could.

The next morning as Wally and Betsy were preparing to leave, Grandma Sophia told them they really must come back when they could. She mentioned Old Town, with over a hundred beautiful Victorian homes to see, a zoo, museums. Obviously, she really wanted them to come back sometime. Grandma Sophia gave Wally's hand a squeeze and softly said to him, "Take care of my girl."

It reminded Wally of another's request. It seemed Minnie said almost the same thing before they left the reservation. All he could say to Grandma Sophia was, "I'll do my best." And gave her a big hug.

Chapter 17

Wally spent his next liberty at Half Moon Bay. Betsy had invited him to go with her to see a special movie; "Inherit the Wind" with Spencer Tracy. She explained it was based on a true story about a Tennessee high school science teacher named Scopes. In 1925 Tennessee had a law prohibiting the teaching of Darwin's theory of evolution in their public schools. Scopes chose to teach it anyway.

They decided to go to the Saturday matinee movie, because it was cheaper. After dinner on Friday night, they went to the bluff to watch the sunset over the Pacific Ocean.

They parked and began walking out toward the bluff. As they walked, they passed a small white church with a tall spire. Betsy explained it was the church her family went to. Her parents were married in that church. She was baptized there as well. It was a small but friendly congregation.

Wally said his family seldom went to church. Nonetheless, as a kid, he would go to church every chance he got. Betsy asked him if he would like to go to church with them on Sunday. "I really would," he said.

They watched as the sun sank lower and lower, and the sky slowly lit up with brilliant yellow, orange, and red color. As they stood on the bluff watching Mother Nature's beautiful display, Betsy summoned up her courage and slipped her hand into Wally's. That simple motion startled and thrilled him, all at the same time. He turned and looked at her. She was looking up at him with such love in her eyes. He knew then that she was his. He gathered her into his arms and held her close, well, as close as you can hold a very pregnant woman. Putting his hand under her chin, he tilted her head up and kissed her; not hard, not passionately, but tenderly, sweetly, a kiss full of love.

So much emotion came pouring out. He was stroking her face and kissing her hair, and murmuring words of love. "I love you, Betsy Miller. I've loved you for a very long time."

"And I've loved you for a very long time," Betsy told him. "I didn't know how to tell you. Remember that day at the ball park when I told you I was pregnant with Nick's baby? You put your arms around me and it felt so good. I felt safe in your arms, like somehow everything would work out. I didn't know it then, but looking back, I think even that day I was falling in love with you."

"That last night in Duluth, remember? We were on the shore by Lake Superior? I wanted to hold you then. It was all I could think of on the plane ride home. I wanted to sit by you and talk to you, but Lt. Good had us arranged in such a way that I couldn't manage to switch without raising some eyebrows." Chuckling, Wally added, "Probably including yours!"

Betsy said "Oh, no. Me, too. It had been such a beautiful night, but the best part was being there with you. When I am with you, everything seems better. I, too, had wished we could have sat together on that plane."

Kissing, holding, stroking, they talked about their love for each other. Wally told her how much he missed her when he wasn't with her. He said he was thinking of her constantly and wondering what she was doing.

The sun was down and it was time to return to the car. It was a slow trip. They kept stopping and kissing. Months of pent-up emotion was pouring out in those kisses and words of endearment. In the car Betsy rested her head on Wally's shoulder. He had both arms around her and they were content. Everything felt so right. They could have stayed this way forever, in their own little world.

Neither wanted this moment to end, but it was time to go home. Much as Betsy loved her parents, Betsy didn't want to share Wally with anyone. They agreed to return to the bluff tomorrow night, after the movie. There was much to talk over, but each wanted some time to think, to absorb, to plan. Tomorrow night in their special place, they would share their thoughts with each other. They agreed not to talk about it until then—not even with Betsy's parents.

Walking into the house and trying to act normal was almost more than they could handle. Betsy would look at Wally, or he would look at her, and it was hard not to grin at their shared secret. Even though they tried hard not to show what was happening, they weren't succeeding. Laura looked at Joe and raised her eyebrows. He winked at her. Both knew the young people would tell them when they were ready.

The next evening, they returned to the bluff. As they watched another spectacular sunset, they planned their future.

Wally started first. "Betsy, I have two questions to ask you. For a long time, I have wanted to ask you this. I love you so much. I always want to be in your life. I always want you by my side. You make me so happy. I want to spend the rest of my life caring for you and the baby and making you happy. Will you marry me?"

"Oh, Wally. I want those things, too. It would be so easy for me to say yes. I want to be your wife. I want to be with you forever. But something is holding me back. How can I say yes when I am carrying another man's child? I have wrestled with this for a very long time. It just wouldn't be fair to you. I can't..."

Wally gently put his finger on Betsy's lips to silence her. "From this day forward, this will be our baby. I will love and care for this child as my own for as long as I live. I don't see it as a burden. I see it as a wonderous gift from you to me."

Betsy's eyes glittered with tears and joy. "Wally, sometimes you absolutely amaze me. I never in my wildest imagination would have believed you could feel this way. I am blown away. I'm speechless! I don't know what to say."

Wally put his hands on her shoulders, locked eyes with her and, speaking very gently, simply said "Just say yes."

"Do you really think we can make it work?" Betsy's voice was hopeful.

"I know we can. We'll figure it out together."

"Then, yes, Wally Allen, I would be honored to be your wife." Betsy continued; a bit puzzled. "You said you had *two* questions to ask me. What was the second question?"

"Betsy, I've been giving a lot of thought to the baby. My mother remarried when I was quite young. My brothers and sister had a different last name than mine. I would have felt more a part of the family if I'd had the same last name. I don't want that for this baby. If after we marry, we have more children, I would like to see them all have the same last name. I'm going to ask you another question, but I don't want you to answer right now. I want you to think about it. Would you consider putting my name down as father on the birth certificate? I could wait until sometime in the future and go through the courts and formally adopt the baby, but wouldn't this be simpler and easier? My thoughts are to do it this way. Please think about it."

Betsy started to say something, but Wally held up his hand to stop her. "Like I said, I really thought about this. As the baby grows, I don't want this to be a source of confusion. The child will always know Nick was the father. But the child will know, by carrying my name, that I love him or her too. I will always hope you stay in touch with Nick's family. And I know you will want this as well."

"Wally, I think that is a splendid idea. What a generous heart you have! I will think about it, as you have asked, but as of right now, I don't see a problem with it.

"Now, to change the subject, do you think we should tell Mom and Dad?"

"I do. I suspect they have already figured it out anyhow."

When Betsy and Wally walked through the front door, both parents looked up expectantly. "Mom and Dad, Wally has asked me to marry him and I have accepted."

Both parents were on their feet before they even realized it. Laura was hugging Betsy and Joe was shaking Wally's hand vigorously. "Congratulations!"

Laura asked, "When?"

Betsy answered, "Well, we really haven't talked about that yet. I would love to wait until after the baby is born. I want to walk down the aisle in a beautiful wedding dress. What do you think, Wally?"

"Whatever makes you happy will make me happy."

Laura was already hauling out a calendar. "Let's see, Betsy. We have a lot of work to do. We have to schedule the church and the reception hall, so we will have to set a date. We have to pick out invitations and get them printed and mailed in plenty of time."

Mother and daughter were bent over the calendar, oblivious to the world around them. There were mutterings emanating from the table they were hunched over. "Let's see, baby due here." Counting 1-2-3. "What about three months? Is that enough time?"

"Oh, yes! June's perfect!"

Joe and Wally exchanged an amused look. Women sure do get excited about such things!

Betsy looked up. "Wally? What do you think?" She pointed to a date in late June. "Will this work for you?"

Wally smiled. "Looks good to me."

Laura said, "Well, that's settled. Late June it is. We'll see what we can do."

The next day Wally went to church with the Millers. He was very impressed. As they walked in, there were two greeters at the door handing out hugs and handshakes. In the narthex there were small groups chatting happily. On a table there were cookies and coffee. There were glass windows, so those in the narthex could see into the actual church itself. Going through one of the doors, a man was handing out bulletins.

Once settled in a pew, Wally looked around. He'd been in many churches, but he really liked the simplicity of this one. The pews were light oak. The walls were white and unadorned. There were regular windows instead of stained glass. There was a plain cross behind the pulpit. Wally thought about how simply Jesus lived. Wally felt Jesus would have approved of this church.

Laura whispered to Wally, "This is where Joe and I were married. Do you like it?" Wally did. "Would you like to be married here?"

"Nothing would make me happier."

After Sunday dinner, the family lingered over pie and coffee. Betsy put her hand over Wally's and said she had an announcement. "Wally has offered to let me use his name as father of the baby on the birth certificate. He asked me to think about that offer and let him know. I want him and both of you to know I have decided to do this."

There was a gasp from Laura, and she was up and out of her seat. She had tears in her eyes as she gave Wally a great big hug. "Oh, Wally! What a gem you are!"

Betsy continued, "I had to think about how I could tell Minnie. And I have a solution I'm sure she will like. I'd already asked her if I could name the baby after Nick. She was delighted that I would do that. If it is a boy, I will name him Nick Cole Allen. If it is a girl, I will name her Nicole. That way the child will carry the full name of Nick, plus Wally's last name. I even have been thinking about a middle name, if the baby is a girl. When I was at the reservation, I met an extraordinary lady named

Lucinda. Her inner strength and fortitude really impressed me. If names can transmit qualities, I would like my little girl to have that same inner strength. If the baby is a girl, I will name her Nicole Lucinda Allen."

When Wally got back to the barracks, the first thing he did was seek out Tom. Grinning from ear to ear, he told Tom the news; he and Betsy were going to get married. Tom, too, got a huge grin on his face, clapped him on the back and said "Congratulations! Woo Hoo!" And he did a goofy little circular dance, with his hands in the air.

Teddy and a couple of his buddies happened to be nearby. "What's all the commotion about?"

Tom said, "Wally's getting married."

"Wally, what did you do? Knock somebody up?" Teddy asked.

At this, Tom and Wally looked at each other and burst out laughing. Wally choked out an answer. "No."

Teddy's jaw dropped open. He looked confused. "You mean you are marrying a girl because you *want* to?" Apparently, this was a new concept to Teddy.

Wally gave Teddy a good-natured punch on the shoulder. "Just you wait, Teddy. Someday some gal will come along sweeter than honey and you won't know what hit you.'

"Not me! The single life is way way way too much fun." Addressing Wally, "Hey, Bud, I'm happy for you."

Next Wally wanted to tell Gunny. The office door was partially open, and Gunny was in conversation with someone. Wally turned to leave but Gunny saw him and motioned for him to come in.

Looking from Gunny to the other man in the room, the Duty Sergeant at Arms, and back to Gunny, Wally said, "The reason I came by was to tell you my good news. Betsy and I are getting married."

Before Gunny could say anything, the Duty Sergeant exploded. "You stupid idiot! Why in the fuck would you want to do that! Don't you know you will have eighteen years of paying for someone else's..."

Before he could finish his sentence, Gunny's fist had slammed down on his desk. Startled, the Duty Sergeant fell silent. "That was a rude and thoughtless remark." Pointing to Wally, but looking at the Duty Sergeant, Gunny said, "This Marine is more of a man than you will ever be. Get the hell out of my office."

Stunned, the Duty Sergeant was frozen in place.

"Right now! Go!"

Red-faced, the Duty Sergeant stormed out of Gunny's office.

Then Gunny turned smoothly to Wally and said, "Sorry about that. Don't take it personally. That guy has a serious case of burnout. I don't know how he has lasted this long. So, you and Betsy are going to get married. I am so happy for you. You are two very special people and you belong together. When will the wedding be?"

"At the end of June. Gunny, I came to ask a favor of you. You have always been so kind to me. Ever since I came here, I have looked up to you as the sort of Marine I would like to be. I would be so honored if you would come to the wedding. Maybe you would even say a few words?"

"I would be glad to come. And certainly, it would be my pleasure to say a few words at your wedding. What about having a military wedding? I can round up enough guys for you, if you want it. Or if there is anything else I can do, just let me know. By the way, how is Betsy feeling? The baby must be coming pretty soon?"

"She's feeling pretty good. The baby is due any day now. Wow! I like the idea of a military wedding. That hadn't occurred to me. You know, Betsy's father also was a Marine. Let me check with Betsy. I'll bet she will like that."

"Wally, you are taking on quite a responsibility. I commend you for it. Not many men would consider what you are doing."

"Betsy is worth it."

"Yes, she is," Gunny agreed.

Next, Wally called his mom. Some unidentified person answered the telephone. "Yeah, she's here. Just a minnit." In the background, Wally could hear people talking and laughing.

"Wally, is that you? Is everything all right?"

"Yes, Mom. Everything is fine. I called because I have some good news to tell you."

"Just a minute, Wally. I can't hear. Hey, you guys, it's long distance. Quiet down!"

Wally heard someone ask, "Is it Wally?" his mom must have nodded, because the next thing he heard was someone saying they wanted to say hello. Then someone else. He had to talk to several people before he could get back to his mom to tell her his news.

"Over the weekend I went to Betsy's at Half Moon Bay. Mom, I asked her to marry me. And she accepted. Mom, I'm getting married!"

"Betsy...isn't she the one who's boyfriend got shot?"

"Yes, Mom, you've got it right. Her boyfriend, Nick, was my best friend. I was the one who found his body. Remember,

Mom? Anyway, that whole incident brought us together and over time we realized we loved each other."

"Just a minute, Wally. Mrs. Price, I know you are listening in. Hang up the phone. This is none of your business." Wally could hear a click.

"Darn party line. Anyway, I don't understand. I thought you told me she was pregnant. Or maybe that was someone else. Honestly, Wally, this place is such a madhouse I don't know if I am coming or going. It addles your brain." Then addressing someone else, she said, "That baby doesn't smell right. Go check his diaper."

Once Wally had her attention again, he said, "Yes, Mom, you've got it right. Betsy is pregnant and due any day now. She..."

"You're going to marry a pregnant girl?"

"Yes, Mom. The way you put it, it sounds like you don't approve. She really is a nice person. I know you will like her once you meet her. She has a nice family, too, and they have been very good to me."

"Oh, no, Wally. How am I going to know whether I approve or I don't approve? I've never met her. It is just a little surprising to me, that's all."

"I know, Mom. I'm sorry there isn't time for you to meet her. But by the time we decided to get married, her pregnancy is too far along for her to travel."

"Well, Wally, you've always had a level head on your shoulders. If you've decided she is the one for you, who am I to stand in the way. My job won't be to judge her. My job will be to love her. If she's the one who makes you happy, then

I am happy too. What more could a mother ask for! When is the wedding?"

"It will be at the end of June. She wanted to wait until after the baby is born. I want you to come."

"Oh, I don't know, Wally. You know how it is around here. Always a lot of stuff going on. It will be hard for me to get away."

"Mom, I know it won't be easy for you to come. It is a long way. But by plane it won't take long. You could come in on a Friday night. The wedding could be in the morning. You could be home by Saturday night. Mom, I'm your oldest son. Surely you can spare one night away from home. For me?"

"I'll see what I can do. No promises. We'll see."

Wally also called his old high school buddy, the guy responsible for him joining the Marines, Zeke McAllister. "Hey, Zeke, I've got news. You are not going to believe it—guess who's getting hitched?"

"Who?"

"Me, Buddy! I'm getting married!"

"Oh, no way! You're gonna bite the bullet?"

"Yep, sure am! In June."

"Well, who'd the lucky gal?"

"Her name is Betsy. I told you about her before."

"You mean the one who's pregnant?"

"That's the one. She's due any day now. We're waiting until after the baby is born to have the wedding."

"Hey, congratulations! She must be a really special gal. I'm happy for you. I hope I get to meet her someday."

"You definitely will. I want you to come to the wedding."

"Send me the details. I'll make it if I can. It'll be good to see you. Hey, Wally, I've got an idea. Why don't you two come out here? It won't cost you a thing. I'll reserve you a cabin. That'll be my wedding gift to you."

"Let me run it by Betsy. It can't be right away, because of the baby. But now you've got me thinking. You know, Betsy and I have never had any private time together, if you catch my drift. Maybe we could get out to see you in a couple of months?"

"Sounds great to me. Call me later and let me know. The cabin will be yours. You'll like it here. Nice and private."

"OK, pal. I've got to sign off for now. Will check in with you later."

On the way back to his bunk, he passed Larry. "Hey, Wally, your garage door is open."

"Oh yeah? You looking at my big V8 engine in there?"

"Naw, I see a scooter with two flat tires."

"Remember, we all shower together. So maybe I have a scooter, but that's better than your tiny skate key."

Everyone within earshot in the barracks was laughing at this good-natured exchange.

That night, since Wally was the driver on duty, he was asked to take Captain Morgan to a meeting. Waiting for the Captain gave Wally some time to think. He was thinking about his proposal to Betsy. Up until this time, he had only himself to take care of. Now he would be responsible for a family; his very own family. Was he ready for this? It was exciting and sobering, all at the same time. With Betsy at his side, he was determined to prove himself worthy of her choice.

Later, back in his bunk to rest, Wally was thinking over his life and all of the different people and events that came together to bring him to this point. Some had seemed quite inconsequential at the time. Life is like a chain, with one link leading to the next.

For instance, fifth grade at Brooklyn School. He was the New Guy in school. The teacher sat him next to Zeke McAllister. What a special friend Zeke would become through the years. Zeke was always the guy with the fun ideas and a zest for life.

When someone came to the fifth grade to talk about the Boy Scouts, Zeke was all for it. "Come on, Wally, let's sign up!" They did. The Boy Scout Code and Wally's Boy Scout leader became a pivotal point in Wally's life; something he could hang his hat on. While some merely recite the Boy Scout Oath, Wally took it to heart. Even now, so many years later, Wally could remember it. "On my honor, I will do my best to God and my country..." From then on Wally did his best to live honorably. He wasn't perfect, but he tried.

When they were teenagers, Zeke taught him to dance. They practiced and practiced. In time, they came to consider themselves almost professional. They even bought matching pointed shoes so they could look cool. One day Zeke decided they were good enough to be on American Bandstand, with Dick Clark. This was a TV program that showcased teenaged dancers. "Come on, Wally, let's go!" They began hitch-hiking. Unfortunately, there was a flaw in Zeke's plan. It was winter. Rides were few and far between. Before long the boys were frozen. They turned around and hitch-hiked home. So much for their professional dancing career.

After high-school, Zeke decided they should join the Marines. "Come on, Wally. Let's sign up!" Zeke thought it would be best to sign up for four years. Unfortunately, Zeke got pneumonia. He got a medical discharge and went to live on a ranch in

Montana. Wally would be staying in the Marines for four years, thanks to Zeke. Not that Wally minded. He thought joining the Marines was a good choice for him.

Nick was his bunkmate in the Marines. Wally felt he would have been lost if it weren't for Nick. Nick guided him and helped him get squared away. He would always be grateful to Nick for all he had done.

And in a roundabout way, Nick brought him to Betsy. Well, maybe not on purpose. Or maybe it was. Who can say? Chains. Wally wondered where this end-link would lead. What would be next in his chain?

Chapter 18

Wally was calling Betsy daily, sometimes even more than once a day, fitting the calls into his duty schedule. Betsy was home now full time. She had quit her job, so she was always there when Wally called. She was spending her time preparing for the baby's imminent arrival.

Wally told her about Gunny's idea of a military wedding. Betsy loved it! She asked Wally to get the details so they could work it into their plans. He promised to do so as soon as possible.

Not long after they had made their wedding plans, Betsy told him she had called Minnie to tell her. She wasn't sure how Minnie would feel about that news. But Minnie wasn't surprised at all. Betsy said Minnie had hoped, even before they left Minnesota to fly home, that the two of them would be together. Minnie told her she could see how much Wally loved her. She also could see what a fine father he would be. Wally told her how Minnie had patted his hand and said "Take care of Betsy." Now he understood she meant much more by that than he originally realized.

Betsy went on to say she'd asked Becca to be her maid of honor. Joe had generously offered to pay for the trip. At first Minnie didn't want to accept, but Joe got on the phone and talked to her. Becca would be the maid of honor, and Annie would be the flower girl. Betsy had talked with Annie directly. She was very excited. They were coming out a few days early to shop for special clothes for the wedding. That would be Betsy's gift to her wedding party.

Betsy said Becca was working on a special gift for the baby. It was a dreamcatcher. Native Americans hang this over the baby's crib. Good dreams will pass through the center hole. Bad dreams get trapped in the web. They are gone by dawn.

On day when Wally finished his duty shift, there was a message for him to report to Gunny's office. Gunny told him Betsy's father had called a couple of hours ago. He wanted Wally to know Betsy had gone into labor and Wally was to call the hospital for updates.

Wally hastened down to the barracks pay phone booths. With shaking hands, Wally dialed the number. The operator patched him through to Betsy's room. Joe answered the telephone. He said Betsy was doing OK. No problems. But the doctor said it might be a while before the baby comes. Wally asked if he could talk to Betsy. Joe cautioned he should only talk for a minute or two. The birth pains were coming quite frequently now. Wally simply told Betsy he loved her and he was proud of her. She told him she loved him too, and would feel more like talking after the baby was born. Joe suggested trying back in four hours.

Four hours seemed like an eternity. Time crawled by. After his duty was finished, Wally normally would eat and sleep. But now he had no appetite for eating and was way too wound-up to sleep. Time crawled by. Wally got a shower. Took a walk. Polished his shoes. Straightened out his locker. Finally, he called back. It had only been three hours. Joe chuckled at his impatience. He said it seemed to him to be taking a long time. But the doctor had reassured them that everything was proceeding normally. There was nothing anyone could do but wait. Over the phone Wally could hear Betsy groaning. It scared him. "Maybe I should come down there?"

"No, Wally, there is nothing anyone can do. This baby will come when it is good and ready. Why don't you try again in two hours?"

This time Wally did manage to wait out the two hours. Joe again answered the phone. Wally could hear something going on in the room. He could hear clanging and people talking. They seemed to be coordinating something. Betsy was groaning. Joe seemed quite distracted. He told Wally the orderlies had come to take Betsy. They were just now putting her on the gurney. He asked Wally to stay on the line a moment. Wally could hear him telling Betsy he loved her. Then Joe held the phone to Betsy's ear so Wally could talk to her. Again, he told her he loved her and would see her soon. Next, Wally could hear Laura softly saying something soothing to Betsy. She murmured something in reply and the noises were quickly receding from the room. Joe talked to him for a moment. Apparently, there was some kind of problem. Joe said it had been hard for them to watch their beloved daughter in so much pain. The baby just didn't want to come. The doctor was going to run some tests and see what could be done. Joe said for Wally to call back in an hour. The doctor told them he should have news for them by then.

Another hour dragged by. Wally called. Still no word from the doctor. Joe and Laura were very worried. But there was nothing to be done but to wait. Joe suggested Wally try again in a half hour. In the meantime, he was going to try and find a nurse.

When Wally called back, it was Laura who answered the telephone. The nurse had just left. Betsy had delivered a baby girl, seven pounds and four ounces. She was twenty inches long. Betsy was in recovery and once she came around, they would be able to see her. The nurse said both mother and baby were doing well. The baby had been breach, and Betsy had a C-section. Joe and Laura were going to see the baby as soon as they hung up the phone. If Wally could call back in couple of hours, they would undoubtedly have more news by then.

By the time Wally called, Joe and Laura had seen both the baby and Betsy. Joe said they would be bringing Betsy back to her room soon. She was awake, but very tired. Joe suggested letting her get a good night's rest and calling in the morning.

Joe said they also got to see the baby in the nursery. Little Nicole had a lot of black hair. They had her next to a little blond baby with bright pink cheeks named "Baby Tuck". Nicole, in contrast, looked like she'd already been to a tanning salon. They said Nicole was a very beautiful baby.

Joe said they were leaving as soon as Betsy got back to her room. They wanted to go home and get some rest, and they suggested Wally do the same. Tomorrow would be a much better day.

The next day when Wally called, it was Betsy who answered the phone. "Oh, Wally, we have a beautiful baby girl! I'm so happy! Are you happy?"

"I'm so excited I can't stand it! I can't wait to see you. And the baby, of course! But especially you. I was so scared we would lose you."

"Yes, I guess I scared everyone, including myself. But it is over now. Blue skies ahead. One thing seemed very comical to me. Here I am completely knocked out. When I come to, there is Mom and Dad telling me I have a baby girl. I'm the one who carried that sweet little bundle for nine months, but I am the last to know what it is!"

It felt so good to hear Betsy laughing and chattering away like old times. It seemed amazing to him. One minute you are struggling to bring new life into the world, and that next you are back to your old self, well, almost. He asked Betsy how she was feeling.

"Sore, of course. I am on some pain medication. I'm not allowed out of bed yet. Tomorrow the nurse will come and help me get up. I am not to try on my own."

Wally asked her how long she would need to stay in the hospital. "The doctor said if all goes well, he will release me on Friday. Mom said if you have liberty you would be welcome to come and stay at the house. Dad can come and get you so you don't have to take the bus."

Wally assured her he would be there. He asked Betsy to thank her parents for their many kindnesses in keeping him informed during that difficult time. He told Betsy to rest so she could get out of there on time. He would call tomorrow. He loved her.

After getting off the phone, Wally called his mom. He told her she was now officially a grandmother. She was delighted with the news. Wally gave her all the details. She asked how Betsy was doing. Wally told her about the C-section.

Again, he asked her about coming to the wedding. She said she'd been doing a lot of thinking about that.

"You know I'd love to be there. I did check on the price of a ticket. Wally, it is almost $300. You know how hard it is to come by that kind of money around here. So, I've made a decision. No, I won't be coming to the wedding. I would rather send you the money I would have spent on the ticket. I know you don't make much money each month, and you are going to need money for the wedding and all the expenses of setting up housekeeping."

"Mom, I'm disappointed that you can't come out for the wedding. But I understand, I really do. I know it is expensive, and I know it is how hard it is for you to get away. What you are telling me makes perfect sense. I love you for being so thoughtful. I'll tell you what. Betsy and I and the baby will come to visit you someday."

After that, the conversation became more general, as Dot filled Wally in on all the news back home.

Wally could hardly wait until Friday, when he would be on liberty, to go to Half Moon Bay to see Betsy and the baby. What a wonderful weekend that was for Wally. When Betsy handed him the baby, little Nicole wrapped her tiny hand around Wally's finger and in that instant, she stole his heart away. He knew he would walk through fire to protect his little family.

Betsy told him she had called Minnie about her new granddaughter. Minnie was very excited about her and looking forward to seeing the baby when they got in for the wedding. Minnie loved the name Nicole, and was on the verge of tears when she heard Nicole's middle name would be Lucinda.

Time went by. Wally was calling nightly and he was so happy to hear Betsy's voice getting stronger and stronger. Every night she had something new to report about the baby. One day when she was giving Nicole her bottle, the baby looked right at her. Betsy said the nurse told her newborns can't see very well. "But, Wally, I swear she could see me! Oh, Wally, I can't wait until you can come again."

At his next liberty, he and Betsy began making some concrete plans for after the wedding. Once they were married and had an actual marriage certificate, they could apply for married housing on base. In the meantime, Betsy would have to stay with her parents and Wally would come on his liberty weekends. Wally said he'd learned once he was married, he would get a small pay increase. Betsy said she had some savings that would help out. Wally told her his mother was not going to be coming to the wedding, but would be sending money to help them set up housekeeping.

Wally also told Betsy about Zeke's offer to put them up at the ranch. They settled on a date two weeks before the wedding. Wally said he would arrange for vacation time so they could stay a week. Laura was happy to take care of the baby for them. It would be the only honeymoon they could have, as they hoped to be moving into their own little apartment on base soon after the wedding. Betsy saw the humor in it all: baby born before getting married, honeymoon two weeks before the wedding. Oh well, much as they would have preferred things differently, that was the way it worked out. Wally promised someday Betsy would have a beautiful diamond, and a real honeymoon. Just couldn't do it now.

One day Tom found Wally. Tom was beaming with happiness. "Sandy's had an offer on her restaurant. Actually, several offers. There was an actual bidding war for her place! She got more than she even was asking for it. She is so excited. She'll be coming out here as soon as she closes on her sale."

Wally was so happy for his friend. "Oh, there's more. We think we've found the perfect location for her restaurant in North Beach. Sandy made an offer on it, contingent on her sale going through. It has been accepted. Oh, Wally, this is going to happen! I can hardly believe it!"

Wally was blown away by this development! He was almost speechless. All he could do was clap Tom on the back and say "Wow! Wow!"

Later he was thinking about Tom's news. It seemed Tom's future and his own future were both starting to take shape. Tom with Sandy at the restaurant, him with Betsy and the baby. When they joined the Marines, they were just two guys without direction. Now look at them. Wally didn't know his future totally yet, but he knew how much he had changed. He was determined to find a way to make a good living for Betsy and their baby. As he mused, he thought how everything could be traced back to Nick and the incident at the back gate.

One day Tom told Wally Sandy was coming in. The sale of her restaurant had been completed. She would be staying with their friend Cara in married housing until they could find an apartment for her.

Tom was going to be Wally's best man. He and Sandy had discussed what they could do for a wedding gift. Now that

Sandy would be in town, she wanted to do all the food for the reception. Her new restaurant would not be usable for a while yet. They still had to close on it, get permits and inspections. But if there was a place where Sandy could cook...?

Wally said there was. The little church where they will be married had a basement with a full kitchen. Those are always inspected by the Health Department, so she could use that one.

Wally was using every liberty weekend at Half Moon Bay now. Little Nicole was growing so fast. She was starting to coo, and she had real smiles. Everyone who saw her thought she was the most beautiful baby ever, but none more so than her proud parents.

Wally had called Zeke and they settled on a date for their stay at the ranch. Zeke was very excited. He said he had a mare who would be giving birth about that time. Wouldn't it be great if that happened while they were there!

Chapter 19

Finally, departure day arrived. Joe drove them to the airport, and Zeke picked them up in Missoula, Montana.

Betsy was tickled with Zeke. What a character! Taller even than Wally, he was beanpole thin. He had a handlebar mustache and a thick shock of unruly hair. He had a deep voice, a firm handshake, and a grin that went from ear to ear. He might have originated in Michigan, but he was the epitome of a true Montana cowboy. He was dressed in his Sunday best, a clean flannel shirt, blue jeans with suspenders, and scuffed-up cowboy boots. He sported a leather belt with a large shiny buckle with an "M" on it. Betsy wondered if the M stood for Montana, or for McAllister.

Zeke's ranch was about a half-hour's drive south. He was four miles deep in a canyon. As Zeke drove, he said he almost had to call and cancel their trip. There had been a major forest fire and everyone but essential people in the canyon had to be evacuated because the road they were on was the only way in and out of the canyon. Everyone was only allowed back in two days ago.

Even as they drove back into the canyon, the air was heavy with the smell of wood smoke. Here and there they could see firemen in grey and yellow suits working on hot spots. They were shoveling dirt over the smoking areas. Overhead a red helicopter with a bucket was scooping up water from the stream and dropping it on the hot spots. Wally thought a forest fire meant all the trees burned down. But here it looked as though the ground was singed and a little of the trunks were blackened. It looked as though the trees would survive, however.

The ranch was a pleasant surprise. It was much more elegant than they were expecting. There was a large main building. Zeke explained the lodge was like a hotel, where they rented out rooms. Inside, there was a good-sized lobby with a stone fireplace, coffee, and snacks for sale. They could also buy postcards and stamps there. Scattered around the lodge were cabins of varying sizes. Some were quite large; three bedrooms, Zeke said. Others were smaller. All the buildings were made of logs. The ranch was very busy during the warm months. The stream nearby offered world-class fishing and people came from many countries to fish there. The ranch closed down in the winter, except for a few permanent residents.

The cabin Zeke had reserved for them was another pleasant surprise. It was one of the smallest ones, but very cute. As Zeke had promised, it was very private, set off by itself, nestled in amongst some very tall pines.

The first thing Betsy noticed when she stepped out of the pickup was the sound of the wind in those pines. The second thing was the wonderful, fresh, outdoorsy smell of the pines. The cabin had a front porch with two rocking chairs on it.

There was a fire pit out front and a stack of split wood ready for their use

Stepping through the front door, Betsy fell in love with the interior. To the right was a sofa that made into a bed. To the left was a table in front of a large picture window that overlooked a meadow. Behind the table was a small wood stove. To the right of the stove was a small kitchen. An eating bar separated the kitchen from the living room area. Behind the kitchen was a bathroom and closet/utility area. Everything they needed and not one speck more. On the table was a bowl of fruit. Zeke had stocked the mini-fridge with a few essentials. Betsy turned and said "Oh Zeke! This is wonderful!"

Zeke gave her his huge grin and said "I know you two will want to go back to Missoula for some groceries. You can use my truck. I will leave you the keys. I will be working around here during the day, so I won't need it. Truck's full of gas. Feel free to use it. I'll check in with you tonight. We'll have a bonfire and nice visit. For now, I have to get back to work." A hug from Betsy, and another from Wally and Zeke was gone.

Wally and Betsy unpacked, then took the truck back to Missoula. They found a grocery and picked up enough food to last the week. One other thing they realized was that they would need some flannel shirts. The air up here in the mountains was definitely cooler than they were used to.

After dinner, while Betsy was cleaning up, Wally was out getting the bonfire going. Soon Betsy joined him. Both were grateful for their new flannel shirts. They were the perfect weight, plus they both were feeling quite cowboyish in them.

There is something relaxing about a bonfire. Sitting there in the flickering firelight, feeling its warmth in the brisk night air, listening to the crackling, they could feel the stress of the day slowly peel away. From the early morning rush to catch their flight to getting unpacked and hunting up groceries and preparing a meal, it felt good to just sit and relax.

Soon Zeke showed up, cigarette in one hand, can of beer in the other. Accompanying Zeke was his faithful dog, Happy Jack. Zeke described him as "one of those Heinz 57 type dogs. A little bit of beagle, some terrier, plus a boatload of unknowns." Happy Jack was a smallish to medium-sized dog, very friendly. He came to Wally, then Betsy, accepted a pat on the head, gave each the sniff test, then took his place beside his master.

Betsy asked how Zeke found the dog. "He just showed up here one day and glued himself to me. Been my best friend ever since."

Betsy wondered how Zeke wound up in Montana on a ranch. Zeke said he'd always liked wilderness. When he was a kid, his dad would take him hunting and fishing in Michigan's Upper Peninsula. When he and Wally joined the Marines, they wound up in California. He got sick and got a medical discharge. Once he recovered, he just started hitch-hiking. His plan was to see a little of the country on his way back to Michigan. He planned on settling in the U.P. When he got to Montana, he fell in love with the state. He found the job of handyman on the ranch and he was content. On his days off, he could hunt and fish. Weekends he'd go into Missoula for some drinking and dancing. He had all he could want right here. Who could ask for more!

Zeke told them a little about the ranch. He said tomorrow he would have some time to show them around. They could visit the barns and also see where he and Happy Jack lived. He said they would have most of the day to themselves, but if they liked, he could take them horseback riding in the evening. Zeke gave Wally a handgun. He said if they did any hiking, be careful of grizzlies. At this time of year, they had cubs and could be aggressive. He also warned them to stay on the paths because of snakes. "The rattlesnakes, well, they warn you usually. But the copperheads are sneaky bastards. No warning at all. They just strike."

Zeke looked at Wally and Betsy. He smiled. "Well, I know it has been a long day for you, so I think I'll just leave you two lovebirds to get some rest." He gave Betsy a hug, Wally a handshake, clap on the back, a wink, and he, with Happy Jack, quietly melted into the darkness

Betsy was yawning. "I'm so sorry, Wally. I think the campfire got me a little too relaxed. Are you about ready for bed?"

"You go ahead and get ready. I'll put the fire out and be right in."

When Wally got in the cabin, Betsy had already transformed the sofa into a bed and she was in it. She'd lit a single candle and placed it on the bar that separated the kitchen from the living room. She was wearing some sort of white filmy nightgown. In the soft illumination she looked lovely. She must have put some lotion or perfume on, because there was a subtle scent of vanilla and roses in the air.

Wally smiled at her and scooted into the bathroom to get cleaned up. Now a dilemma. What to wear? Boxers? No boxers? Shirt on? Shirt off? He hadn't thought this through. He decided to go the safe route. Boxers and a shirt. A quick sniff under the arms. Passable. Check teeth and hair in the mirror. OK Take a deep breath. Here we go.

It was nine steps from the bathroom doorway to the bed in the tiny cabin. Wally covered that ground in record time, lifted the covers, and quickly slid into bed. Now what?

Betsy solved that problem. She reached over and drew him to her, turning him on his side and up against her. She moved her hand up Wally's back and tangled her fingers in his hair. Bringing his face to hers, she kissed him. At first the kisses they shared were sweet and tender. They became firmer, harder, seeking, demanding. Her leg slid between his legs. Then it was gone. She rolled him onto his back and straddled him. Off came the nightgown. Wally gazed up at her candlelit body. Everything about her was exquisite. Her breasts were perfect. He reached up and gently caressed them. She lay down on top of him and was kissing him passionately. Wally rolled her onto her back. Sitting up, he stripped off his boxers. Betsy helped him with his shirt.

Again, she drew him to her. He was ready. Gently he entered her. He could not believe how glorious she felt. For Betsy, having Wally inside her brought her happiness beyond measure. She'd wanted him for so long. The thrusting was coming faster and faster. Betsy was squirming with delight. He was thrilling her beyond her wildest dreams. She wanted him so badly, all of him. Wally exploded deep within her. Then it was over. He stayed inside her, kissing her lips, her eyes, her forehead, her nose, covering her with little feathery kisses over and over.

Betsy was stroking his face, running her fingers through his hair, caressing his back. He was hers and she was his. Completely. Both had tears of happiness.

They spent the night locked in each other's arms. Skin against skin. Wally loved the feel of that warm little body against his. She loved his strong arms wrapped around her. She realized she always had—even from that first time in the baseball field. She felt safe. Protected. Loved.

After breakfast they sat at their little table across from each other, holding hands. They were drinking coffee and looking out of the picture window. Someone had hung a bird feeder on a tree just outside the window. They were watching birds come and go. A chickadee flew down and perched on the feeder. He didn't come to eat. He looked in the window at them, cocking his head this way and that. Betsy remembered the little chickadee at Nick's gravesite. Could Becca have been right? Was this Nick's spirit bird? Was Nick watching over them? Was it possible? There is so much we don't understand about this world we live in. It is just as easy to believe in spirit animals as to discount that idea. Betsy chose to believe.

There was a knock at the door. It was Zeke, and of course, Happy Jack at his heel. Betsy fixed Zeke some coffee and he joined them at the table. She commented on how peaceful it was sitting here looking out of the window. Zeke told her of an author who spent the previous winter in that very cabin, writing her book. She could have afforded any cabin, but she chose this one, precisely because of its isolation. She welcomed the winter. She loved the howling wind in the pines, the snow gathering on the trees and piling up in drifts on the ground. She loved the quietness that follows a big snow, loved being snowed in, snug in her sturdy little cabin. No distractions, she said. In the spring her book was completed.

Once Zeke left, Wally and Betsy strolled to the main lodge. They purchased post cards. They sat on the sofa by the fireplace and wrote their respective messages to send to their families. They found Zeke did not exaggerate when he told them how beautiful the interior of the lodge was. The entire inside was made of logs, even the exposed rafters, visible because of the cathedral ceilings. The stone fireplace rose all the way to the ceiling. There was a nice fire crackling in the fireplace. Comfortable overstuffed chairs and the sofa circled the fireplace. Underfoot was a colorful woven southwestern-style rug. Windows were generous in length, allowing views of the forest beyond the lodge. There was a wrap-around porch with rockers to relax in. Betsy couldn't believe how peaceful it was here at the ranch. She missed Nicole, but she was so happy they took time from their hectic wedding preparations to come here.

After mailing the postcards, they returned to the cabin. Betsy packed a picnic lunch and they spent the rest of the day exploring some of the hiking trails. They stopped at one point for lunch. Betsy spread out a blanket. After lunch, Wally looked at Betsy. She saw the desire in his eyes. Without a word being spoken, she held out her arms.

After dinner, Zeke came by. He showed them his little cabin, similar to theirs. He showed them some of the fancier cabins. One wasn't occupied, so they peeked in the French doors to see the living room. It had a stone fireplace and was very elegantly furnished.

Zeke took them to the barns. He showed them the mare that soon would give birth. It was his own mare and her name was Kitten. Zeke had three horses all saddled and ready for them. For the next hour they rode on trails through the forest. Betsy had only been horseback riding twice before. Her horse was very gentle and she was loving the experience.

The next day they again were sitting at their table with their after-breakfast coffee. Again, they were quietly appreciating the misty morning and the birds happily chirping, when they saw a most amazing sight. The evaporating mist revealed a doe in the meadow nursing her fawn. To be treated to such an astonishing sight took their breath away. They discussed why she would choose such an open spot at a time when she was so vulnerable. Wally came up with the best probable explanation. He noticed the doe was about ten feet into the meadow from the tree line. She was centered in a spot where the trees formed a "V" shape. In that way she could see danger no matter what direction it came from and she had two good ways to escape to cover. They marveled at how clever she was.

In the late afternoon, Betsy and Wally decided to just sit and relax on their front porch. As they came out onto the porch, they startled a little chipmunk and he skittered off with an "eek, eek, eek". As they sat rocking and talking, the chipmunk would run by. Each time he would announce his presence with another "eek, eek, eek". So, of course, Betsy named him Eek. She went into the cabin and came out with a slice of bread, peanut butter and a table knife. She tore off a bit of the bread, smeared peanut butter on it and placed it on the far end of the porch. Eek eyed it suspiciously. Finally, curiosity got the best of him. He zoomed in, snatched it, and then consumed it at a safe distance away. Eek didn't wait as long for his next piece.

Betsy was having fun feeding the little guy when Zeke came striding up hurriedly. "Kitten is having her baby. Would you like to see the birth?" Wally ran and grabbed the keys to the truck and gave them to Zeke. He drove to the field where Kitten was giving birth. Just as they got there, she dropped the colt. Zeke pulled over to the side of the road and they parked there, watching. The colt was struggling to get to his feet.

Atop a hill on the opposite side of the road was a group of horses. They looked up when the truck arrived, but soon returned to their grazing. All except one horse. He was watching them. Every muscle of that horse was on the alert. When they parked, he left the group and came down the hill at a full gallop. He came right over to the barbed wire fence. He pulled up short at the fence and looked at them menacingly. Betsy knew if they tried to get out of the truck, he would come right over that fence. He looked from them to the mare and then back to them. There was not the slightest doubt he was protecting the mare at this delicate time. It was such an extraordinary moment, how the male would protect his mare and her colt. It brought tears to Betsy's eyes. How admirable and brave animals are, if only we had the time to pay more attention.

Zeke said, if she wanted to, Betsy could name the colt. He told her to think about it. Wally laughed and said Betsy was very good with names.

That night when they met Zeke for their nightly trail ride, Kitten was in the barn with her colt. Zeke asked Betsy if she'd thought of a name yet. She had. "You know, Zeke, he is a beautiful buckskin color. How about if we name him Bucky."

Zeke loved it. "Bucky it is."

Early on Saturday Zeke showed them a cement pond. He explained they raised trout there on the ranch, then, when they were ready, the trout were released into the stream. Beside the cement pond was a cement-block building painted yellow. The sunny side of that building was covered with mayflies. Zeke showed Betsy how to pick one off and throw it over the water in the cement pond. To her astonishment, a trout came leaping out of the water and grabbed the mayfly. Betsy and Wally spent the next few minutes feeding mayflies to the trout. It was amazing to see how high they could get the trout to leap, and fun to see which trout would successfully nab the mayfly.

From there, Zeke took them to the stream. Standing on a high bluff overlooking the stream, they saw another spectacular sight. Far downstream on the other side, a mother grizzly was fishing. With her were two cubs. The cubs were not paying much attention to Mom. They were too busy playing with each other, batting and tumbling, chasing and scrapping beside the stream. Zeke said she must be a new mother. After the first year, grizzlies typically only birth one cub. The three of them stood watching the bears until the mother finished fishing and ambled off, her cubs scampering behind.

Too soon the week was over and it was time to go home. It had been a wonderful week for Betsy and Wally; a week of rest and relaxation, lovemaking, horseback riding, and lots of nature. They told Zeke they would see him in a week at the wedding. They couldn't thank him enough and they promised to return when they could. Zeke took them to the airport.

Chapter 20

On the way home, they talked about their plans for the upcoming week.

Betsy would be finalizing wedding preparations. Minnie, Becca, and Annie would be coming in on Thursday night. They all would be shopping for wedding clothes on Friday. Betsy had already selected her choices earlier. It was just a matter of getting the correct sizes. The rehearsal and dinner would be Friday night. The wedding was Saturday afternoon. The reception followed immediately in the church basement. The Coles would be leaving on Sunday.

In the meantime, Wally and Gunny would be organizing the military part of the wedding. Tom's friend, Cara, had found a soon-to-be vacated one-bedroom apartment in married housing on base for Wally and Betsy. Wally had already applied for it and was accepted. All they had to do was sign the papers the following Monday, after the wedding, and they could move in that same day. Betsy's parents were giving them some furniture. Wally would be taking the third week of his four-week liberty allowance that Marines were given annually so they could shop for whatever else they would need for their apartment.

Finally, the big day arrived. Everything was ready. Two Marines, in their dress blues, served as ushers. Since Wally had no family able to attend, his fellow Marines were seated on the groom's side of the church. Some were wearing their dress blues; others were just dressed in the best civilian clothes they might have.

Minnie was escorted down the aisle. She proudly carried her beloved grand-daughter, Nicole. Minnie chose to represent Wally's absent family and was seated in the front pew on the groom's side. As she sat there, she looked around the church with approval. The florist had decorated perfectly. Two bouquets of mixed white flowers flanked the altar. The main-aisle-ends of the pews each held a large white bouquet of satin ribbon. That was it. The effect was simple, but tasteful.

Laura left the room when the preparations of Betsy and her bridesmaids were completed. She was the last to be seated, just across the aisle from Minnie.

The organist began and a hush came over the room. A clear and lovely voice began to sing an Etta James song "At last, my love has come along..."

Wally, Tom, and Zeke took their places to the right of the altar. Wally and Tom were wearing their dress blues. Zeke had somehow managed to come up with a decent fitting suit for his tall scrawny frame.

Laura noticed with amusement that Wally's knees were shaking so badly the entire fabric covering his legs was trembling. It looked almost like he was dancing in place! Laura hoped he could get through the ceremony without fainting.

The ushers rolled out the white carpet and the wedding procession began.

Becca came first. She was wearing a slim-fitting floor-length pink satin gown. Her long black hair was piled high on her head, with two wispy tendrils spiraling down in front of her ears. Tiny flowers were tucked into her hair. Minnie gasped at how grown-up her daughter looked as she slowly and gracefully made her way down the aisle and took her place to the left of the altar. Her mother smiled proudly at her.

Sandy followed, attired identically to Becca. Her brown hair was styled in the same fashion as Becca's. But, being Sandy, she had beads and feathers adorning it instead of the tiny flowers.

When Tom saw her coming down the aisle, he had to blink to believe his own eyes. He always thought Sandy had a natural beauty, but he had never seen her dressed up or wearing makeup. The transformation was astonishing to him; he couldn't take his eyes off her! He thought his heart would burst; he was so proud of her.

Next came a very proper flower girl in her frilly pink dress. Her hair was in a grown-up upsweep, with the same tiny flowers. Annie was being very solemn and businesslike with her important job. She carefully portioned out her flower petals to the right and to the left. She was so cute there were audible "awwws" as she walked up the aisle. Taking her place beside Sandy, she flashed her mother a huge gap-toothed grin (she'd lost another tooth by then} as if to say "I did it!"

The air of anticipation was almost palpable in the little church as the organist struck up the wedding march. Betsy seemed to float down the aisle on her father's arm. Her floor-length dress was white satin, with a flare below the waist. Her hair was in an upsweep, similar to her bridesmaids, with the same tiny flowers. She was carrying a bouquet of white roses. Wally thought she was more beautiful than he had ever seen. She was absolutely stunning!

Wally was so nervous he didn't remember much about what Pastor Bill Burnia said during the wedding ceremony. He was worried about getting the "I do's" right and not dropping the ring, and in general not making a fool of himself.

He remembered Pastor Bill began with a few words of welcome. He talked about how Wally and Betsy met and came to love each other. Wally remembered looking over at Minnie at one point. She was looking at him with such joy on her face.

Minnie was beaming with happiness. She knew almost from the first that these two were meant for each other. And she knew in her heart little Nicole couldn't have asked for a better father. Minnie thought about how the wisdom of the ancestor spirits was so much greater than human wisdom. They always know what is best.

The vows spoken by the young couple was a particularly moving part of the ceremony. Betsy spoke her vows with such passion, it brought tears to Wally's eyes. Her face, looking up at his, was absolutely radiant. When it was time for Wally to recite his vows, he was so choked with emotion he had to struggle to get through them without breaking up. He could see Betsy was just as emotional. Had they looked at the assemblage, they would have seen many dabbing at eyes and blowing noses.

At the same time, Tom was looking over at Sandy. His heart was overflowing with happiness. She looked at him, and there was unspoken understanding between them. it was almost as though they, too, were pledging their love for each other.

Tom handed Wally the ring and he placed it on Betsy's finger. She then placed Wally's ring on his finger. Wally remembered looking at their two hands joined, and the rings really brought it home for him. They truly were one, now and forever. When he kissed her, all the love he held in his heart came pouring out and into that kiss. For a brief moment, the world faded away.

Following the ceremony, the new Mr. and Mrs. Allen made their way down the aisle and into an anteroom to complete their paperwork. The guests mingled outside in front of the church. Twelve Marines assembled at the foot of the church steps in two lines of six each, facing each other. When Wally and Betsy emerged from the church, Gunny gave the command and the Marines drew their swords and crossed them in the air. The newly-married couple passed underneath the crossed swords and upon reaching the other side, were greeted with a shower of rice from the wedding guests.

Everyone then went to the basement for the reception. Sandy had prepared a spectacular dinner, with prime rib, turkey, and ham. During the dinner, Becca reviewed how she and Betsy had met and become close friends. Tom spoke about what a loyal and caring friend Wally was. Gunny spoke about how Wally was a man of great honor and integrity and how he was proud to know such a Marine.

After dinner and cake, there was dancing. First the bride and groom. Then the bride with her father. Then the groom, first with Laura, then with Minnie. Soon everyone was dancing. The young female attendees were especially delighted with the Marine presence. The Marines were delighted with all the young ladies, as well.

It was time for the bride and groom to make their exit. They waved to everyone, walked out the door and into their future.

Epilogue—15 years later

Becca: Received her Doctor of Jurisprudence degree from the University of Minnesota-Duluth, and is currently working as an advocate in the Bureau of Indian Affairs in Washington, D.C.

Annie: Made a career change. She had long since abandoned her plan to become a paleontologist. She is currently enrolled in the pre-med program at the University of Minnesota Medical School. Her goal is to eventually open a medical clinic on the reservation.

Rolly: Joined the Marines, as did several young men after Wally and Tom's visit to the reservation.

Minnie and Lucinda: Both with empty nests, the two cousins now live together in Minnie's house.

Zeke: Still lives on the ranch. He has authored several magazine articles about horses.

AJ: Married his German girlfriend and has remained in the Marine Corps. He currently serves as a Gunny.

Tom and Sandy: Married, and now own three very successful restaurants in the area. It so happened that Sandy's style of restaurant was very popular with the local students. Each evening poets and would-be writers would read their works. The readings would be followed by intellectual discussions. Tom and Sandy started at the right time and place for the type of restaurant they wanted. It was the start of the Beatnik era, which in time would morph into the Hippie era. They are looking to franchise in other university towns.

Wally: Works in his father-in-law's insurance agency. Joe showed him how to invest in real estate, and he lives quite comfortably with Betsy and Nicole in Half Moon Bay. One day he absent-mindedly reached down to his sock to retrieve his packet of cigarettes. Then he chuckled; he'd quit smoking years ago. As sometimes happened over the years, he had that same flashback: John sitting on the curb, John taking a cigarette from somebody. Why did that always bother him? Why? His brain was trying to tell him something. Something important. What? The lump. That was it! The lump in his sock. If that lump was his cigarettes, why was he getting a cigarette from someone else? What if that lump wasn't his cigarettes? What if that lump was the glove the prosecution never could find? *What was that lump?*

Betsy: She, Wally, and Nicole visited the reservation for the one-year anniversary of Nick's death, at which time the Cole family's one-year period of mourning was officially over. From there they journeyed to Michigan to visit with Wally's family. Wally's mother was happy to meet her new daughter-in-law, and overjoyed to meet her new granddaughter. Nicole would be their only child.

Nicole: Visited her grandmother faithfully every summer on the reservation. Remained very close to her Aunt Becca. This past summer Becca took her to Washington. The fifteen-year-old was impressed with Becca's office, her apartment, her closet with lots of fancy clothes for business and parties, her lifestyle, mixing with so many important people. But she most admired Becca's mission. Becca's people were her people. She is considering obtaining a law degree eventually and joining Becca in Washington.

John: Re-enlisted and was sent to Vietnam, where he was killed in a fierce gun battle. Most say he died a hero. Under heavy fire, he went into the field and rescued several wounded, even though he was wounded himself. Eventually he was shot and killed. A few say it was almost like John wanted to die. He just kept going until gunfire brought him down.

Teddy: Got a job as a streetcar conductor on Market Street in San Francisco. One day a very frail lady struggled up the steps. She was so weak, he had to help her. With tremblng hands, she opened her worn purse, withdrew the needed coins and dropped them in the box. Only then did she look up. Although Teddy didn't recognize her, she knew him. "Teddy! It's me—Angie!"

Teddy was shocked by her appearance. She was skeletal. Her once-abundant hair was almost all gone. "Here, sit behind me. We can talk."

They reminisced about the people they knew and the things they did. "Those were good times, Teddy." Angie said wistfully. She was quiet a moment, as though thinking something over. Then she straightened up, coming to a decision.

"I'm dying, Teddy. The doctors tell me I haven't long. I have something I've kept for a very long time. I think you should have it." She began rummaging around in her purse.

"You're dying!" Teddy was shocked. "What's wrong?"

"The doctors don't know what is wrong with me. I was living in New York City and I got sick. At first, they thought it was pneumonia, but it isn't responding to any known medicine. So, I have come home to die." Angie found what she was looking for. She withdrew a very tattered, worn, dirty paper that had been folded over many times. She gave it to Teddy. "Here, read this when you get a chance." Angie reached her stop and got off. "Good-bye, Teddy."

Teddy slipped the little packet into a pocket in his shirt and forgot about it. Two weeks later he remembered. Curious, he pulled it out and read it. It was a note John had written to Angie long ago.

"I told you I'd move on. I told myself I had to let you go. Honestly, it was the hardest thing I've ever done. But I had to do it. For me. For my heart. You hurt me so badly. How could you cheat on me? I worshipped you. I would have given you the sun, the moon, and the stars, if it was in my power. I even killed for you. But you changed me. I knew I could be strong enough to let you go. I knew it, and I did it. Because I am the

only one who knows how much you hurt me. Now I have to figure out how to go on without you. And I have to figure out how to live with what I've done. I'm not even sure I ever can. The court martial set me free, but I will never be free."

Teddy immediately set about trying to find Angie. He finally found her apartment, but no one answered. A neighbor, hearing his hammering on the door, stuck his head out and told him Angie died a week before. She'd been cremated and the Neptune Society had scattered her ashes in the Pacific Ocean.

It was one of the few times in his life that Teddy cried. He bought a single long-stemmed yellow rose, took it out to the dock, and cast it out on the water. Silhouetted against the sunset, he stood and watched the tide take it out to sea.